Charlotte

A South Landers Novel

Virginia Taylor

LYRICAL PRESS
Kensington Publishing Corp.
www.kensingtonbooks.com

First Electronic Edition: February 2016
eISBN-13: 978-1-61650-927-9
eISBN-10: 1-61650-927-9

First Print Edition: February 2016
ISBN-13: 978-1-61650-928-6
ISBN-10: 1-61650-928-7

Printed in the United States of America

A marriage most inconvenient…

After losing his first love in childbirth, Nicholas Alden knows with a great certainty that he must never be a father. But to be a husband is a very different matter—mandated by South Australian society, necessary for his family name. So when he meets beautiful social climber Charlotte, he believes he has found a wife he can keep at arm's length. He is terribly wrong.

Born on the wrong side of the sheets, Charlotte hopes Nick can prop up her reputation long enough to secure a suitable match for her beloved cousin. She assumes that is all she can ask of her new husband—until they succumb to a night of uninhibited passion. Her heart is won in his embrace, but he doesn't know the truth of her scandalous parentage. If he did, all would be lost.

Still, somehow, Charlotte dares to hope that her match of convenience could become something more. It is a reckless gamble, but the prize—a marriage of blazing lifelong desire—is one worth any risk…

Books by Virginia Taylor

South Landers
Starling
Ella
Charlotte

Published by Kensington Publishing Corporation

To RJT, all my love, forever

Author's Foreword

In 1998, after I joined RWA, I was asked to be an online moderator. Me. An Aussie. I have no idea why and I bless my luck because during those years when the online groups kept romance writers all around the world communicating, I was part of the dedicated team of 'enablers' led by the amazing Claudia Yates from the RWA links to the WoWlinks. I would like to thank (in alphabetic order): Lori Alpert, Teresa Eckford, Jamie Leigh Hansen, Deborah Lawson, Deborah Ledgerwood, Reb Paisley, Robin Perini, Alicia Rasley, Hannah Rowan, and Eliza Shallcross for showing me how to keep my cool, how to phrase my words inoffensively, how to be tough when needed, and how to listen and solve problems—in other words, how to be a grown-up.

I'm not sure about 'enablers.' I wrote 'fixers' first but that read like a hit squad. I thought the word should sound a bit more helpful than that.

Prologue

Adelaide, South Australia, 1865

Nicholas Alden wandered down the torch-lit path to the middle of the garden, a stone paved area surrounded by clipped hedges. Glancing around, he chose the only available seat, an uncomfortable looking bench. A piano tinkled in the distance, competing with the overriding voices in the ballroom and a screeching violin or two.

He took a long draught from his wine glass, glancing briefly at the flickering stars before trying to shut out the world. The light clip of footsteps caused him to open his eyes. A hazy shape dressed in white stood in front of him—ah, yes, the beautiful, well-behaved debutante who'd sat beside him during the pre-ball dinner. He lifted his eyebrows in query, again appreciating her lovely figure, her porcelain skin, her huge eyes—and the slender fingers that moved to either side of her neckline grasped her exquisite gown and ripped.

He brought his glass to his lips and quaffed while she stood, her gown asunder and her face expressionless.

"You have my attention," he said, hoping she would pull aside her chemise. A view of her pretty white breasts would likely be enjoyable.

She stared straight at him, opened her lovely mouth, and screamed, almost hitting a high C.

He massaged his forehead. "Was that really necessary?"

Her perfect face softened momentarily. "You know it was. It had to be done, and I'm sorry, but I'm in trouble." She sat beside him, her hands neatly clasped in her lap. "But if you help me, I'll help you. I know about you, you see."

"The whole world knows about me." Giving a long, deep sigh, he stretched out his legs and crossed his ankles. *He* didn't have a reputation to lose. Her attempt to compromise him would do her no good at all.

"If someone doesn't marry me soon, I'll be in dire straits."

He covered a yawn. "I'm afraid you'll have to find someone else. I'm not a marrying man." The next act of her tired scenario would now play out, but not her way.

"I know, but you're just right for me. If only... Oh, I could bear a disgraced life for myself, but not for two of us. Mr. Hawthorn is a cad to have ruined...."

His hazy mind latched on to the name Hawthorn. Footsteps pounded along the slate path. She kept talking, talking, talking, while he concentrated on Tony Hawthorn and his wife. The man had seemed perfectly matched. Who would have guessed?

Nicholas had barely lifted his chin from his chest before the beauty's plain companion, Miss Someone, appeared, making far more noise than the beauty. She grabbed the foolish creature into her arms.

"Your gown, your gown," she wailed, as if more worried about the cost than the reveal.

Her recriminations continued while Nicholas polished off every last drop in his glass. Predictably, others arrived, among them his friend, Luke. Nick's head ached even more. He wanted them all to go away.

Strangely, the beauty didn't make any more fuss, and she kept saying the whole thing had been an accident—not his fault. Before he knew where he was, he was grabbed by the arm and told by Luke he would marry her. Annoyed, he swatted Luke away.

He needed another drink, and he'd already decided the beauty's offer would suit him.

Chapter 1

Charlotte Alden bounded off the central stairway. The morning sun glittered red through the leadlight panels surrounding the main entrance. Bursting with her news, she sped across the hall to the library. Sarah, her only relative, sat sprawled on the lush carpet. Tumbled books surrounded her, and she rubbed her head.

Charlotte stopped. "What happened?"

"Nothing." Sarah glanced up with a frown.

Charlotte breathed out. "I thought the books had toppled off the shelves and hit you."

"I've been moving them around." Sarah pulled a pencil from the knot of her apricot hair and chewed the end. "I was wondering how I ought to sort them."

"You normally do your wondering on a chair."

"The floor's larger than the book table. What do you think? Should I file these by author or subject? I've tried each, and I still don't know which is best."

Charlotte picked up the nearest book and examined the cover. "Don't tell me you're going to read each one first."

"I couldn't possibly. If you wanted to read a story, how would you choose one? Yes, I know. You don't want to read a story."

Charlotte laughed. "When would I find the time?" She watched her cousin pick up a book and scan the contents. "Our visiting cards have been printed," she said, trying to sound casual. Now married into a wealthy family, she could give Sarah her chance to find a husband, one who would love her and give her adorable children for Charlotte to dote upon. "We will be expected to make morning calls soon."

Sarah moved two books to a pile of five. Outside, three squawking rainbow lorikeets fluttered past the window.

Charlotte waited, hoping for interest. "Perhaps in the next few weeks?"

"Perhaps," Sarah said, holding up a book covered with pale orange watered silk and marked with exquisite oriental writing. "Look at this one. I'm keeping it aside for later."

Charlotte took the volume. "It's full of illustrations. Is it Chinese?"

"It's from Japan. Look closely at the pictures."

"They're lovely, Sarah. The ladies are wearing such beautifully patterned fabrics. Look at this clever design. Such intricate...oh." She clapped the pages together.

Sarah giggled. "I'm sure your father-in-law doesn't know he owns this, or he wouldn't have let me catalogue his books."

Charlotte couldn't blink. "I didn't know people printed such things."

"Why not? If people do them."

In the last picture Charlotte had scanned, the sight of the man's naked body had shocked her, let alone the female lying beneath him with her legs apart. "They do?" Her mouth dried.

"You should know."

For a moment, only the ticking of the clock broke the silence in the room. "But I can't discuss that, of course," Charlotte said, a slight constriction in her voice.

Almost two weeks ago, desperate for financial security, she had married Mr. Nicholas Alden, the only son of Mr. Alfred Alden of Alden House, Burnside, and Alden View in Stirling. A careful selection, Nicholas had the requisite income to support Sarah and herself, but Charlotte had chosen him because the façade of their marriage would benefit him as well. He had no interest in females. Adelaide's bustling society, however, didn't know that.

"The luckiest day of your blessed life was the day you met him," Sarah said with envy in her voice. "I wish a man like him would fall into *my* lap. Rich and indulgent. What more could a woman want?"

Charlotte tapped her forefinger onto her chin. "I'll admit the appeal of a man knocked unconscious with a cricket ball is hard to resist, but you know he didn't propose because of my skills with a cold compress."

"Just the opposite." Sarah made a face. "After you were caught with him, half naked."

Charlotte shrugged. "A gentleman would offer marriage, and he did."

But no more than marriage, of course. Nicholas had not, up until now, proved he remembered her name, which didn't bother her a bit. He had never laid one of his misleadingly masculine hands on her. However, not even Sarah, her closest companion, knew Charlotte had to use her knowledge of his secret life before he agreed to marry her. Like the rest of the world, Sarah assumed that Nicholas was simply a too ardent suitor.

"And soon we'll find the perfect husband for you as well."

"One who, I hope, will propose to me in the proper way."

Hearing the reproof in her cousin's tone, Charlotte nodded. "Decorum certainly has its place." She moved to drop the Japanese book on Sarah's pile, but at that moment, a presence loomed in the doorway. Embarrassed by the material she held, she hid the book behind her back instead.

Nicholas Alden was beautiful. Wearing his crisp brown hair fashionably disheveled, he stood propped against the doorjamb. His wide shoulders and lean hips made his unbuttoned evening jacket and his waistcoat of brocaded emerald look especially stylish. Charlotte experienced her usual intake of breath disguised by her carefully oblivious expression.

As if he had all the time in the world, he crossed one elegant ankle with another, aiming a thick-lashed impartial glance at Charlotte. "Are you stealing a book?" His voice was deep, and his tone, as usual, bored.

She breathed out. "Of course not."

"What are you hiding behind your back?"

"A book I was about to give to Sarah."

"But seeing me made you change your mind?" With a suspicious expression on his face, he moved toward her.

She took a step back, trying to pass the palmed pages to Sarah who glanced at her with a look of puzzlement.

Nicholas reached out to take the book. Charlotte swung her arm around, evading him. He grabbed her instead, holding her body against his, reaching for the book, which she lifted high over her head, even farther away from him. Not for the world did she want a man with his bent to think she would scan titillating pictures. Face-to-face with him, she noted his mocking expression.

"Come now." His breath had the aroma of mint. "Let me see."

"Let me go."

His mouth tilted. "No." He settled his body closer to hers. The long length of him fitted against her as intimately as her undergarments. His hand slid to the small of her spine.

Inexplicably, her body relaxed against his, and his eyes changed. The blue-green froze. The moment expanded into a silent challenge, which she realized she shouldn't even try to win.

"Take it." She swallowed. Her whole body thrummed with excitement, and she hoped he couldn't tell that he had such an embarrassing effect on her.

"Oh, that I could, my tempting treasure," he murmured. Sliding his hand along her arm, he reached his objective. Suddenly, he let her go. He opened the book and turned page after page while she watched, her face hot.

"You were about to give this to Sarah?"

"I was about to put it onto the pile." Her voice sounded thready.

"You said you wanted to give it to Sarah. It's hardly suitable for a young female, is it?"

"I, um, no."

He touched the tip of her nose with his finger as if reprimanding her. "I'll be taking luncheon with you today."

Sarah rose to her feet. "That will be nice. If Charlotte wants me to have the book, I'll take it." She stared wide-eyed at him, her hands pressed prayer-like in front of her mouth.

"Certainly not. If my wife needs to amuse herself with these illustrations, I'll keep the collection safe for her in our rooms." He left with the book.

Sarah fanned her hand in front of her face. "That was a little risqué. You shouldn't let him fondle you that way in front of others, though, Lolly, no matter how he feels about you."

"I could hardly stop him without embarrassing us both." Charlotte placed her cool palms on her cheeks.

Sarah gave a resigned shrug. "I expect most women wouldn't want to stop him. He's the catch of the year."

Charlotte nodded. "A landed fish."

"A landed gentleman, which is far more important. You were born lucky."

"I know." Charlotte gave a rueful smile. She was the luckiest woman in the entire colony.

Nicholas could have repudiated her after she'd proposed her bargain. He could have resented her and made a snide remark, but he had resigned himself to marriage with no more than a close inspection of her face and a terse nod. She would never let him regret his generosity. Never.

"I couldn't have done better if I'd tried."

A crease formed between Sarah's eyebrows. "A bad beginning with a good end. But if I had such a handsome husband, I wouldn't let him out of my sight."

"'We think caged birds sing when indeed they cry.'"

"What?"

"It's something I read long ago. It had some meaning for me then, but I've forgotten the context. If Nicholas is staying, I must see the housekeeper and organize a more extensive meal. What would you like?"

Sarah waved a dismissive hand. "A peach. I'm not very hungry today."

"But you'll join us anyway?"

Sarah nodded and resumed sorting through the books, her way to contribute since she'd always talked of herself as a burden. Heaven knew she'd never had Charlotte's advantages—education at an expensive school and an opportunity to take her pick of the eligible bachelors. In a fair world, the cousins would have had an equal upbringing and an equal opportunity in life. Sarah could have that now.

Charlotte left for the housekeeper's room, still surprised by her body's untoward reaction when Nicholas had snatched her into his arms. Perhaps he would have preferred a man, but marriage protected him from accusations of the unimaginable act of *gross indecency*, now only a criminal offence rather than a capital one. She could certainly be loyal to a man who would never claim his husbandly rights, for in exchange she had security, the opportunity to be useful, and the chance one day to be a loving aunt. Since she didn't plan to exploit him again, one day he would like her, too.

Nothing she could do from now on would be as bad as compromising him.

* * * *

Nick changed quickly. He had spent the night with his gloriously infertile mistress and he needed daywear. For the past two weeks since his marriage, he'd spent every night with Beth, not wanting to be tempted by a stunningly beautiful, young wife who he could take if he wished. Judging by today, she would let him, despite her amusingly convenient assumption that he was a daisy.

He had married the most admired debutante of this season. Added to a pair of wide blue eyes was a captivating smile, a charming voice, and the sort of elegant curves that made a man's palms sweat. His body craved the marital rights he wouldn't take, but he couldn't let a devious twenty-year-old tempt him to risk siring a child again.

After attiring himself more suitably in brown striped trousers and a red tie, he walked down to the breakfast room.

One of the maids, bearing a tray full of food, stopped and smiled. "Mistress is having luncheon served in the dining room today, sir."

With a tilt of his eyebrows, he changed direction to the indicated place, a vast area blessed with two sets of multi-paned Georgian windows. The sun beamed in, lighting a room furnished mainly in heavy mahogany furniture and dull pink velvet. For the last few months, he and his father had eaten in the breakfast room, a smaller annex closer to the kitchen. Apparently, his young wife had greater pretensions.

"Good of you join us," his father, Alfred, said, his face set on harsh lines.

Like Nick, Alfred was tall. During the past years, his neatly trimmed beard had begun to fleck with gray, though his hair was still dark. Dressed as a country gentleman, he wore buff trousers and a brown jacket. "Can the racing fraternity spare you?"

Nick moved to the foot of the table. Charlotte, her dark hair perfectly knotted on the nape of her neck and wearing a smart layered crinoline, sat on his father's right. Plainly dressed Sara sat on his left.

"There's no meet today, otherwise, as you know, I wouldn't be here."

"Serve yourself from the side-table." His father eyed him. "There's food aplenty, though this little miss"—he indicated Sarah—"never eats luncheon."

The waif contemplated the empty plate in front of her, her mouth firm. "I'm not hungry. I said I only wanted a peach."

Nick rose to his feet and jerked the bell pull. "We'll have a peach," he said to the maid who answered.

"The peaches is preserved, as Cook told the mistress."

Nick caught Cousin Sarah's catlike glance. "Won't that do for you?"

Sarah nodded and heaved a sigh.

A manservant stepped into the doorway. "Your pardon. The coachman wants a word with Mr. Nicholas."

"Could you relay the message?" Nick shook out his table napkin.

"He says not."

"Send him in, then."

The coachman, Bookmaker Harvey, a stubby knowing fellow with gray side-whiskers, who had apparently been standing just out of sight, smacked his hat on his moleskins as the manservant retreated. "Got this letter here, Mr. Nicholas. And a horse."

"You're not considering bringing a horse into the house." Alfred almost rose to his feet.

"Got the horse outside. Got the letter here in my hand."

"Stay where you are. The ladies won't want your great dirty boots in the dining room."

Nick eyed Harvey's well worn but clean boots. "I'll see the letter." He perused the page signed by his friend of twenty years and massaged his forehead. "Walk the horse. I might send her back."

Alfred frowned. "Who would send you a horse?"

"Tony." Nick quickly scanned the papers that came with the letter. "He says Blue Bobbin jumped into the wrong paddock and met with an unsuitable mare." He lifted his glass of wine and finished half.

"Bound to happen." Alfred reached for the salt. "A ruddy great stallion like that. He belongs to Tony Hawthorn," he explained to Sarah and Charlotte. "Bred by his father. Been dead eight or so years—his father not the horse. He made a tidy sum on the stallion at the racetrack, Tony that is, and he put him out to stud. That's, er..." Glancing at Sarah, he cleared his throat. "Used him for breeding purposes."

"And in the intervening years, Tony has made a fortune from him. I've made a guinea or two as well." Nick finished his wine and refilled his glass. "His progeny are the best blood stock in the country, except, Tony says, for the mare outside. Her sire had a pedigree a mile long, but her dam was a hack. Tony thought Charlotte might like the mare for a riding horse." His jaw clamped.

Sarah gasped. "A horse. Charlotte, you've always wanted a horse of your own."

Charlotte sat unmoving. "Yes, I *have* always wanted a horse of my own. I happened to mention that once in conversation with Mr. Hawthorn."

"He is calling this a wedding present." Nick watched her with narrowed eyes, hoping she would have the good taste to reject the gift. Hawthorn ought to know better. His delightful wife would surely be hurt if she knew he was handing out gifts of livestock instead of leaving well enough alone.

"Is a horse a common wedding present?"

"Would you have preferred rubies?"

"I would rather have a horse than anything else in the world."

"And so, we will accept the gift, although you can hardly expect to ride."

Her eyebrows drawn, Charlotte met his gaze. "If you won't let me ride, I see no point in having a horse."

Nick, shrugging, turned to the coachman. "Stable the mare with the others."

At that moment, the fruit arrived. Cousin Sarah decided to out-stare her plate.

Nick glanced at her. "Not to your taste?"

She gave him a placating smile. "I'm sure it will be delicious."

Nick wondered why he had bothered. He didn't care whether she ate or not. Nor could he maintain interest in a conversation with his wife that appeared to be going nowhere. He quaffed his wine, made his apologies, then left, arriving at his club in the city center some half hour later.

Dixon, the owner, greeted him. "Lookin' for a meal or a bout, sir?"

"More like a fight," Nick said, still annoyed that he had been forced to accept Tony's reprehensible gift.

Dixon inclined his head and indicated the large gymnasium sited down a flight of stairs. Most of the light came from the high windows, leaving the walls lined with punching bags. A few were being treated to a pounding. Two boxing rings filled the center of the area. Currently, both rings were being used, and Dixon's bruisers were either idling or skipping the ropes to warm up for a bout with any likely club member. "You ain't been here for some weeks. How's your condition?" Ben, his usual sparring partner, asked.

"Middling."

The man grinned. "Best you work off your choler with a bag rather than me, then, Mr. Alden."

Nick nodded curtly and left for the dressing room where he stripped down to his smalls. When he returned to the main area, he bandaged his fists and worked up a sweat. He needed a drink but, apparently, Dixon had decided to serve only watered ale today. Nick downed two, which barely moistened his throat. Still irritable, he aimed a high hard punch at his bag, which was grabbed by two large hands.

A head appeared to one side—a head filled with carroty hair and brighter sideburns surrounding a strong-boned face usually described as interesting. "Work, you fairy. Stop playing at boxing."

Nick aimed a punch close to Luke Worthing's nose. "What did you call me?"

"Daisy. Sprite. Girly-boy." Luke, a friend since schooldays, dropped his hold on the bag. "Bastard."

"Your fortnight in the country didn't do much to improve your vocabulary." Nick shot a dismissive glance at Luke's hardy body. "Do a round with me. Though, perhaps you'd rather join me upstairs for a drink. A good sustaining bottle or two will solve more problems than a pounding."

Before Nick could take a step, Luke grasped his upper arm and swung him around. Encouraged by the color of his hair, Luke had a quick temper. "Not *my* problems. I don't drink to forget. I remember. And I remember exactly what you said on your wedding day, you bastard," he said, his voice oiled with anger. "You'd *known her for a couple of months.* Why in hell did I never know that?"

Nick shrugged.

Luke moved a step back, legs apart, his big hands clenched on his hips. "You made a fool of me," he said through his teeth. "She never even let me put my hand on hers."

"Apparently, one man at a time is enough for her."

"Apparently, when she no longer wanted to *know you*, you decided to force her."

"Do you want everyone to hear you?" Nick held Luke's gaze.

Luke snorted. "I can't imagine why you saw the need to mishandle her. The fact that you've consumed most of the grape-stock in the colony would excuse you to others, but not to me. Your behavior was disgraceful."

"The dear creature forgave me. Accept it."

"Whenever you appear, the dear creature sees nothing but a face that sends angels into spasms of jealousy." Luke half turned, a disgusted expression on his own face. "I hope you've saved her reputation by this marriage."

"Unless you've been gossiping, I presume so."

"Gossiping about what?" Luke's mouth clamped.

"Exactly." Nick unwound the bandages on his fists.

"I should have broken your damned nose that night instead of slinking off." Luke clenched his hands at his side. "But she already has enough people talking about her. Even now I can't believe she'd been conducting a secret relationship with a soak like you."

Nick raised his eyebrows. "Believe what you like. It makes no difference to me. Now, I'm off to find a bottle. I haven't seen a tall enough glass today."

Luke jammed his hands into his pockets, hunching. "Do you plan to play the faithful husband?"

"I don't intend to embarrass her."

"I ought to beat you to pulp."

Nick twisted his mouth. "Wait until I'm falling-down drunk, and you might have a better chance."

He left his friend staring daggers after him and strolled upstairs for more convivial company. Charlotte couldn't have forced him to marry her, despite deliberately involving him in a compromising situation. He didn't believe in honor or duty.

He did, however, believe in justice. His family deserved an heir. His great-grandfather in England had been an only child, as had his grandfather and his father. Nick, as well, was an only child, not that his mother hadn't tried to rectify this situation. She had conceived four babies after him. All had died before birth. His mother had died with the last.

If Nick turned up his toes without issue, his father's great effort in making his fortune in the colony of South Australia would be entirely wasted. The least Nick could do was continue the family line, though with a twist. Charlotte was already carrying an heir, but not of Nick's faulty seed.

The gift of the horse and the attached story of the wandering stallion had finally confirmed Nick's reluctant suspicion that the next Alden heir had been bred by hardier stock, that of Tony Hawthorn.

Chapter 2

Charlotte happily took the role of Nicholas's dutiful wife in front of others, but at night when he left to amuse himself elsewhere, she occupied his private sitting room, not because she wished to be alone but because doing so served two purposes—while covering for his extra-curricular activities, she could work on hers.

After her modest debut last year, she'd tried hard to find a suitable husband, and despite the pittance she'd had to spend on her gowns, she'd needed to dress well enough to pass the scrutiny of her well-to-do friends. She'd made do mainly because she had a talent for sewing. However, the awaited sale of her mother's tiny house would give her only possession to her husband, leaving her without a penny of her own, which, as a married woman, she wouldn't have in any case. She made a face to herself.

Although Nicholas and his father had accepted her cousin into their home, they couldn't be expected to clothe her, too. Charlotte liked making gowns for herself, and she longed to make a few for Sarah. Sarah had not been interested in the fabrics saved for her eventual come-out, but Charlotte suspected she would change her mind given the change in her circumstances.

After placing her loose wedding ring on the small table beside her, she settled into a fireside chair to sew. Tonight she meant to finish a new bodice for her blue crinoline. She worked on a panel of striped red until her fingertips hurt. This tiny change would make the too-often seen creation look new, and, after one last seam, she planned to retire.

A floorboard creaked in the hallway outside, and the door opened.

"You're still awake, my delicate delight?" Nicholas, his tie loose and his waistcoat unbuttoned, entered their rooms, holding a bottle by the neck.

Every time she saw him seemed like the first time. She needed to glance away to regain control of her expression. Although she knew enough not to judge a man by his looks, no woman could resist the lure of the unobtainable. Despite his dishevelment, from the top of his gleaming hair to the toes of his crafted shoes, her husband was gorgeous. His manly body made a lie of the thick girlish eyelashes surrounding his bluish eyes.

"Barely awake." She put her wedding ring on her middle finger where the band didn't slip around as much and faked a yawn. He would want his room to himself. Her bedroom opened from a door on one side of the room and Nicholas's opened on the other.

She offered him a careful smile. "Did you enjoy your evening?"

He placed his bottle on the drum table by his comfortable armchair. "Not at all. Join me." He indicated the drink. Without waiting for her answer, he took two glasses from the bow-fronted cupboard beside the fireplace.

She hesitated, folding her sewing. The last time they had been alone was in the Hawthorn's garden after which he had told her he would marry her only if she agreed not to interfere with his pleasures. At the same time, he had mentioned he would not interfere with hers. Today, he had almost forbidden the first, riding, and at the moment he was interrupting the second, her one skill, making do.

He began to work the cork out of the bottle. "Tell me. Were you tipsy on the night we met?"

"No." She knew he referred to their second meeting, for the first had been during the day. "Just desperate."

He glanced at her, his mouth a cynical twist. "Was I a random pick or planned?"

"Very much planned. I thought we would suit each other."

"This supposition gleaned from a few words at dinner?" He glanced at her. "I must have been more sober than I suspected. And you would have taken Luke if I hadn't...ah, conceded?"

She shook her head, for she would never have taken Luke Worthing. Better that she found a man who wouldn't love her than settle for a man whose love she could not return.

Nick glanced toward the opening door. Vera, Charlotte's maid, held a silver tray.

"Good. You've bought the cheese," he said. "Leave the food on the table there." He indicated the bottle. "And thank you. I shouldn't have disturbed you."

Vera bobbed a curtsey and left.

"You and I made a bargain." Nicholas poured two drinks and handed Charlotte one. "I won't have a problem sticking to my side as long as you remember you may certainly not sully the Alden name. You know what that means, don't you?"

"I must behave like a lady at all times." She gazed into the amber-colored depths of her glass. "And I intend to, for I plan to use your name to introduce Sarah into society." She kept her voice even. "I'm as vested in respectability as you."

"Let's hope not. My vesting days are long past. Make sure yours are not."

"I wouldn't break my word."

"You have never given me a single reason to trust you."

Irrationally hurt, she put her glass on the table. "I know. I wronged you, but no one could have forced you to marry me. You made that decision. I will never plot against you again. I promise. And I think I ought to retire."

"Have your drink first."

"It's too late in the day."

Nicholas up-ended his glass. "And you are quite determined to keep up your guard."

"Not so," she said before she could stop herself. "I just don't like brandy."

"You are so *very* young." He sounded tired. As he poured himself another drink, he skimmed his gaze over her white evening gown, which tonight she wore with a looped over-skirt of emerald green, shot silk taffeta. "And so very expensive."

She inclined her head, taking his words as a compliment to her constant refurbishments. "My costs are small."

"Sarah's costs are small, not yours." He leaned back in his chair, and after stretching out his long legs, he crossed them at the ankle. The fit of his fine woolen trousers emphasized his firmly muscled thighs, and with his taut belly and wide shoulders, for a moment she saw him as overwhelmingly male. Her insides reacted with an unwelcome clench, and she quickly averted her gaze.

Nicholas sighed, emptied his glass, and filled yet another. His fingers tapped against the stem of his glass. "Don't let me keep you."

"I begin my days just past dawn." She didn't raise her head. She couldn't when she wanted to return her gaze to his muscled thighs.

He finished his third glass of brandy and stood, holding out one hand. "Come here. Vera will have hung up her apron. I'll unlace your corset for you."

She stood, walked over to him, and presented her back. His fingers worked on her gown and the row of lacing beneath. Her skin quivered where his knuckles brushed, and she wished she could say something bright and interesting. His breath stirred the tendrils of hair on her nape. A warm shiver ran down her spine, but not a word formed in her brain. Finally, he turned her to face him.

Settling a forefinger under her chin, he stared into her eyes. She held his gaze, but her throat dried. Then he turned, poured himself a small amount of brandy, swilled the liquid around his mouth, and swallowed. With no particular expression, he stepped forward and pressed his mouth against hers. The pressure of his lips moved hers apart. His tongue tickled over her lips and insinuated inside. She tasted his liquor, fruity and shocking.

She jerked back, inexplicably excited. "Why did you do that?"

"Why not?" His eyes turned smoky as he stared into hers. His lips curled with weary amusement. He placed his glass on the table, and without another word, left.

Her gold band slipped over her finger knuckle, dropped to the floor, and bounced under a side table. She snatched up the ring, resolving to keep the carelessly bought trinket safe until resized, and then marched into her bedroom, her heartbeat erratic.

Two weeks married and she'd just been tested or teased, and she'd certainly been titillated. Her husband might not be as accepting of his marriage as she thought, but she couldn't make their vows disappear. He could have refused her hand. She would never have revealed her knowledge, and she'd made quite clear she only meant to be his cover.

She drew a deep breath. Somehow she would show him that she could be his perfect wife.

* * * *

Charlotte spent the next morning with Mr. Alden's man of business, signing over the ownership of her tiny house to her new husband. After that, she added to the week's menus, inspected the faulty stove in the kitchen, freshened the flowers, and skimmed the mail.

Finally, the silver salver held visiting cards. Three. One took her breath. *Eleanor Hawthorn,* the wording said, with an address in Toorak Gardens. Charlotte's heart raced. She changed into her riding habit and, with the card in her hand, sped to the library.

Sarah stood on the top of the tall ladder.

"I received a card from Mrs. Hawthorn today," Charlotte said, holding aloft her reprieve.

"So, someone knows you're alive and well."

"It means she has forgiven me for the disturbance at her ball."

Sarah made a wry face. "The disturbance?"

"It also means we can pay a morning call on her. We don't have to leave a card and hope she doesn't cut us."

"All these silly society rules. You visit her. I'm busy."

"We want to introduce you into society." Charlotte clasped her hands in front.

"I'll never take. I'm plain and poor."

"You won't say that when you're dressed the way you ought to be."

Finally, Sarah turned around. "I promised to make order of these books. When I've finished, I might put my mind to looking at the fabrics you've saved for me."

"Therefore, you should let me help you."

"Right. Hand those books to me in alphabetical order." Sarah pointed to the pile beneath the ladder. "Travels. So dull. They deserve a place out of reach."

Charlotte sat on the floor and found the order Sarah wanted. "Would you learn to ride, Sarah? Then you could come out with me."

"You know I'm not interested. You like riding, and I like reading." Sarah accepted the first few books. "Which is strange, really, when you're the one who had the expensive schooling. It only goes to prove that if you want a clever daughter, you shouldn't waste your money. Home education, which your mama gave me, is far more efficient."

"Mama didn't send me to Miss Main's School for an education. She wanted me to have the right contacts, as you know. And it wasn't her money she wasted."

"My mother was your mother's sister. She must have had the same elderly relative who left your mother that trust fund. I've often wondered why she was so favored, other than that she was beautiful."

Charlotte made a face. "And you look so like my mother that people often mistook you for her daughter."

Sarah shrugged. "Similar coloring."

"I don't know why you can't see how lovely you are. As for the trust fund, we'll never know why my mother was so lucky." Charlotte's cheeks warmed. Lying didn't come naturally. She could hear the constriction of her tone. "And if I hadn't had those social contacts from my expensive school, I wouldn't have been in a position to see Nicholas or receive an invitation to the Hawthorns' ball where he...um, proposed."

"I don't think Mrs. Hawthorn is wonderful to have forgiven you. You'd done nothing. She forgave Nicholas instantly—mainly, I'm sure, because he was completely unrepentant." Sarah laughed.

Charlotte dropped her gaze. "And so we're back to the beginning of the conversation. For you to take advantage of my marriage, we'll need to go out into society."

Sarah stopped pushing books onto the shelf. She sighed. "Just you and I? It would be so much better if Nicholas joined us."

"I have no reason to suppose he won't. As I said, he's a gentleman."

"Not born, but bred," Mr. Alden said from behind her.

She turned. "Instinctively noble. I couldn't want a finer husband."

Mr. Alden nodded. He looked like a rougher casting of Nicholas, with similar blue-gray eyes, a heavier nose, a bulkier chin, and slightly protruding ears. In all, he was a good-looking man, although over fifty. "I couldn't want a finer son."

With nothing to add, she pretended an interest in the books she held. "I expect we'll go to Stirling after Christmas."

"I do, but Nick doesn't. You will have more influence on him than I. I'll leave you to your work. You ladies are doing a first-rate job, first rate." He backed out of the room.

Sarah giggled. "He's as intimidated by books as you are."

"No doubt." Charlotte completed her task as fast as she could because she wanted, in the very least, to see her own horse.

But by the time Sarah was satisfied with her placements, the sun was beginning to sink. Charlotte knew she would have to change for dinner. However, never one to let a plan go begging, she collected her crop and hastened to the hall. She just cleared the steps into the garden when Mr. Alden joined her. "Off for a stroll before dinner?"

"I had planned to visit the stables."

"I've just come from there on an errand, but it seems Nick got there first."

Without knowing why, Charlotte experienced a wave of fear. "I hope... I do still own a horse?"

Mr. Alden gave her a glance of astonishment. "Why in the world not? Quite the contrary. I thought I would check if we had a suitable hack for young Sarah so that she could accompany you. Nick already arranged for her to use his bay gelding—a steady enough ride for a lady."

"Oh, she'll be...delighted." Charlotte's mood swung from apprehension to hilarity in a single breath. She wondered how Sarah would evade the generosity of the two gentlemen, but she suspected her cousin was up to the task.

"I'm quite delighted, too, with you. When Nick first told me he planned to wed you, I was mightily surprised. I didn't know he was acquainted with any young ladies. But then I heard about your friendship with Sir Patrick's daughters, and that explained all."

"I met Nicholas while I was staying with the Graces in Stirling," she said, not quite able to meet his gaze. "A cricket ball hit him on the side of his head, and he was quite stunned for a while. I tended to his wound."

While he'd been recovering consciousness, Nicholas had muttered the secret that had decided her to marry him.

Mr. Alden nodded. "I remember the bruise. The hit put him off kilter for days, or maybe meeting a beautiful young lady did that. Seems to me, he should have courted you openly, though I suppose, with his reputation…" He cleared his throat. "Now, has Sarah decided to remain with us?"

"I thought Nicholas had explained she has no one but me." Charlotte's heart thumped. "Neither of us have any other known relatives."

He rubbed his hands together. "Which is very convenient. Sarah offered to catalogue my books, and I'm finding her to be great company. I only asked because, even now, I know very little about you other than you were brought up alone by your mother after she was widowed some weeks before you were born."

She adopted a tragic droop of her shoulders. "And she died last year. If I have any other family, none has come forward. Mama's only sister was Sarah's mother, and Sarah's parents died of a fever eight years ago. We're all the other has."

"Not so. You also have Nick and me, doubling each of our small families. On another matter." He lifted onto the balls of his feet. "After you signed over your house this morning, I arranged with my man for you to have an allowance separate from Nick's. He has his own budgeting system, one that doesn't carry over from month to month. My money is his money, but it's easier if I manage the incidentals."

She gave a small smile. "He said he didn't know if he could afford me."

Gossip mentioned Nicholas's as one of the wealthiest families in the colony. She'd heard his father had come to this utopia called South Australia with only enough money to buy a plot of land. As a tradesman, he had built a successful business making furniture and had expanded this into a series of factories while the population kept growing. Now he had orchards in the hills, even more employees, and an even larger income.

His mouth relaxed. "You'll have six hundred pounds a year."

She gasped. Her house had sold for half that amount. "That can't be right. That's far too generous."

His eyebrows met at the top of his nose. "Not at all. Being married has already changed my son. I couldn't be happier, or more surprised that he thought of a hack for Sarah. I expect the next thing you'll do is persuade him give up his shoddy companions."

Her gaze wavered. She wanted to please this admirable man, but she couldn't make a promise that would counteract another promise. "If you'll forgive me for saying so, I don't think I have the right."

"Regardless, I'm sure any influence from you would be one for the better. Now, I have a gift for you in my study if you'll follow me." He made a sweeping gesture toward the front door.

After a regretful glance in the direction of the stables, she followed him into the house. In his study, a paneled room crammed with dark, heavily carved furniture and curtained in red, he swung a large painting of ships at sea out from the wall and exposed a safe. After moving a few articles, he lifted out a flat velvet box, which he put into her hands.

Her lips parted as she drew out an intricate necklace glittering with rose-cut diamonds. "How incredibly beautiful."

"It belonged to Nicholas's mother. Let me fasten it for you." He stood behind her, his fingers careful on her nape while he found the catch. When he had finished, she turned to face him, holding her pounding chest.

"A beautiful necklace for a beautiful woman," he said, his voice gruff. "Now, off you go. I'll see you at dinner."

She placed her hands on his shoulders and a quick kiss on his cheek and headed for her shared suite of rooms, thrilled to her very core. She'd never owned a piece of jewelry other than the oversized ring Nicholas had offered her at their wedding ceremony and her mother's gold cross. Her steps light, she moved to the gold-leafed mantelpiece mirror, shifting to reveal the glitter of the stones.

Nicholas's bedroom door opened, and he emerged wearing a red and black striped waistcoat beneath his black tails. "Is it the thing to wear diamonds with a riding jacket?"

She laughed. "It ought to be, but I'm just looking at the necklace, not really wearing it. Your father gave it to me."

His mouth hardened. "There's not a man you can't twist around your finger, is there?" Straightening his evening jacket, he left the room.

She turned back to the mirror. The necklace, a chain of smaller diamonds graduated from a large central diamond, was the most beautiful article she could imagine. The face above looked pinched and disappointed.

There *was* a man she couldn't twist around her finger. Her husband. He didn't want to be in the same room with her, nor in the same house.

She neither interested nor amused him. This hurt despite the fact that she deserved no better.

Sighing, she turned from the mirror and concentrated on the six hundred pounds a year Mr. Alden had put aside for her. Quarterly, she would have one hundred and fifty pounds, of far more use than the regard of a husband who had no reason to like her. Yearly, she now had twice the worth of the house she'd had to sign over to Nicholas. She undid her necklace and slid the cool weight from hand to hand.

Nicholas strode out of the house before dinner, as usual, and she wished he would take the time to get to know her. She might have pushed him into marrying her, but he would have had to marry someone eventually, either that or be known for what he was. A woman who knew what he was could never be disillusioned—and Charlotte was quite determined to be the best wife possible, ever supportive, and as present as she needed to be.

She finished off the alterations to her morning gown, knowing that a visiting card from Mrs. Hawthorn sat on her dressing table. A push here and there, and smiles and deferments, and Charlotte would ease Sarah into the opportunities she had been denied all her life.

She only needed to scrimp and save for another year, and the generous allowance from Mr. Alden could be used for a purpose far more worthy than finding a husband for her cousin.

Chapter 3

Slashes of red and gold lit the blue of the dawning day. The heady stench of ammonia wafted from the steaming piles of manure that stood outside each stable. Charlotte strolled to the first stall and saw only clean straw spread across the floor. She finished the last bite of the toast she had appropriated from the servants' breakfast table and walked to the next stall, similarly empty. She breathed in the more pleasing aroma of fresh grain.

"Mornin', mistress," a male voice behind her said.

She turned and saw the coachman, Harvey, chewing a strand of straw. She gave him a smile, which he returned.

"Have you finished your breakfast already, coachman?"

"Didn't have no breakfast. Like to save meself for later. You must be lookin' for that new mare of yours?"

"Could you direct me?" She wore her old riding outfit—a tailored black skirt and jacket of emerald green. Three lush green feathers, salvaged from a fan of her mother's, refurbished her flat black hat.

"They leaves the livestock in the yard while they cleans out the stables. She's a testy creature. Are you thinkin' of takin' her out?"

Charlotte turned in a half circle, spotting a small, bare, fenced area. Eight or more horses stood flicking their tails or nuzzling into various buckets. "I want to see how she does in Victoria Park."

"She'd be too much for a lady to handle."

Charlotte shook her head. "I have wrists of iron. Unless the mare has a mean streak, I'll manage."

"Mr. Nicholas won't thank me if you get hurt." He glanced toward the house. "Hey, Makepeace!"

Makepeace, the tall thin groom, approached with the stable boy, having apparently finished breakfast with the Alden servants. He lifted a hand in acknowledgement of Harvey without a change in his perpetually glum expression.

"Mistress wants her mare." The coachman used a voice of authority.

"Mornin', mistress." Makepeace turned to the stable boy. "Rob. Bring over the new chestnut."

Rob was a lad of about sixteen with a gapped-tooth grin. "Right, you are." He removed his hands from his tatty trouser pockets. Most of the dirty work would be his. "Likely she'll be thrown, though." His smile broadened.

For the next five minutes, under the eagle eye of the coachman and the groom, Charlotte put the mare through her paces, letting the strong-willed chestnut show off her training. After Charlotte finally agreed to be accompanied, Rob saddled a stocky dun-colored gelding and rode behind her to Victoria Park, a short distance away in the reserved lands surrounding the rising city of Adelaide.

As soon as they reached the riding path, she pushed her hatpin firmly into her hair and urged the mare into a canter. The fresh morning air streamed past her face, and she deliberately emptied her mind.

Galloping hooves thundered behind her. She would have enjoyed a race with Rob, but she doubted the placid gelding could gain on her spirited mare. Not easing off, she let the animal have her head. The pounding came closer and closer. Astonished, she turned and saw Antony Hawthorn's big black thoroughbred ranging near. She forced a courteous smile as the lean dark-haired rider touched the brim of his hat. He reined in. Manners compelled her to do the same.

"I thought she'd be right for you." Mr. Hawthorn's white teeth flashed as his horse sidled impatiently. "She deserved a fitting owner."

"I'm glad you see me as one." Gathering a wary breath, she patted the neck of the sweating mare. "But you couldn't know that Red Robin and I suited. I decided to call her Red Robin. I hope you don't mind. No one told me if she had a name. Actually," she said, firming her jaw, "I didn't ask."

"No, I don't mind." Mr. Hawthorn was as tall as Nick, but his hair was darker and his eyes bluer. Although as striking as Nick, instead of perfectly chiseled features, he had a large and straight nose, a dented, squared-off chin and an inflexible mouth.

"She is yours to name as you wish. But I *did* know you suited. I saw you ride Daphne Grace's horse in that challenge after the cricket match in Stirling. You and the other young ladies proved very successful in winning."

She glanced at him. That day when she had first met Nick, four months ago, Mr. Hawthorn had thoroughly scrutinized her. With hard eyes, he had looked from her to his younger brother, who had introduced them. He had asked her surname, not once, but twice, causing her insides to quake.

"We were given little competition. The gentlemen had no intention of beating us, even if they had to rein in their horses."

"Speaking of which…" He watched Red Robin flirt skittishly with his arrogant black and indicated the track, clearly expecting to ride ahead with her. "You haven't called on Nell yet," he said in his abrupt voice, referring to Eleanor, his wife. "I'm sure she would like to see you."

Offering him a polite smile, Charlotte kept apace with him. Mrs. Hawthorn had been as inquisitive about Charlotte's background as her husband, though in a far more charming way. "She was kind to me at your ball. She found a maid to sew up my ripped gown after the unfortunate incident with Nicholas in your garden. Then she insisted that you partner me in a dance. She didn't indicate by word or deed that blame was due to me for the scene."

"Nor was it." He drew his dark eyebrows together. "Nick's behavior was reprehensible. It's unfortunate you were forced to marry him."

"It's unfortunate that people think I was forced. The incident could have been skimmed over easily enough." She adjusted a rein, knowing he'd wanted her off the marriage market for his younger brother's sake.

James Hawthorn might have been hot on her trail, but he'd never been on her list of prospective husbands. Her mother had mentioned the Hawthorns as one family she need not try to cultivate, being far too willing to scrutinize antecedents. "Mrs. Hawthorn left a card for me, but I haven't yet settled into the Alden household. A new bride…" She gave the helpless shrug that usually served her well. "I'll be making morning calls in a few weeks. And thank you for Red Robin. I do love her."

He gave her a searching glance. "I'm glad." He tipped his high crowned hat and left at a gallop.

She would have liked to ease her tension the same way, but she heeded her mother's advice not to act out her emotions. His presence had made her shoulders ache, but since he had not said a word out of place, she had at least confirmed that her marriage to his childhood friend kept her within the bounds of courtesy. Taking her horse into a canter, she realized she had lost Rob.

Wagons bearing fresh vegetables trundled along the main road, delivering their goods to the kitchens of the houses in the area. She finished her circuit and spotted Rob sitting on his horse by the perimeter fence.

"You won't enjoy my morning rides," she said to the lad. "You don't need to come with me, you know. It's only a few blocks to the house."

He looked unsure, and she resolved to evade him in the future. The proprieties would not be served by him waiting by the fence, and if she had to ride beside his slug, she would not have momentary respite from her thoughts, let alone serve the requirements of her spirited mare.

If she rode this early each morning, no one would know she rode alone.

* * * *

Nick arrived home in the early afternoon, tired and out of sorts. He'd barely slept last night, not because of his mistress, Beth, but because of the damned mare Tony had given Charlotte. The easy passing off of incidental progeny had recalled to Nick Tony's words of three years ago.

Leave the trollop and her problem for her husband to deal with, he had said to Nick.

Nick, however, had gritted his teeth and done his duty. In those days, although annoyed with himself for having sired a child during an irresponsible encounter, he thought he should try to right the wrong. He hadn't known he would pay for his mistake for the rest of his life. Now, as the husband who didn't want any interference from the father of the baby, he could see the ironic twist.

He joined the family in the dining room for luncheon, greeting all, noting again that his wife was extravagantly dressed while her sharp-boned cousin wore her usual drab gray. He wondered what Charlotte, a beautiful but ambitious nobody from nowhere, hoped to gain by launching Sarah into society.

Helping himself to a plate of cheese and ham and a tankard of ale, he said to Sarah, "Another day. Another plate of food to watch."

She sighed. "I'm not hungry. I ate a huge meal last night."

"So, you really only come to meals to see others eat?"

Sarah looked toward Charlotte, possibly expecting support.

Nick leaned back and waited.

Charlotte appeared to spot a crumb of food on the red-striped bodice of her new morning gown. Apparently, her appearance absorbed her more than her cousin's plight. If Sarah was now his responsibility, he had no intention of treating her as a poor relation, or of pretending concern. "I was thinking you might like a trip up the Torrens River. But I don't want you fainting from hunger."

Sarah's eyes narrowed. "I've never fainted in my life."

He folded his arms.

After scrutinizing his face, she sighed. "But a bite of cheese and ham never goes amiss." She quickly arose and helped herself to a thin slice of ham and a shaving of cheese. Although each appeared to try her appetite, she ate, her old/young face creased with apparent satisfaction. "I've never been in a boat."

"Perhaps I should look after Sarah today, Nick," Alfred said gruffly. "She might like to visit the museum. I think you should be alone with your bride."

"What sort of man would want to be with one lovely lady when he can be with two?"

Charlotte laughed, and when he glanced at her, she made a wry face. "I wasn't certain for a moment that I was invited as well. When do you plan to leave?"

"Within the next ten minutes."

When Charlotte joined him in the hall a full half hour later, she wore a concoction of red roses and blue satin ribbons on her head, which highlighted her stunning blue eyes. With her figure still slender and curvaceous and her posture perfect, she presented a lovely picture. Nick gave her a mocking salute, annoyed that her looks had the ability to stop his breath.

Sarah had added a straw bonnet with green ribbons that did nothing for her coloring. Nick suppressed a sigh. Until she was suitably outfitted, she couldn't be presented.

* * * *

The city of Adelaide had been built along the southern edge of the Torrens River, which eased past in a gentle curve. These days, grass grew down the banks, and the reed beds only existed on the sides of the water. Native ducks nested while two long-necked, black swans soared overhead, their graceful bodies in unison. Nick rested the skiff's oars on his thighs so that he could take a swig from his silver hip flask. Before rowing back to his starting point, he needed a drink.

Charlotte, who sat with Sarah in the front, leaned forward. "Would you mind if I took the oars for a while?"

Noting the exasperation on her face, he took a longer draught. He could certainly manage to row both ways, primed or not, and he skimmed the boat along until he realized she still supposed him to be a daisy and consequently unable to perform ordinary male tasks. Experiencing a moment of sheer mulishness, he slowed, deliberately under-dipping with his left oar. The skiff veered. The ladies grabbed onto the sides, their eyes wavering. The opportunity to enjoy himself came rarely, and so he kept at the oars, loose-jawed and circling.

Charlotte slid her parasol under her seat, stepped along the planking, and sat beside him, taking the closest oar with a reprimanding lift of her eyebrows.

Offering her a wide-eyed smile, he stood and wobbled to the position beside Sarah. He leaned back, resting an effete wrist against his forehead, awaiting Charlotte's reaction.

She stared at the training teams of rowers who glided past with barely a ripple, and back at him. After a few moments of sucking air though her teeth, she began to row, her success markedly lacking.

"Wake me if we reach the sea," he said, his voice unsteady.

"We'll be lucky to get back to the boat ramp," she said, watching the river flow past. "I miss more water than I catch."

"Perhaps I could help, too." Sarah closed her parasol.

Charlotte shipped one oar. "It's harder than it looks, but I assume it's merely a matter of reach."

Sarah scrambled over to the rowing seat. She took one oar from Charlotte. On her first stroke, she almost overbalanced. "This is hard," she said, aiming her words at Nick. "I thought you were teasing before, but perhaps you really couldn't manage."

"It's a learned skill," he said, trying to sound aggrieved. He sat up, wondering if Sarah had his measure. He half smiled at her, and her next stroke skimmed the water. She fell backward.

He leaned forward, grabbing at the dropped oar. "Right, ladies, thank you for the lesson." Indicating with his head that Sarah should move, he took her place. "You, too," he said to Charlotte, who stood, teetering, until he managed to still the boat.

"I think between us, we barely managed five full stokes." Charlotte daintily repositioned her crinoline.

"You tried, which is more than most women would do." He could test the patience of a saint, which his wife certainly wasn't, no matter how composed she tried to appear.

"We did." Charlotte's face momentarily lit up. Her eyes focused on his bare forearms and quickly shifted. "And now it's back to the house for us."

"Waiting for morning callers," Sarah said dolefully.

"Morning callers are not an event you wait for." He began to exert himself at the oars. A trickle of sweat ran down his back, and he realized he was out of condition. "They're an inevitability you do your best to avoid."

"Not while we have Sarah to launch."

"Like a ship." Sarah trailed her fingers in the water.

He caught Charlotte's gaze. "Are you aware you've been gossiped about?"

"I assume there would be a small amount of speculation about our marriage." She held her parasol as upright as her chin. "I'm certain I can put most of the gossip to rest. Please don't feel the need to concern yourself in our affairs."

"On the contrary. As my wife, your affairs are mine." He edged the vessel alongside the riverside jetty, wishing he had bitten his tongue. As his wife, Charlotte could not have affairs. None. Not until after her baby was born and, even then, she needed to be discreet.

However, she'd been exactly that until the Hawthorn's ball, which had landed him with her and her dependent cousin, steeling him in his determination not to attend society functions forevermore. She had courted the scandal she had to face. He steadied the rocking vessel. "If I were you, I would drop by to see Lady Grace for your first morning call. She will set you right."

"That's what I planned do. Lady Grace has been such a good friend, not a friend, more like a parent in absentia, or a mentor—"

"And if you plan to present Sarah," he interrupted, "she'll need a new wardrobe. We'll shop for gowns today."

Sarah stood, staring at him. "New gowns? Today?"

Her face a picture of surprise, Charlotte clambered out. After a pause, Sarah more carefully followed her cousin. Nick tossed a few coins to the boatman.

He took draught long enough to almost empty his hip flask and, with the two ladies, strode the path toward the bridge where the coachman waited. Harvey spotted them and sped to the brougham, holding the door open while Sarah and Charlotte bundled in. Nick took his seat opposite the ladies.

Sarah fixed him in the eye. "Are we really meaning to shop for new gowns? Where?"

"We'll try Seymour's Emporium where we can buy ready-made. A good dressmaker will take weeks to gown you suitably." He felt in his pocket for his flask, wondering why he had volunteered to bore himself to death.

"What's not suitable about the gown I'm wearing?" Sarah scanned her gray gown as if she'd never seen the repellent garment before. "I look like a respectable companion."

"Do you think that's your role?" He unscrewed his flask and shook the last few drops into his mouth.

"It has always been my role." Sarah's lips thinned. "Although, I suppose now I'll have many opportunities I didn't previously."

"A social life, Sarah," Charlotte said, sounding determined. "You will meet all sorts of people."

"Perhaps with the right clothes I won't be an unimportant shadow with nothing of interest to say."

Charlotte's face froze. "You were never that. Surely you didn't think so?"

"Your friend, Mr. Worthing, thought so."

"Why would you care for his opinion?" Nick massaged his neck, shooting a glance at Charlotte. "The man can't see the woods for the trees. Sarah should be dressed in pretty gowns like you. Why should she wear half mourning when you see no need?"

"Mama died almost a year ago." Charlotte smoothed the backs of her gloves. "I couldn't afford to hide myself away."

"I didn't attend social functions." Sarah clutched at her reticule as the carriage rounded a corner. "So I didn't need pretty gowns."

"Every pretty girl needs pretty gowns."

"We had no money for non-essentials, Cousin Nick," Sarah said, her face stiff.

"Those days are over." His head ached. Nothing eased the ache but a sustaining drink, but he had emptied his flask. He leaned back and closed his eyes.

* * * *

For the first time since their marriage, Nick ate an early dinner with the rest of the family. He followed Charlotte up the stairs to their sitting room. "Sarah looks very smart in her new gown. In a few years, you will be fighting off her suitors."

Charlotte stopped and studied his expression. "In a few years? How old do you think she is?"

"Seventeen, eighteen." He frowned. "How old is she?"

"The same age as me. Twenty, almost twenty-one."

He nodded, strangely relieved. "Good. You can chaperone each other." This would leave him free to avoid her. He didn't plan to fall into the clutches of Tony's former mistress—or any other woman for that matter. One woman had died because of him. Once was enough.

"I'm glad you helped her choose her gowns. She wouldn't have taken my advice as well as she took yours, though I'm surprised by your knowledge of female fashions."

"You're not surprised. That's what you expect from a man like me." He fluttered his eyelashes and made a pout of his lips.

She blinked at him, looked away, and walked ahead into their sitting room. Her posture was perfect, and her skirts swayed gracefully. "Your father thinks I can lead you astray."

The line from her neck to her shoulder looked eminently kissable. He straightened his shoulders. "He won't when he discovers why I married you."

"I thought he knew. He said something... Are you going out?"

He sighed. "Can you give me any reason to stay?"

She sat on the couch. "Perhaps. A game of cards?"

He frowned at the unexpected suggestion. Playing cards with a callow twenty-year-old would cause him to nod off in half a minute. "You wouldn't be able to play anything too complicated, I imagine."

"Of course not, though I'm rather good at Casino."

He rubbed his fingers over his chin. Casino might be a child's game, but players needed good observation, a better memory, and an ability to infer. "I would beat the drawers off you."

She gave him a mysterious smile. "I might beat the drawers off you."

His mind led exactly where he didn't plan to go. He swallowed a measure of his waiting brandy, needing to moisten a suddenly dry mouth. "I can picture it now, both of us sitting here naked."

"Just picture yourself naked." Her cheeks pinked.

He searched for cards in his desk and tossed the deck to her. After sitting on the floor, she tucked her legs to one side and inexpertly shuffled the cards. He didn't say a word as he moved to the carpet with her. Just thinking about the word "naked" was enough to send his imagination on a journey he would never travel, or certainly not while his wife was pregnant. He wouldn't risk her baby. Using another swig of brandy to help, he concentrated on her placement of the cards, anywhere but at her nubile body.

She dealt the hand with laborious concentration. After the first game, he discovered he needed to try. She won easily. Child's game or not, he didn't expect to be beaten by an inexperienced twenty-year-old when he had been gambling for years.

Provoked by her greedy grab when she collected her cards, he lost all coherent thought of the game, and she won the second round, too. The third had begun to go the same way when he saw her hide a card beneath the pack. Now having noticed, he concentrated. She cheated constantly.

Intrigued, he leaned back on one elbow, assessing her. Her shuffles looked awkward, but a woman with her extraordinary looks could cheat and expect to be forgiven even by a man who had his own cynical opinion to deal with.

"Do you play poker?" he asked, flicking his cards toward the deck.

"A little. Probably not as well as you."

"We ought to find out sometime, fancy fingers, but not tonight." He rose to his feet, realizing she had kept him speculating over her talents in bed for well over an hour.

Speculation would lead nowhere. He wouldn't touch a pregnant woman even though he had married her. Best she continued thinking him a sodomite.

Resigned, he went again to Beth.

Chapter 4

Charlotte stared at the lion-head brass knocker on the black door and held tightly to Sarah's hand. "Ready?"

Sarah nodded. The pale yellow crinoline she wore in no way resembled the hand-me-downs she had formerly insisted on wearing, and her little hat in shades of blue sat elegantly on her strawberry blond hair. Nick's taste in women's fashions was a joy. His insistence on paying was a relief.

Charlotte lifted her hand and gave a hesitant rap. She barely had time to step back before the door swung open. A manservant in a black suit inclined his head in query.

"Mrs. Nicholas Alden and Miss Sarah Page," she said in her most pompous voice, and she smiled.

His eyes twinkled back at her, and he indicated the hall of the town house owned by Sir Patrick Grace and his wife Frances, Lady Grace. The outside was modest, a bluestone single story surrounded by a wide tessellated veranda roofed to keep out the sun. Fresh flowers sat on the hall table. With shaky fingers, Charlotte removed her card from her reticule, but a small and very pretty woman, likely in her middle forties, appeared from the back of the house. She wore a gown of olive green with a fussy bodice and looped skirts.

"Charlotte, my dearest. Come in. The girls will be so pleased to see you, and you too, Miss Page. Dennison, tell Miss Daphne and Miss Emily that Mrs. Alden is here." Lady Grace, smiling happily, waited while the servant made his stately exit to the back of the house, and then she ushered Charlotte and Sarah toward a set of double doors.

"Emily is here, too?" Charlotte asked.

Lady Grace seemed fluttery and insubstantial, but she rarely missed a trick. She had three daughters of her own. Her eldest, Daphne, had been a good friend to Charlotte, not only at school. She had also spent holidays with the Graces and attended informal functions with them while staying at their country house in Stirling not long after her mother died.

"Emily is with us for the week. Her Mama thought she could trust her to us. Hubert is very glad of it, and I will be glad when they finally marry. I'm not certain long engagements are a good idea."

"You met Hubert at the Hawthorn's ball," Charlotte said to Sarah. The ball needed to be mentioned if Charlotte were to pass the test. "Daphne's brother, remember?"

Sarah nodded. "I met the whole world at the Hawthorn's ball."

Lady Grace laughed. "The whole world was there. Nicholas told Antony he had made his ball the success of the season. What a dreadful man your dear husband is."

The hallway thundered with feet. Female chattering burst into the room. At least three voices greeted Charlotte at once. She had her waist clutched by Theodora Grace and her cheek kissed by Chrysanthe Grace, who said, "Such a scandal you caused. Isn't it wonderful!" She turned and nodded at Sarah.

"Did I cause a scandal?" Charlotte's gaze met Lady Grace's.

"You? No. I'm afraid we'll have to attribute the blame to Nicholas, which then makes the event a mere titillation. Society has seen his disruptions more than once, and if he can ignore gossip, his wife should, too."

Charlotte stilled, not certain how to hear the word "disruptions" in relation to Nick, whom she judged to be too indolent to bestir himself.

"He can surely be excused," said Emily Downing, a pretty young lady of twenty years with fair hair and a shy smile. "He must have been mad with love for you to rip your gown that way."

Charlotte smiled, her mind easing. The incident had established Nick as a man mad with love for a woman. However, she didn't want him also known as a cad when he hadn't done a thing but stare at her when she'd begun screaming and tearing at her gown. "He didn't mean to."

Daphne, dressed in pink with a single strand of pearls around her neck, turned to her younger sisters, who stood, eyes wide. "Out. None of this is for your sticky noses. You've seen Charlotte doesn't look any different now that she is Mrs. Alden."

Theodora swirled and left.

Chrysanthe crossed her arms. At seventeen, she didn't like being treated as a child. "I don't see why I can't hear everything you hear."

"Go," her mother said.

Chrysanthe, nose in the air, marched off, while Emily and Daphne took a seat. Daphne sat beside Charlotte on a buttoned gold couch. The room looked smart, the windows dressed with draped and fringed green velvet, and the single chairs upholstered in blue brocade.

Lady Grace pulled the bell cord. "We'll have tea," she said to Dennison.

"Tell us what really happened," Daphne said, her eyes wide with curiosity. "Did he rip your bodice?"

Charlotte focused on her short white gloves. "Certainly not. He kissed me and somehow caught my bodice on the button of his jacket sleeve. He ruined my lovely gown, and that's why I screamed. Sarah came at the gallop."

"I ran," Sarah said with indignation. "Only great hefty horses gallop."

Charlotte winced. "I meant you arrived immediately. Anyhow, no harm was done."

"We hope," Sarah said. "You don't deserve to have your reputation in tatters because Nick was so very ardent."

"Now that we know the truth, you needn't worry, Charlotte." Daphne reached out and patted Charlotte's hand. "We won't let anyone say you shouldn't have been out in the garden with him."

"Thank you, Daphne, but the incident really wasn't his fault. I should have told him to go away." Charlotte tried to relax, but her fingers intertwined and clenched together. "But I just couldn't." She tried a soulful look.

Lady Grace gave a shake of her head and a *tsk*. "Nicholas should know the difference between a well brought up young lady and those he, er... Sometimes his mind is somewhat clouded but least said, soonest mended." Her smile looked hopeful.

"Poor you. I'm sure you never wanted to marry Nicholas Alden. It's such a shame." Daphne again patted Charlotte's hand.

"I don't mind at all being married to Nick." Charlotte paused and gave an unplanned mischievous smile. "Would you?"

Both Daphne and Emily returned the same smile.

Emily said, hands clasped under her chin, "I would have to say *no* if he asked me, because I'm betrothed to Hubert."

Being Hubert's sister, Daphne nodded her approval. "I couldn't manage him, but, oh, I could look at him all day. He makes my heart ache."

Charlotte continued to smile. He made her heart ache, too. She could dream of him being the sort of man who would actually attempt to inveigle her into a dark garden, or even just snatch her into his arms without wanting to see which book she held. Or she could face reality, which she had every single day of her life. "Did you hear Mr. Hawthorn gave us a horse for a wedding present?"

"It's just like Tony," Lady Grace answered. "Or James. Those two are almost interchangeable. I've never seen a pair who look so alike, and as for gifts... They are very generous with their money."

"In my opinion, it was a very unfortunate gift," Sarah said, her voice doleful. "Because now Cousin Nick thinks I want to ride, too. He offered to teach me when I said I couldn't."

Charlotte laughed. "Sarah is being droll. She knows how lucky she is not to be left to me. I'm too eager to ride myself to have the patience to teach someone else."

"Nick was always a very kind young man, quite angelic, to match his looks." Lady Grace picked up her embroidery frame. "He and Antony, and James, too, had the run of our country property when they were young. I remember when—Daphne, was it you or Zanthe?—perhaps it was Hubert.... No..." Lady Grace rattled on.

Charlotte sat back and drank her tea. Nick had been right about whom to see first. This family not only gave support to each other, but to others as well. Charlotte had missed each and every one of them, and now, as before, she could enter society clutching to the Graces' coattails.

* * * *

Nick regretted offering to teach Sarah to ride. Because of his commitment to the racetrack, the odd cockfight, various boxing matches, a jealous mistress, and a deep thirst, he could only find time to be with Sarah in the mornings.

This unseasonably hot morning, for Sarah's fourth riding lesson, he had arrived home an hour since, hung-over, dry-mouthed, and with an aching head, which Sarah's antics didn't help. He hadn't imagined that an intelligent female could have such a short attention span.

"Keep your foot in the stirrup, Sarah. You have little enough to balance you in a side saddle."

"The horse jolted me." Sarah leaned over, shifting her skirt so that she could rub her leg. "I'll try to concentrate."

Nick strode over to the stable-yard pump and wet his head. This morning, Sarah had forgotten to check her saddle-girth, she'd stared elsewhere while he'd adjusted her stirrup leather, and she'd dropped her crop twice, causing him to bend to retrieve it, exacerbating the throbbing of his brain. Having two young females in the house kept a man busy, what with buying various knickknacks and making sure they didn't jumble their brains with artistic erotica.

Taking a few calming breaths, he returned to his pupil, who sat staring into the distance and swinging her crop too close to the horse's ears. He put his hand over hers, stopping her movements. She made a face at him.

"Perhaps rather than having me perform a task to which I am patently unsuited, you should be taught to ride by Charlotte."

"I don't think she has the time," Sarah said, a wary expression on her face.

"Not in the morning, Mr. Nicholas," called Rob, leaning on his broom. "She rides in Victoria Park."

Nick scowled at the lad. "If my wife is in the park, shouldn't you be with her?"

"I would be, but I can't keep up with her on that there thing." Rob glanced at the horse tethered by the post. "Let alone, she makes sure I don't."

Nick turned to Sarah. "If she's in Victoria Park, you ought to be with her. It's an opportunity to practice riding."

"I wouldn't be able keep up with her."

"She would hardly be galloping around the race track."

Sarah stared at him as if he were crazy. "She's very skilled, Nick. I'm quite sure she isn't bothering with a collected trot."

Nick's head throbbed. He grabbed the reins of his horse and swung into the saddle.

"Where are you going?"

"To Victoria Park," Nick said, hearing the irritation in his tone. "You two are being deliberately obscure. If my wife is in the park, not chaperoned, I want to see exactly what she is doing."

"I'll come with you." Sarah swung her crop back and forth.

"And yet you couldn't go with her."

Sarah narrowed her eyes. "I didn't learn how to ride at a fancy school. I was taught the three Rs only. If I don't have her skills, it's because I never had the opportunity to learn them."

Nick massaged his forehead. "I'm giving you a chance now, princess."

"Which I am taking."

"In that case, join me by all means." He opened the stable-yard gate.

Sarah urged her horse close to his. "Just don't go into a gallop until we get there."

Nick heaved a breath and eased his horse into a controlled canter along the side of the road. Sarah stuck to him like a shadow as they passed through the tree-lined streets, her plain straw bonnet wobbling on her head. Within minutes, they reached the grassed area of the park where, between the trunks of the few remaining eucalyptus trees, two riders had angled their recognizable horses and appeared to be engrossed in conversation.

"She's with Mr. Hawthorn," Sarah said with interest. "Imagine her seeing him here?"

"Not so strange," Nick said, his shoulders stiff. "He lives in Toorak Gardens, just over the road."

"So he does. Do you mean to join them?"

"I do, indeed," he said through his teeth.

As they closed the gap to his wife and the father of her baby, the couple separated, Tony riding in the direction of his house and Charlotte heading around the track long ago cleared of the native scrub. Tony waved as he spotted them, but he didn't stop. Nor did Charlotte. Nick saw his devious wife skimming the grass on a rangy horse that was surely not born of a misalliance.

He had agreed to marry her so that he could have her child. He hadn't agreed to be continually cuckolded, nor would he be. "Yes, she rides well," he said to Sarah, his jaw rigid. "You're right. We won't catch her today. Let's go."

His temper grew with each hoof beat on the way home.

Chapter 5

Nick followed Sarah into the main hall. She ambled upstairs to change out of her riding dress and he stood, spine tense, tapping his crop against his boot.

The front door opened. His father strode inside, stripping off his gloves and placing his hat on the hall table. "Will you be here for luncheon?" the older man asked. "If not, you should be. That wife of yours has come up with some mighty clever new ideas."

"Clever ideas indeed," Nick said grimly.

"Concerning our daily fare." His father eyed him askance.

"Not my daily fare." Nick didn't intend to eat with his wife. He intended to lay down the rules to her.

"I would like a word with you if you have a moment." His father indicated the direction of his study.

Nick baulked, crossing his arms. "Could this wait until later?"

"Of course," his father replied. "But what I have to say won't keep you more than a few moments."

Nick stiffly inclined his head. He followed Alfred into a den of leather and carved cabinetry, where he sat, legs lengthened, his fingers tapping impatiently on the cushioned arms of a custom made study chair.

His father rested his behind on his polished cedar desk, his hands folded in front of his appalling waistcoat of tan worsted. "What plans do you have for the future?"

"None." Nick glanced through the window behind his father, watching a gardener show his young son which weeds to pull. The lad looked at his father as if the world turned on his words while he yanked up the wheatgrass blown in from the north.

Alfred studied his fingernails. "I hoped you might reconsider your decision about managing the business."

Nick shrugged. "Ah. So you plan to go back on your word?"

"A man without occupation is like a rudderless ship."

"Without occupation? I drink and gamble. I couldn't be busier."

"I thought marriage might modify a few of your habits."

Nick shook his head. "Not a one. I'm set in my ways. A total bore."

Alfred's eyebrows drew together. "What about *that woman*?"

"I still keep *that woman*."

"Despite recently acquiring a very lovely wife?"

"Why change?" Nick shifted his position, checking the crease of his trousers. "I married her because she told me she was expecting."

Alfred squeezed the top of his nose. "Forgive me for being old. When you said you had met her *before* the night of the ball, I thought you were making the incident that night more explicable—not more disreputable."

Nick checked his fob watch.

"In that case you had to accept the consequences. Again."

"History has a habit of repeating itself." Nick rose to his feet.

"At least your wife is a lady."

"No more so than Clara."

"Clara was another man's wife. It bothers me that a son of mine can see no difference."

Nick walked to the door, uninterested in this conversation. Once, he'd been young. Now, he was as old as time. Once, he'd hung on his father's words, too, but those days had passed. Another reprimand couldn't make a dent in a man who would never forgive himself. "There is no difference. Both conceived out of wedlock, yet you have decided Charlotte is a lady and that Clara was a whore." He paused, gazing straight through his father, remembering being in this study four years ago, listening to his father berate him.

He'd been back in South Australia for three months after his years at Cambridge. That day, he'd needed support for a decision that even now he would make again. "When you heard about Clara's pregnancy, and not from me, you cut me off without a penny." He remembered his gut-wrenching despair, the anguish of the callow youth he had been who had believed he could right a wrong. His mouth twisted into an involuntary grimace.

"I thought that would remove you from her clutches. I didn't expect you to run away with her."

Nick stared straight at his father. "She needed my support as much as I needed yours."

"Regardless, you managed." His father crossed his arms over his waist.

Nick noted the defensive move and wished this discussion over with. "Yes, I managed. I had to. I earned a small amount gambling and an even smaller amount working as a coal hauler. An arts and humanities degree didn't set me up for a job."

"A degree is useful for a man who wants to run a business."

Nick rested his hand on the doorknob. "We've been through this."

"When you have a family, you'll see things my way."

Nick smiled, sourly amused. "I'll have a family within six months, I'd say."

His father shook his head, his mouth ruefully tilted on one side. "She's not breeding yet. Telling you she was expecting was somewhat unethical, but the lie shows she wanted you."

Nick scrutinized his father's face. "The lie?"

Alfred tugged at his beard. "Your mother bore five children and, ahem, I think I would recognize the look females get at that time." He lifted his shoulders.

Nick stood, unable to focus for a moment, and then he drew a jerky breath, tightened his mouth, smacked open the door, and left.

* * * *

The housekeeper, Mrs. Wishart, had expressly told Charlotte *she* would relay any changes in the menus to the cook. However, the cook had been in Mr. Alden's employ since Nick was a lad, and Charlotte not only enjoyed hearing tales of the younger Nick but she also wanted his food preferences considered.

Risking the wrath of the house tyrant, she sat on the big central table among various pots, saucepans, and spoons, swinging her legs. Cook had her back to the door, stirring gravy over the old-fashioned smoking stove. The scullery maid clanked a set of greasy dishes into a bowl of suds.

Charlotte raised her voice to read the recipe Cook wanted the kitchen maid to begin. "Take one pound of currants and one pound of raisins, finely chopped."

Thomas, the manservant, polishing the silver, glanced over her shoulder. With a widening of his eyes, he lost his grip on his tray.

Over the resounding crash of the metal, she shouted, "And leave to soak in brandy."

Her last word echoed in the hush-filled room.

"A fate to be desired," said a cool voice. The kitchen doors swung slowly back and forth behind her husband.

Nick's dry wit surprised her. She laughed. "Certainly, for raisins," she said, tilting her nose in mock reproof. She let the recipe book flop onto the black skirt of her riding outfit.

With a flick of his head, he indicated her exit through the quivering doors. "I must speak to you, my fragile flower, if you can be spared from your kitchen recitals." He gave Thomas a cold glance. "Now."

Charlotte slid off the table, her cheeks warming. "I don't normally spend my time in the kitchen, but I found this recipe for Cook." She nudged Cook's back. "Cook, tell him I'm hardly ever here."

Hands on her ample hips, Cook turned and grinned at Nick. "Mistress is hardly ever here. Mrs. Wishart expects to have mistress's orders for the kitchen relayed through her."

He lowered his eyebrows at poor Mrs. Wishart, a woman who'd had his best interests at heart since he was three years old, and made a sweeping motion with his arm that sent Charlotte scuttling ahead of him through the doorway.

The echo of Cook's merry laugh followed her along the passage, where she stopped, quite conscious of her less than spotless appearance. "Where would you like to speak to me?"

"The drawing room will do for my purpose."

She brushed a quick palm across her mouth and cheeks, checking for food traces, and led the way. "I wanted to speak to you, too, but not, I think, in front of the others during luncheon."

In the drawing room, hunting, fishing, and shooting scenes hung on the walls. Various side tables stood crammed with ivory carvings of elephants, monkeys, snarling tigers, and writhing dragons. Two ornately mirrored credenzas sagged under the weight of a porcelain collection. Although Charlotte had been told not to interfere in Nick's life, she'd been given so few rules that she wanted to obey at least one. She hoped that eventually she would be allowed to brighten the room. The chairs needed refreshing with a color other than the currently used dull pink velvet. The clutter oppressed her and closed her in. Most appalling were the fashionable stuffed birds in the glass-fronted cabinet. Turning away from the dead creatures, she took a seat in the curtained window nook, watching her husband expectantly.

Hip propped against the back of an over-stuffed armchair, Nick crossed his legs at the ankle. "Don't encourage Thomas. I know he's handsome, but he gets enough attention from silly young females."

She averted her gaze from his powerful body, deciding to ignore his unwarranted reproof. *He* might think Thomas was handsome, but no one could be less interested in handsome young men than she. The only man who had ever made the slightest impression on her was her elusive husband. Thoughts of his recent kiss led her to clear her throat. Her voice slightly constrained, she said, "A certain amount of our mail is addressed to us jointly. I've been opening those I assume are invitations."

He nodded, tapping his hand impatiently on the chair.

"One was an invitation to join Mr. and Mrs. Hawthorn for a regatta on the Torrens."

"From Tony and Nell?" He stiffened his pose. "If it were from anyone else, would we be having this conversation?"

She stared at him, mystified.

"You've been seeing Tony."

She blinked. "I can hardly avoid him. He rides in the park the same time as I."

"I want you to change that arrangement."

Her neck stiffened, and she folded her arms. "Then perhaps you could arrive home earlier in the mornings and tell *him* to ride elsewhere."

His lips curled with disdain. "You want *me* to confront him?"

"Everyone knows you were forced to marry me. How do you think it looks when I ride with him while my new husband is entertaining himself elsewhere? I'm trying to shield you from gossip, not court more. If you and I ride together, or if we appear together at the regatta, we will eventually bury the gossip and appear to be a normal married couple."

He stared past her to the window. "I haven't been to a regatta for years. It's the sort of mundane event that I despise."

"So, should Sarah and I stay at home, too? Should the world know our marriage is a sham?"

"The world doesn't give a jot about our marriage. And this is not the subject I brought you here to discuss. I need the truth from you. Are you increasing?"

She stared at him, half smiled at the absurdity, and glanced down at her waist. "I hope not."

His jaw firmed. "Breeding. Up the duff. With child. Expecting. In an interesting condition. Stop me when I use a word you understand. Knocked up. In a family way."

Her cheeks heated with annoyance. "I knew what you meant, but I've only been married for three weeks, and you haven't... You *know* you haven't..."

"At the ball, you told me you were in trouble. You said it was because of Tony."

"And so it was." She drew her eyebrows together. "I needed to marry, and he steered his brother away, which would naturally lead to others—"

"You thought he might let you marry James?" He gave her an incredulous look. "James? Anyone but James, if you and Tony planned to go on."

"To go on?" She stared uncomprehendingly at him.

"To think I would continue to countenance your relationship is reprehensible enough." His face was rigid.

"Reprehensible?" She put her fingers on her lips, suddenly grasping his allusion. "You thought I was expecting Tony's *baby*? And you married me? I'm at a loss. Why would you do that?"

He gave her a glance of disbelief. "Tony is married."

She stood, her hands loose and her mind a blank. "I don't know what to say. I'm shocked. Amazed. No one—" Her voice cracked and started again as a whisper. "No one would have married me under those circumstances. And there I was, thinking we had made a bargain, while you were only being kind."

He made an impatient gesture with his hand. "So, you're not increasing?"

She slowly shook her head.

He closed his eyes for a moment. Seconds passed before he drew a long breath and focused on his shoe-tip. Finally, he straightened. "If you're telling the truth... Nevertheless, you will stay away from Tony in future, and don't bother with the wide-eyed, hurt look. You can't fool me the way you have my father. He only gave you my mother's diamonds because he thought I had feelings for you."

"And that's what everyone is meant to think," she said, not about to let him sidetrack his amazing act of generosity. "And must continue to think, because if you married me for such a selfless reason, I certainly must keep my word to you."

"Your word? Ah, yes. You promised to be my understanding wife." For reasons unknown to her, he looked furious. He reached out and roughly grabbed her by one arm. Before she could react, he swung her in a tight embrace. "And I'm certain you will understand this."

He dropped his mouth over hers, his hands settling under her breasts. His body pressed hard up against hers. He was hot and big, and he smelled of the outside and the park and the wind. Her heart sped up. He shifted his thumbs and stroked her nipples. Her body arched into him. She fought to control her need to fling her arms around his neck. Not even a rush of conscience stopped her lips softening under his and her fingers sliding into his hair.

After a breath-stopping few moments, she forced herself to turn her head aside. "No. You don't need to do this. You don't have to pretend with me."

"Am I pretending?"

"You don't want me. You know you don't. You only want to find out what being with a woman might be like."

"And why shouldn't I, with my own wife?"

She drew an astonished breath.

"But of course I don't need to *do this*." His expression tight, he stepped back. "As you know, I find my pleasures elsewhere. You don't honestly think I intended to make love to you?"

She stared at his beautiful stony face, her insides jumbled. "What else should I think when you touch me that way?"

His eyes narrowed. "Perhaps you would be better served if you decided on your own thoughts."

He strode off, leaving her standing with her arms hanging by her sides, staring after him, very much afraid that if he knew the depth of her physical attraction to him, his repulsion would keep him away from her forever.

* * * *

Disgusted by his interplay with his wife, Nick strode into Dixon's through the paneled main hall and across the carpets of patterned red that dulled the sound of the male footsteps entering and leaving. The club had standards to maintain, discretion being the foremost.

A waiter with the misshapen nose of an ex-boxer grinned at Nick as he ushered him to the dining area. The man paused resignedly when Nick took a bottle of wine from the racks on the way in.

Nick spotted Luke, his red hair glowing in the midday light of the window, sitting alone like the perennial bachelor he claimed to be. Nick joined his friend. "Too early for you to have a drink with me?"

"Take a seat. I have a client to see at two, so I'm in no rush." Luke leaned back in his chair. Having attended Cambridge with Nick and Tony, Luke had been accepted to the bar in South Australia, the only one of the threesome to study law. He dressed like a solicitor in a dark cravat, a starched shiny collar, and a discreet jacket, not without style but perhaps without grace. "I haven't seen you around lately."

Nick, dressed like a gentleman of leisure in checked trousers and a dull yellow waistcoat, examined the label on the bottle he had appropriated.

"I'm a creature of habit. If I'm not here, I can be found at the racetrack, almost any inn, or a selected few sporting events. Even, sometimes, at a low boxing match. You could find me if you wanted me."

"How fortunate I don't want you." Luke half smiled.

Nick turned to the hovering waiter. "Get me a corkscrew and a couple of glasses, Ned. And bring back a menu. I'll be eating with Mr. Worthing."

The waiter nodded and left.

"So, your wife got a filly of Blue Bobbin's?" Luke unfolded his table napkin.

"Where did you hear that?"

"It's doing the rounds. Tony hasn't passed on a good horse to anyone, previously."

"The horse was a wedding gift."

Luke examined Nick with unreadable brown eyes. "What did he give you for your coming of age?"

The waiter returned, offered Nick a menu, opened the wine, and poured a glass for each man. Luke had already ordered. Nick made his choice and the man left.

"He gave me the same as he gave you," Nick said, taking a healthy gulp of his wine. And another. "A fob watch."

"Has he spent any more than tuppence on you at any other time?"

"You know he hasn't, and I don't want to hear anything you might be insinuating. The Hawthorn family likes Charlotte, and rightly."

Luke nodded. "She's a very lovely woman, and I'm not insinuating a thing. I'm simply letting you know how gossip is moving this story along. Tony is being connected with Charlotte."

Nick took another gulp. "No one could be less suited to him."

"And no one could be more suited to Tony than his wife. Tony wouldn't do the dirty on Nell. No one with a sound head would, and I'm not casting aspersions on *your* beautiful wife."

"I'm glad to hear that chivalry is not dead." Nick scrutinized his friend, but Luke sipped his drink with a nonchalant expression on his face. Nick swilled down his.

"Will you be attending Nell's picnic?"

"At the regatta? I think I should be there to warn off the predators, and my wife appears to think she needs to be seen in my company."

"Seems reasonable enough. Another female has. Why not your wife?"

"More gossip?"

Luke lifted his fair eyebrows. "I saw you with my own eyes."

"*Own eyes,*" Nick repeated in a derisive tone. He had seen Tony and Charlotte together with *his* own eyes. Normally, Tony didn't ride with any lady other than his wife. Tony had also warned his independently wealthy younger brother to keep away from Charlotte. And the gift of the lovely mare. Why that? The family kept most for their own breeding program.

By the time Nick had finished his second glass of wine, he believed Charlotte was not carrying Tony's child, but he still wouldn't countenance her meeting her lover. Tony had invited Charlotte and Sarah, both comparative nobodies, to attend the Hawthorn's pre-ball dinner, an event usually confined to family and close friends. That alone singled her out for gossip.

By the third glass, Nick realized that Charlotte needed him as her cover more than he needed her for his. As a matter of fact, he didn't need her for his. He was no more a sodomite than Luke, or any other of his cronies.

Without a doubt, Charlotte had been willing to grant wifely favors to him because she wasn't pregnant. Then, should she later find herself in a predicament, her husband would assume he was the father, which put Nick in a quandary. He had married Charlotte because he wanted her baby, who apparently didn't yet exist, and then he had forbidden her to go to her lover again. Perhaps he should have left well enough alone. Not likely. He appeared to have developed a disturbingly possessive streak.

He stifled a sigh and refilled his glass. Now that gossip had linked Charlotte to Tony, he had no choice but to put a stop to further talk. Inconvenient or not, he would have to attend the regatta.

* * * *

Much later, after a good pounding of the bag in Dixon's lower rooms, Nick turned the key in the lock of the door of the so-called "other female," Beth Blocker.

Hands on her hips, Beth's shapely form appeared in the doorway of the front room. Widowed four years ago and proven barren, she was the ideal mistress for Nick. She waited for him to enter the dimly lit passage of the comfortable house he rented for her in the city.

"A new gown, my lovely? Is there any special reason for this finery or is your splendor meant to bamboozle me into paying for it?"

"You paid for the gown weeks ago, Nicky," she said, biting off her words. "Don't try your tricks with me. You know very well we planned to go to the theater tonight. I expected you at six, and it's almost eight now. The show starts in a half hour."

Lifting her chin, he planted a quick kiss on her pursed mouth. "I would be better entertained here."

"But I've been looking forward to going out."

"I'll take you to Spenders later."

"Are you drunk?"

"What do you think?" He slid a thumb across her cheek.

She flicked her head aside. "You are drunk."

"Not drunk enough to leave your lovely body unappreciated."

She put her fingers on his mouth. "I want to show off my new gown. Take me out, Nicky," she said in a cajoling voice. She slid her hand to his abdomen and lower, smiling. "But keep this. I'll need your appreciation later."

Few men saw Beth as a beauty, but her features appealed to Nick. Her body—firm, lithe, and amenable—was her greatest asset.

He angled his hips against hers. "If that's your best offer, perhaps I ought to go home."

She twisted in his grip. "Why did you marry her? You can't love her. Oh, I know you want her, but I also know you haven't had her. You let her tease you rigid, and you expect me to give you satisfaction. Until you married, you didn't expect instant relief. We talked occasionally. We went out occasionally. These days, you're barely in the door before you throw me on my back."

"Isn't that what I pay you for?"

"I'm not a whore. I'm your mistress."

He released his grip. Turning his back and trying to control his unexpected shakiness, he stared at a dark oil painting on the wall, wondering if he had paid for the gloomy scene depicted by an untalented and apparently depressed artist.

"Your wife is the subject of gossip," she said, her tone hectoring.

"My wife is none of your concern."

"I heard she was given a valuable racing horse by one of the richest men in the colony. I heard you let her keep it. Everyone is saying—"

"I don't care what everyone is saying." He faced her. "I don't want you repeating tales about my wife."

She tossed her head. "It's clear that she doesn't take care of you the way a wife should, and it makes me wonder why. You're rich, exciting, and unavailable. The last would make you all the more attractive to a young lady. By wedding you, she would have impressed her friends. But instead of making certain of you, she is driving you away."

"Rich, exciting, and unavailable? That's how you see me? Or more rich than exciting?" He smiled deliberately and, moving toward her, placed his hand on the back of her neck, drawing her into him.

"I'm insane about you, Nicky. Insane." She flung her arms around him. "But you don't feel the same way about me."

"You don't know how I feel about you." He touched her lips with his. Once, twice, and she relaxed. When he settled his mouth against hers, she reacted with fervor, and he pressed her against the wall.

He couldn't wait; he didn't intend to let his wife tease him. She had acquiesced to being taken, but if he had, she would resent him and rush all the more quickly to Tony. Whereas Beth wanted him, and until he ended his association with her, would accept no one else.

Within a few seconds, Beth had lifted her skirts and twined her legs about his hips. He needed no urging. Beth was a woman his age who, although she might not always understand him, shared his hobbies, drinking, gambling, and rutting. With her cries of passion and her heels on his buttocks, she suited him and she satisfied him. Again and again.

Chapter 6

On the day of the regatta, the sun shone hot and high. The past week had been one of disappointment for Charlotte. Today she should be triumphant, side by side with her husband and presenting her cousin to society. Instead, she walked down the grassy banks of the Torrens River beside a man she hadn't seen for days and whom not only appeared to despise her, but also seemed determined not to enjoy her company. She might understand his attitude had she been bearing a child, but she wasn't, and in all likelihood never would.

Knowing the Hawthorns had erected a pavilion near the bridge, Charlotte soon spotted the structure. Eleanor Hawthorn, a blue-eyed blond with Nordic features, stood to one side of the draped opening, her arm raised high and waving. Nick reached the tent-like arrangement first, snatched Mrs. Hawthorn into his arms, and planted a kiss on her cheek.

"You look magnificent," he said, leaning back and smiling.

Mrs. Hawthorn patted her pregnant belly and laughed. "Like a laden barge heading to port. Charlotte, how lovely to see you here. And Sarah, too. Do come in out of the sun."

Charlotte closed her parasol and glanced at the spread on the table: tiny sandwiches, whole fish, sliced hams, cheeses, fruits, jellies, and tarts. "Has no one else arrived yet?"

Mrs. Hawthorn fingered her choker of pearls. "Everyone went down to the river to watch the first race. They'll be back here to eat soon."

"Who won?" Nick idly pulled a grape from a bunch. This morning, he had arrived home late, and he had quickly changed into a dark blue jacket and light trousers. As usual, he looked striking.

"Tony's team. James rowed in your place." Mrs. Hawthorn turned to an auburn-haired lady who appeared from outside with a belly that looked as near term as Mrs. Hawthorn's. "Do you all know Mrs. Amelia Penrith?"

Apparently, Nick did, and he shook the lady's hand. Next, Lady Grace drifted into the tent, followed by Daphne, Hubert, and Emily Downing.

Charlotte greeted Emily and the Graces, and Daphne aimed a smile at Sarah.

"You look lovely today, Sarah, if I may call you Sarah," Daphne said, examining Sarah's new pale blue gown. "Just as lovely as you did the day you came to call."

Sarah glanced at Daphne. "Thank you. Looking nice is a change for me, but a habit for you. I do like your hat, Daphne. Is it designed by Madame Fleur?"

Daphne nodded, causing the bouquet of pink silk peonies on the side of her shady straw hat to jiggle. "Mama's taste matches Madame's. You must sit with us, Sarah, so that we can gossip about everyone who isn't here."

At that moment, in a welter of voices, four jacketless gentlemen dressed in white shirts and cream trousers arrived, boisterously slapping each other on the back.

Nick took two glasses of champagne from the servant who was circulating with a silver tray and passed one to Charlotte. Draining his glass, he aimed a disinterested face at the group. "You won?"

"Did you arrive too late to see our resounding victory?" Tony Hawthorn put his arm around his wife's waist.

She passed him his jacket and introduced Amelia Penrith's husband to Charlotte and Sarah while Luke Worthing aimed a faked punch at Nick's midriff.

"We won without you," Luke said.

Nick shrugged. "Why wouldn't you?"

"With me as their handicap?" James piled his plate with salmon. Tony Hawthorn's younger brother had the same dark hair, blue eyes, and cleft chin. "According to them, they would be sure to lose if they had to replace you with me, despite the fact that I also had a Cambridge blue."

Surprised, Charlotte turned her head to Nick, who tilted his eyebrows carelessly.

Her chin lifted. "My husband has hidden talents, rowing in circles being the least of them." Stiff-faced, she brought her champagne to her lips and actually sipped the ghastly liquid.

Mr. Worthing stared between her and her husband. "Very much the least," he said, buttoning his russet jacket. "He's ex-rower. His other activities leave him no time to practice."

She carefully placed her almost full glass on the table. "He had an opportunity to practice not two weeks ago."

Nick turned. "But I was sadly out of condition." He picked up her glass. "As you saw."

Charlotte eyed him. "Acting is another of your accomplishments."

"And drinking, yet another." He took a mouthful of her champagne.

"Which was the only reason why I..." Charlotte glanced around. She sounded exactly like a nagging wife.

"I know. You don't approve of my drinking."

Mr. Worthing frowned. "No one does. You've made drinking into a competitive sport and one you're more likely—"

"Luke is out of sorts with Nick." Mrs. Hawthorn gave Mr. Worthing a chiding glance as her guests gathered around the table and loaded their plates with food. "He wanted their old team to row today, but Nick wasn't interested."

"I suspect he's sorry now the team has won." Charlotte kept her tone cool.

Mrs. Hawthorn laughed.

"Not a bit." Nick polished off the dregs of Charlotte's drink. He stared in the direction of the river. "I'm glad to hear I'm replaceable."

"Not easily replaceable, though." Mrs. Hawthorn glanced to the opened side of the tent where Sarah stood with the single ladies. "Luke, have you met Charlotte's cousin?" She beckoned Sarah.

Mr. Worthing stood with his eyebrows raised as Sarah approached. "Miss Page and I have met, yes."

Sarah stared at him blankly. "Surely not?"

"A number of times," Mr. Worthing said, jutting his jaw. "I'm a former suitor of your cousin, but possibly you missed me in the crowd."

When Sarah's eyes narrowed, Charlotte said, "She's joking with you, Mr. Worthing. I'm sure she danced with you at the Hawthorn's ball."

"You'd best call me Luke. Your husband does. What do you plan to do, Miss Page, now that you are on your own?"

"I'm not on my own and I plan to find a terribly rich, terribly handsome, terribly clever husband for myself."

"In that order?"

"Strictly," she answered, clearly more interested in the arched stone bridge, which had filled with carriages bearing onlookers. Toward North Adelaide, the church spires competed with the tall chimneys.

"I'm safe, then. I'm far more clever than I am rich." Mr. Worthing's face creased with a satisfied smile.

Sarah's expression closed.

"I imagine the next race will begin soon." Charlotte glanced at Nick.

"Nick, if that's so, could we go down to the river to watch?" Sarah said, stepping behind Luke Worthing.

"As you wish, princess." Nick scooped his arm around Sarah and within seconds was absorbed into the crowd.

Charlotte rubbed the back of her neck. During her schooling, she'd been taught who to seat with whom around a dining table, she knew the precise placing of the flatware and plates, she could correctly line up a series of wine glasses for each course, and she could make a bunch of weeds into a formal table arrangement. She'd been groomed as the perfect wife for a successful man—but her husband neither knew nor cared.

"Princess?" Luke put out his hand. "Let's get out of here."

She took his arm. She'd always been very careful around Luke who had shown a clear interest in her, as had James. However, James had mumbled something about Tony and suitability, and he had become a graceful dancing partner, which had relieved her of the responsibility of turning him down. Luke, her only other option for marriage, had worried her by acting with an unwarranted possessiveness. Then, when Nick had supposedly attempted to ravish her, Luke stood back and left her holding her torn bodice. If he'd cared for her, he would have defended her.

After she had positioned her parasol, Luke wove her down the bank of the river. Soft-leaved trees partly obscured the view on the other side. People brushed past laughing and chattering. Two small boys chased each other around men's legs and women's skirts. One grabbed for balance at the waist of a woman holding a cloth-covered basket and almost toppled her.

"Over there," Luke said, pointing. "Nick and your cousin if I'm not mistaken." He steered Charlotte toward the couple, and with a determined clamp of his jaw, he reached around Sarah, spun her around, and walked off with her.

Nick lifted his eyebrows and stood staring after the two. "A nifty move," he said, turning to Charlotte, "but unnecessary. His chivalry is misplaced. I'm sure you would rather be gossiping about gowns with the other ladies."

She glanced away. "I didn't give you a chance to prove your skill as a rower. I was presumptive."

"Or presumptuous."

"Is there a difference?" She caught his gaze.

"Presumptuous means being an ass." He jammed his hands into his trouser pockets.

She laughed, wryly amused by his subtle insult. "Then I was being presumptive. Which means 'taking for granted.'"

"You're implying *I'm* presumptuous. An ass." He inclined his head, and his lips relaxed. "Touché. Now let's watch the race. The finish rope is over there. The skiffs will cross within minutes. The Port Adelaide team is ahead by a good length."

"They look equal." She wanted to hold his arm, but she didn't dare touch him.

"That's the angle. See that. Two lengths."

A tug around her waist jerked her sideways. Her parasol bounced onto the grass as beery breath blew over her face. A stocky stranger loomed over her, leered, and tightened his arm around her waist. She put her palms on his chest and leaned back. "This is rather embarrassing."

He grinned. "Not for me."

"Charlotte," Nick said in a bored voice. "Do leave the poor gentleman alone. I'm sure he would like to go and watch the race elsewhere."

The man sniggered. "Who's the dainty flower? Your sister?"

"He's my husband and he's a very, very jealous man," she said, using her firmest voice. "So you'd best let me go before he—"

"—hits me with his pretty parasol." A blast of stale onions came with a derisive laugh.

"Take your hands off my wife, *now*," Nick said in an irritatingly calm voice.

The man snorted. "'Cos a toff says so? I think not. She likes me. And I like her."

As she twisted, he lurched backward into Nick, said, "Oof," and tumbled onto the grass. Nick passed over her parasol, which had closed. Trembling, she reached for him and clutched his arm with one hand. He began to move her away, but on her second panicked step, the man grabbed Nick by the shoulder and spun him around.

Nick raised both palms in a gesture of surrender. "Don't push your luck. Charlotte, return to the pavilion."

She stood watching two more males in rough twill trousers move to stand behind her assailant. "Not without you," she said shakily.

"Leave," Nick said in a hard voice. He scanned the crowd behind her. "Your presence is not required. Take her, Luke."

Her breath short, she half turned.

Luke grabbed her by both arms. "Leave Nick to deal with this." He lifted her into the crowd.

She found her feet and slapped at his encircling fingers. "Nick will be beaten to a pulp by those...ruffians. Let me go back to him."

He put his arm around her waist and tried to move her up the bank. The pushing bystanders occupied every inch of space. "A sight I'd enjoy, but there are only three of them."

Tony's head appeared above the crowd. "Luke. Leave her be."

Hot cheeked, Charlotte twisted out of Luke's grip. He recaptured her, his hand around her shoulders. "I'm following Nick's instructions, though I would have preferred to stay and watch."

Charlotte's eyes hurt. "You're heartless."

"Is Nick fighting?" Tony tried to see over the heads of the crowd.

"He's found an acceptable outlet for whatever eats at him."

"With how many?"

Luke laughed. "Only three."

Tony made a wry face at Luke. "I'll referee. Charlotte, Nick won't need help, and he won't thank any of us for offering. Don't worry about him, he's... Ah, here he is."

Charlotte flung herself at Nick, squeezed her arms around him, and pressed her cheek against his chest. When he winced, she let him go, hoping she hadn't exacerbated an injury. Her throat thick with guilt, she examined his handsome, unmarked face.

He cleared his throat. "My apologies. I shouldn't have dragged that out. I'll have the lout apologize to you, too."

"I thought they would macerate you."

Nick inclined his head. "Thank you for caring."

"You should have left when I did."

Sarah appeared. Arms crossed, she moved to confront Luke. "May I presume you forgot me?"

"I must have." He scratched his ear. "Good Lord. Who could credit it?"

Sarah gave him a glare, which softened when she glanced at Nick. "You were wonderful. I truly hope those bullies can't swim. He's incredible, isn't he, Charlotte?"

"I tried my best to avoid fisticuffs," Nick said in a lofty voice.

"Didn't want a fight?" Tony glanced sideways at Nick. "You probably started it."

"On my word, I didn't, did I, Charlotte?"

"No." She noted the laughter lurking around his mouth. "You did your best to avoid a fight as you said." Stupidly unsteady, she walked into the empty tent.

Nick followed her inside. "I suspect I should have laid that tub of lard at your feet."

"Should I suspect you could?"

"Of course."

She faced him, furious. "I ought to push *you* into the river. Why are you so determined not to let me know a thing about you?"

He ran his knuckles from her cheek to her jaw. "My life is an open book. Should you wish to turn the pages, you could."

"End this, Nick." Tony stood, blocking the entry. "If you embroiled your wife for your entertainment, apologize."

"He didn't embroil me," Charlotte said as Nick's palm slid to the center of her spine. "He again showed me the folly of erroneous assumpt—"

Nick's mouth dropped over hers. Arching her into his full length, he lifted her hand onto the side of his neck, flattening her palm onto his sun-warmed skin. He smelled of spirits and clean linen, and she melted, curling her fingers into the crisp hair on his nape. Her eyes closed as his tongue teased inside her lips. He tasted male and thrilling. His size and strength excited her, and his hand dropped to her behind, spanning her bottom, raising her higher against him. She wanted to clutch him, and hold him, and never let him go.

Then he lifted his head. "Is that the sort of apology you meant?" he asked Tony, his mouth disdainful and his eyes hard. "Or do you think I've forgotten she's *my* wife?"

She turned.

Tony stood, hands at his sides, his face stiff.

A hollow formed in the pit of Charlotte's belly. She dropped her grip on her husband and stepped back. He had kissed her only because he thought Tony was watching.

"No one has forgotten she's your wife," Tony said. "And so if you have finished apologizing, I'll let the others in."

Nick smoothed the front of his trousers, buttoned his jacket, and found Charlotte a canvas chair, where she sat straight-backed watching Nell hurry toward her, followed by Mr. and Mrs. Penrith.

"I just heard what happened." Nell sat beside her and took her hands. "I'm so sorry you were put through that dreadful experience."

Charlotte stared. "Oh, by that awful man. You must think I make a habit of being accosted."

Nell laughed. "You were certainly accosted at our ball, but Nick has redeemed himself by tossing the next aspirants into the river. You're so sweet to make a joke of this. Nick could be exactly the right husband for you if any more men try to...er, oh, dear. You can make a joke of this, but I shouldn't."

"Of course you should," Charlotte said as her cousin sat by her other side. "That's exactly what the gentlemen have been doing. Did you manage to see the race, Sarah?"

"Most of it, despite being deserted by Mr. Worthing. What do you think?" Sarah clasped her hands neatly in her lap. "The Downings have invited us to a musical evening. Emily says it will be dull, but everyone will be there. And I told Daphne we will be attending Lady Grace's supper dance."

"Lady Grace should have received our acceptance already."

"*Our* acceptance?" Nick asked, hovering around. "You didn't include me, I hope."

"Not specifically." She looped a curl behind her ear, appalled that he let everyone hear him reject a respectable invitation.

"Because I have another engagement." He shot his white cuffs and joined a noisy group of males who appeared to have been waiting for him outside.

She glanced at Nell, who lifted her shoulders with a rueful smile.

"Men," Charlotte managed to say indulgently.

Nell nodded. "It takes patience to train them."

Charlotte steeled herself. "I need to go as a chaperone for Sarah."

Nell patted her hand. "None of Nick's friends expects him to run tame in the first few weeks of marriage." She indicated the group outside. "He has built up quite a following in the past year."

Charlotte glanced outside, wondering if his young followers were the type of males he preferred. None, of course, were as attractive as he. They looked rather sporting and careless in their attire. As she watched, one tried to box with Nick, who ignored him. As Nick's wife, she understood when the lad left with slumped shoulders, though she now knew better than to care.

"Are you and Mr. Hawthorn planning on attending the Graces' supper dance too?" She laughed when Nell demonstrated her answer by glancing down at her huge belly.

Charlotte was glad, *glad*, that Nick had not been prepared to escort them to the Graces' function. Without a perpetually sozzled husband in tow, she would manage far better, and if he tried to manhandle her again, she would give him a hearty shove.

She gave Nell a sideways glance. "Could one of your charities use my sewing skills? I find that having servants has left me with too much time on my hands."

"My dear," Nell said, her smile wide. "I've never heard anything quite so wonderful. Amelia…"

While the other two ladies enthused about having another helper, Charlotte squared her shoulders. She was now an independent wife, and tomorrow she planned to see a man about a house.

Chapter 7

Smoke furled at head height, masking the dim lights in Spenders, the most popular gambling rooms in Stepney, a seedy area close to the city of Adelaide. The drunk, the sober, the clean, and the unwashed stood four deep around the gaming tables. Nick glanced at the finger-marked roulette table, wondering if he wanted to place a bet.

Mrs. Beth Blocker, her brown hair upswept, dressed in a pink satin crinoline and long white gloves, leaned forward to place a sovereign on the table. "Red seven," she said to the croupier, a man with sloping shoulders and a sharp nose.

"Imagine seeing you here," said a sardonic voice behind Nick.

He turned, eyeing Luke, dressed formally in black trousers and a tailed jacket. "Imagine seeing *you* here."

Behind, a group of young bloods noisily disputed a game of faro. Two ladies of the night in ankle length gaudy gowns wandered around the room, scanning for likely customers.

"Do you plan to introduce me to your friend?" Luke stared through the gloom at Beth.

"Mrs. Blocker, Mr. Worthing," Nick said curtly.

Beth smiled and Luke raised his eyebrows. With a shrug, she turned back to the wheel. When her money went into the pile in front of the croupier, she put out her hand. Nick filled her palm with more gold coins.

"A never ending pastime." Luke watched the wheel spin. "It surprises me that this doesn't bore you."

"Did you enjoy the regatta on Saturday?" Nick blew a ring of smoke into the fog above their heads. Yellow nicotine stains patterned the ceiling.

"Certain aspects," Luke answered casually. "I might have enjoyed it more if you'd had the trouncing you deserved."

"I don't suppose you'll ever see that."

"What I do see is a married man with his mistress."

Nick shrugged. "I don't hide her."

"What does Charlotte think about Mrs. Blocker?"

"Charlotte doesn't think anything about anything."

"She doesn't know." Luke faced Nick, his expression serious. "But she'll hear if you can't be a little more discreet."

"I can't be."

"Curse you, Nick. Why didn't you escort your wife to the Grace's supper dance tonight instead?"

Nick lifted his glass, checking the level. "Not that it's any of your business, but I'm sure my lack of availability won't spoil her pleasure."

Luke gave a snort that could have been a laugh. "I wouldn't know about her pleasure since Miss Page is staying overnight with the Graces. She didn't need Charlotte's chaperonage."

Nick drew his eyebrows together. "Charlotte didn't attend the supper dance?"

"She accepted an invitation from Tony instead, according to Miss Page."

"She's with Tony?" Nick's blood began a slow boil. The kiss at the regatta should have ended Tony's insane pursuit.

Luke pursed his lips. "What sort of husband doesn't know how his wife amuses herself?"

Nick gave a deliberately offensive leer. "I may be a very understanding husband, but I won't leave Tony to ride my wife whenever he chooses." A punch at his shoulder caught him by surprise. So, too, did the shocked expression on Luke's face.

"Rephrase that. You won't leave Tony to ride *with* her whenever he chooses. Say it," Luke demanded in a set voice.

"Damn you." Teeth clenched, Nick raised his forearm and blocked Luke's next blow. "You won't get another hit in, and you know it. You caught me by surprise the first time. I hadn't realized you were so loyal to Tony."

"Tony doesn't need my support. Charlotte does. You should be defending her against gossip, not spreading it. You can't honestly believe Tony would have an affair with your wife."

Nick bared his teeth in a hard smile. "Tony is accustomed to taking whatever he wants."

"If he is seeing her, he probably thinks she needs support. I certainly do. And I intend to be her friend if she will have me as such."

"Perhaps you would be better off befriending a wife of your own."

Luke gave a scathing laugh. "Damn you, too. I was befriending her until you snatched her from behind my back. If I ever have an opportunity to serve you the same backhanded turn you served me, I'll take it."

"You've always had the same opportunities as I have." Nick stepped back and hid his expression by flicking ash from his shirtfront. "But I've yet to see you take one." He reached over, circled his fingers around Beth's elbow, kissed her bare shoulder, and, despite her vehement protest, guided her to a Hackney waiting outside. He left her at her front door and went home.

His wife had a lesson to learn.

* * * *

Charlotte entered her lamp-lit sitting room, stripping off her long gloves. For the first time in her married life, Nick's bedroom door stood agape. She veered as his shadow appeared, blocking all but a halo of light from his room. "I'm sorry. Did I wake you?"

Nick yawned, rubbing his hair into a tousle. Beneath his gold brocaded dressing robe, only his white toes showed. "I was dozing. What's the time?" His sleepy gaze examined her face.

"Around midnight." She reached for the bell-pull near the fireplace.

"No, don't disturb Vera." He moved toward her, his face expressionless. "I'll help you."

"She'll be waiting for me to summon her."

"I told her she could retire an hour ago."

"I'm happy enough to leave her to her rest." She turned her back, lifting the curls off her neck, waiting for him to undo her gown as before. "In fact, I told her I can manage alone, but she would have none of it. I've managed alone for twen—"

"We can talk while you're undressing." He put an arm around her and steered her into her bedroom.

She broke his hold. She had no intention of disrobing while he was in her room. Their marriage of convenience did not allow such an intimacy. Staring at him, she dropped her reticule onto her dressing table, followed by her silk shawl.

However, ignoring her silent rebellion, he spun her around and began on the buttons at the back of her gown. "Where have you been tonight?" His breath stirred the curls on the nape of her neck. A shiver of apprehension cooled her skin.

"At the Hawthorn's house. I meant to accompany Sarah to the Grace's supper dance, but Daphne invited her to stay the night. I saw my presence as superficial."

"Superfluous. You could have gone, nonetheless. I doubt you would have suffered a dearth of dancing partners while Luke was there."

She glanced at him over her shoulder while he concentrated on her buttons. "I would have been quite bored, you know, standing around when I had other things to do. Then Nell sent a message via Tony asking me to join her at home and I was reprieved." Holding her loosened red and white bodice to her chest, she stepped behind the dressing-screen, nervous that he might follow. When he didn't, she began to disrobe.

"How long have you known Nell and Tony?" His tone sounded set.

She stepped out of her gown. "Six months or so. I met them in Stirling while I was staying with the Graces at their country property."

"Hmm. Just after Nell announced her interesting condition. He loves her, Charlotte. He'll cut you when she's had the baby."

She paused, considering. Although she would happily be cut by Tony, she liked Nell. Despite Charlotte being some years younger and not about to be a mother, they shared a common interest. "I don't think he will. It would look so very rude, wouldn't it, while I enjoy Nell's good graces?" Slinging her gown over the screen, she peered around the carved edge. Nick was sitting on the side of her bed, staring in her direction.

"Everyone enjoys her good graces." He frowned. "She is one of the most sensible women you could meet. Usually," he added with a puzzled lift of his shoulders.

"Um... My nightgown is under my pillow. Would you mind handing it to me?"

"You won't need it." He swung his bare feet onto her bed, leaning back against the carved headboard and crossing his arms over his chest.

"I don't know you well enough to appear in front of you in my chemise."

"You're married to me, for God's sake. I'm sure I won't be the first person to see you partially disrobed."

Her cheeks hot, she came out from behind the screen, snatched at her nightgown, and took the garment back with her. Breathing hard, she removed her chemise, donned the lacy gown, and chin raised, she moved out to her dressing table. In silence, she began removing her hairpins. She slapped a handful onto the polished satinwood while she watched him in the mirror, wondering why he stayed if he only wanted to be disobliging. His gaze connected with hers in the reflection. He looked...lonely.

"Any time you want to join me, or us, you only have to say so. You are included in every invitation I accept," she said, reluctantly.

"I wasn't included tonight."

"You weren't even home when I received the note."

"And what would have happened had I borne you company?"

"You would have been mightily bored. Amelia was there, too, and we mainly talked about babies."

"What did you contribute?"

"Very little. I don't know anything about babies." She began to brush her hair.

"Only how to make them."

She stood and turned to face him. "Thank you for waiting up for me, but I think I'll go to bed now."

"Is that a dismissal?"

"Stay if you wish," she said, knowing he wouldn't. She put her brush down, walked to her bed, lifted the covers, and slipped in. "I used to talk to Sarah at night, and I found that very comforting."

His lips pursed. "So, I can stay if we talk about gowns?" He lifted off the bed and removed his dressing robe. Beneath, he wore trousers, but his chest was bare, the smooth white skin stretched tight across his muscles.

Without a doubt, she had married a man she could happily gaze at from dawn to dusk. She drew a long breath. If he meant to share her bed, she could talk to him, and perhaps eventually they would become…friends? She didn't need his heart.

"Sarah and I didn't discuss gowns. She isn't interested in fashions. We simply chatted about life and our hopes and dreams."

He climbed in and turned to her, scrutinizing her face. "Which I mean to do. My first hope is that you won't see Tony again."

"You're saying you don't want me to go out into society?" she asked, her chest beginning to thump.

"I don't want you to go out into *his* society."

"If you think he is talking about you or questioning me about you, you're mistaken. I don't think he has ever—"

"The man's not a fool. Of course he—"

"Well, I don't want you to go out gambling." She folded her arms.

"What?"

"And I don't want you to drink so much. I'd like you to come home a little earlier occasionally, and I think you ought to help your father." She firmed her jaw.

"Help my father do what?" He sat forward, his face rigid.

"He wants you to learn how to run his businesses."

His lips compressed. While he focused his frowning gaze on the opposite wall, she touched his forearm.

"Surely you know that."

"He has made an occasional mention," he said in a heavy tone. He swiveled away and turned down the lamp. His upper body brushed against her. Surprisingly, he dipped his head and pressed a kiss on her lips.

"You're not cross?"

"I'm not sure." He kissed her again.

Her hand lifted to his shoulder, but before she had time to turn her head, he gave her a third kiss. This one lingered until surprise left and pleasure began, and guilt. She'd meant to shove him away if he'd tried to kiss her again, but instead she flattened her palm and pushed against him but so half heartedly that he seemed not to notice. He put one hand behind her head and the other on the curve of her spine. Despite knowing he couldn't be enjoying this, she accepted his experimentation in breathless silence. When his hard male part pressed between the juncture of her legs, her treacherous body lurched with hope, or desire, and she couldn't fight her need to be held by him, nor her need to touch him.

She folded her fingers around his heavy male part, which appeared to be bare. The intense pleasure of the intimacy heated her into a full body blush. Her heart thudded in her ears, and she breathed heavily. For a moment, he didn't move, but then he pulled back against her palm. Guiltily, she dropped her hold.

He exhaled with a hiss. Then he gave a short harsh laugh. The bed trembled as he rolled over, presenting his back to her. While she agonized about him being repulsed by her touch, his breaths grew deeper. He seemed to have fallen into a sound sleep.

Although she had accepted that she would never experience the pleasure of the flesh, she ached for the unknown.

Chapter 8

Pre-breakfast gallops were not Nick's style, but last night he'd slept without waking. Perhaps having an early night helped. Perhaps sleeping with his wife helped. When he slept with her, he knew where she was.

He reached the parklands. Despite the cover of the trees, he spotted Tony riding his big black alongside Charlotte, impeccable in her tailored outfit and her green-feathered hat.

"Good morning," Nick shouted, determinedly loud enough to set a family of magpies fluttering.

The couple reined in. Tony turned and tipped his hat.

Charlotte showed a face covered with black netting. "Good morning, Nick," she said in a constrained voice as his horse sidled up to hers.

He had expected nothing more. Her stealthy movements in the dawn light had awoken him, and he had remained ostensibly asleep in her bed. After she'd left, he hastily donned his clothes and strode to the stables, intent on catching her at her sneaky little game.

"Escort Mrs. Alden home, Rob," he said in a curt voice to the young groom who accompanied him. "I want a few words with Mr. Hawthorn."

"It's not necessary." Charlotte shifted her reins to her other hand.

"Didn't you promise to love, honor, and obey me?"

Charlotte nodded slowly, and without further ado, she moved her horse to Rob's, which baulked.

"This here pony don't like Red Robin." Rob's mouth turned down. "Mortal enemies, they is."

"Nevertheless, you will accompany my wife home."

"I'll ride in front, Rob," Charlotte said, her posture precise and her instructions to her prancing horse invisible. "The dun never minds following."

With a resigned shrug, Rob left behind Charlotte. Nick leaned over to control his horse that showed a willingness to bite Tony's, acting out his rider's desires.

Before Nick could form his words Tony said, "I hear you want Charlotte to cut herself off from society the way you have."

"Not all society. Just you."

Tony's lips stretched and turned down at the corners. "Nell says our occasional morning meetings are causing talk. Normally, she rides with me, but with our baby due soon, she just isn't up to it."

"I've been accused of being disreputable, but you take the prize."

Tony frowned. "The talk doesn't bother me."

"The talk bothers Charlotte's husband."

"Why? She and I ride together in full view of the world."

Nick gave a snort of disgust. "You should have set up Charlotte in a house of her own before I married her. You can surely afford it."

Tony looked down his nose at Nick. "She was already in a house of her own with her cousin, which is far more acceptable to society."

"In what way could that possibly be acceptable?" Nick asked, his voice tight with fury. His horse lunged at Tony's black, which reared.

"Steady on."

Tony fought his nervy horse while Nick backed his. After some seconds of skirting each other, the horses finally calmed enough to stand nose to nose, breathing heavily.

"Miss Page is a perfectly respectable chaperone," Tony said.

"Do you usually set up a mistress with a chaperone?"

"Steady on," Tony said again, but this time to Nick. "You implied on your wedding day that you and Charlotte had a previous liaison. If she was anyone's mistress, she was yours, information that completely surprised me."

Nick narrowed his eyes. "On the night of your ball, I asked why you were so set on marrying her off to me and you said—let me let me think of your exact words—you had an 'interest' in her. If you weren't tupping her, what was the interest that you refused to discuss when I asked you?"

Tony's black shifted restively. "At that stage, I was interested in averting a scandal. You were found with her in my garden, her gown ripped from the shoulder to the waist. You refused to explain yourself." He shook his head. "What society saw was a young innocent virgin whose reputation had just been shot to pieces, nobly protecting the reputation of a drunken sot."

"Nobly," Nick repeated, twisting his mouth. "Sometimes I wonder if she is as ingenuous as she seems."

Tony rubbed his chin. "You wonder? Don't you know?"

"We've had few *conversations*," Nick said, hoping to imply a more intimate relationship. He could at least set himself up as competition for Tony.

Tony examined his expression. "How much do you know about her?"

"She's a respectably born orphan educated with the daughters of the best families, with whom she associates. She has no great fortune and a dependent cousin." Nick offered a satisfied smile, hoping his glibness hid his ignorance, which he'd only just realized. When he'd agreed to marry Charlotte, his only thought was gaining an heir.

"She went to Miss Main's school with Daphne. And that's about as much as I know, too. Whenever I try to get more detail from her, she smiles politely and changes the subject."

Nick slapped his crop on his boot. "You should ask her in bed. With the lights out, she tends to confide."

"*What* did you say?"

"Talk to her before you tup her."

"You're tempting me to take a swing at you."

"Try by all means," Nick said through his teeth. "Luke managed to take me by surprise last night. Perhaps you'll have the same luck."

"Not while you're watching me." A slight crinkle formed around Tony's eyes. "Take it from me, I'm not tupping your wife. I have my own."

"You need to remember that while you're with mine."

"I remember it every minute of every day, and I bless my luck." Tony took a deep breath. "Though, you're right. Charlotte is *exceedingly* beautiful. When I first saw her, I was completely floored."

"And yet you bless your luck to be married to Nell?"

Tony raised his eyebrows. He was, unlike Luke, hard to rile. "She was with James, and they both turned toward me at the same instant." His gaze held Nick's for some five seconds, and then he lifted a hand from his reins in an open gesture. "James told me he meant to court her. Charlotte had completely bedazzled him." He paused. "I thought it best to find out who she was."

"And who is she?" Nick asked in a contemptuous tone.

"Fortunately, after a few more words with James, he came to his senses." Tony cleared his throat. "He has another female on his mind, and until he can put her out of it, he's not a candidate for marriage, and so I told him."

"You're not his guardian."

"Sometimes I'm simply the pup's voice of reason." Tony held Nick's gaze. "As in times gone by, I have been yours."

Nick glanced at a group of gray box trees swaying in the wind. "You want me to believe you're not having an affair with my wife."

"I'm *not* having an affair with your wife. I'm in love with my own."

"What, then, is the reason for your interest in Charlotte?"

Dark clouds had begun to gather. Tony cleared his throat. "A whim. She was a beautiful nobody who was turning the heads of all my friends. I couldn't see a reason why my wife shouldn't befriend her."

"Hence her invitation to your ball?"

"She had acceptable references—the Graces and the Downings." Tony shrugged. "I suspect she could have had Luke had she not been compromised by you."

"Luke wouldn't marry a woman who'd been tupped by one of his friends," Nick said with a twisted smile. "He's a straight-laced lawyer."

Although the three had studied together in England, Luke had been the only one who had needed to take a profession seriously. At times, Nick envied Luke's independence.

"Or," Nick said, "he wouldn't if he knew."

Tony nodded. "I appreciate that you made *quite sure* he did know you'd had her previously."

Nick's mouth clamped. His hasty lie about a previous dalliance with Charlotte had been meant to prepare Luke for a six-month baby after her marriage. "So, do you now expect me to sanction your meetings with my wife?"

Tony gazed across the park. "We ride together. Nothing more. Our horses are from the same stable and have the same breeding. We share a love of horses that few do. I see no harm. While you are agreeable, the gossip has no teeth." He turned his horse toward home. "I like Charlotte. She doesn't gossip, she doesn't sermonize, and she doesn't insist on constant attention. She's interesting in that she's so self-contained."

"An attribute I appreciate in a woman," Nick said, realizing he spoke the truth. Certain aspects of Charlotte's personality were commendable, but he preferred to look no deeper. He desired her and that was damnable enough.

Tony guided his horse to the riding path. "She has others, though she's so darned beautiful that it's almost impossible to see past her features." He laughed, urged his horse into a gallop, and disappeared.

Puzzled by the laugh, Nick took his horse up to a slow canter. Unfortunately, he believed Tony, a friend since early school days, a serious boy who had managed to tolerate Nick's frivolity long enough to learn appreciation for the lighter moments in life. Luke completed the trio of contrasts with his pugnacious nature, his quick judgments, and his staunch support.

However, if Nick believed Tony, he made a mockery of his own future. He had married a woman for a baby that didn't exist. He had reviled the same woman for taking a lover who also didn't exist. Now he was stuck in a world that didn't exist for him, the respectable world of men with wives.

However, Charlotte hadn't tricked him into marriage. She might have ripped her clothes and screamed for aid during the first ball of the season, but only the erroneous impression that she carried Tony's baby had decided Nick to marry her. She'd suggested that a fair exchange for his hand and fortune would be in not exposing him as a sodomite, more gently worded as *if you help me, I'll help you.* If either of them had tricked the other, he had done so, letting her think he wouldn't be a husband to her for the wrong reason.

He wouldn't touch a virgin bride, which he was beginning to believe she was, but only because of his intention to never again father a child. When she discovered the truth about his sexual preferences, she would be humiliated and know that not only had she been accused of lying and suspected of adultery, unjustly, she had also been rejected. This was a cruelty he now doubted she deserved.

She wanted wealth and social success. The first she had gained with marriage, but the second she could only gain with his compliance. He suspected he owed her that, if only for her honoring their invalid bargain.

* * * *

Charlotte watched Nick's face at breakfast, but his expression was unreadable. She would curl up and die if he had mentioned her mythical pregnancy to Tony for she herself would never have said a word about the confusion she had caused in her husband's mind. Though, if Nick had, she would bluff her way through somehow.

She began a light conversation that his father changed to property matters. Nick ignored this, his preoccupation apparent. He ate a large breakfast and sipped slowly from his tankard.

Finally, he rose to his feet. "What do you say to a night at the theater?" he asked, including his father in his gaze.

"The whole family?" Charlotte hid her surprise. She had expected at some time to be chided. Apparently, Nick's conversation with Tony had concluded satisfactorily, and she and Nick had made another bargain— she would evade Tony in the park, no loss for he made her tense, and Nick wouldn't go out every night to gamble. She hadn't expected the bonus of Nick as her escort, a clear indication to the world that her husband was content with his marriage, a must if a nobody were to be a social success.

He nodded, pausing. "Sarah, too, if she arrives back today."

* * * *

"The Queen's Theater?" Sarah said later that afternoon as she picked through her new gowns. "A supper dance last night and now this. I thought I would be your companion for the rest of my life, but you really are launching me into society. You're amazing, Charlotte, truly."

Charlotte shook her head. "It's none of my doing. This was Nick's idea. I assume he is no longer tempted to rip my gown at social functions, and we may now be seen together."

Sarah laughed. "I expect he's been quite embarrassed."

"No doubt. Are you planning on wearing the pink gown?"

"Probably." Sarah shook out the silk gown patterned with sprigs of tiny cream roses that Nick had bought for her. "Do you know what we will see?"

"A farce, I believe. I have some ribbon for your hair that will look delightful with that gown. Now, tell me who you danced with last night."

"Oh, everyone," Sarah said airily. "It wasn't too formal, you know. Rather than having a dance card to fill, we were pulled onto the floor by our partners: James Hawthorn, Hubert Grace, Ralston Hunter, Luke Worthing—you know the crowd."

"It sounds like a romp." Charlotte adopted a severe expression. "Young people these days simply don't know how to behave. In my day—" A slipper hit her shoulder. She laughed and left the room.

That night, she changed into the first gown she had purchased in more than two years. The generous allowance Alfred had granted her, strictly budgeted, covered the cost of the creation after she had hired a certain building.

She stood in front of the mirror while Vera tightened the corset and tossed the full burgundy skirts over her head. As the maid dealt with the buttons at the back, Charlotte said, "Help Miss Sarah when you've finished."

Vera left while Charlotte ruffled the pale orange trimmings on her gown, knowing she could change them to purple and have an entirely new creation. She smiled. Habit died hard. Too late she noticed the pink satin ribbon meant for her cousin's hair had been left on her bed. After gathering up the tie, she walked toward Sarah's room. The door stood ajar.

"Did you have a nice stay away, miss?" Vera asked.

"Very. I had such fun dancing and flirting."

"But you're glad to be home."

"Home? I've never really had a home."

"Go on with you. If this isn't your home, I don't know what is. Mr. Alfred fairly dotes on you."

"He does?" Sarah said in a voice that sounded surprised. "Well, I fairly dote on him, too."

Charlotte tapped on the door and entered, somewhat shaken. Sarah had shared Charlotte's home for the past eight years, and Charlotte had not been aware that Sarah didn't consider that to be her home as well.

"You left Miss Sarah's ribbon in my room, Vera." Charlotte checked Sarah's face, which looked softer. Her eyes were bright, and her mouth curved upward.

"Lovely," she said, as Vera entwined the pink ribbon in her curls.

"Miss Sarah looks like one of them foreign princesses, don't she?"

"I'm not certain about foreign, but I'll accept princess," Sarah said, patting the thick apricot roll of hair at her nape. Delicate curls edged her face.

"I've never seen you look more beautiful, Sarah." The pink Sarah wore brought out the red highlights in her hair and the peachy smoothness of her skin. "You'll turn every head tonight."

Sarah gave her a cynical glance. "Only if I'm standing beside you."

"Tosh," Charlotte said lightly. "You merely have to look in the mirror to see how lovely you are."

Sarah turned to her cheval mirror and examined her looks. "I might be putting on a little weight. That helps, I think."

Charlotte nodded. Now that Sarah didn't fuss all the time about her food, her skin had smoothed out a little, too.

Charlotte left the room in an optimistic mood. Both her life and Sarah's had changed for the better, which was almost as much as she needed—but not all. She also needed a certain amount of security.

When Nick joined them in the dining room, he wore tails with a black and white silk waistcoat that showed a belly flatter than a board. His narrow trousers set off his lean hips and showed the curve of his thigh—her breath shortened and she raised her gaze to his light brown hair brushed back from his chiseled face, knowing she had never been more physically aware of a man in her life.

Other than last night in bed, she had been in Nick's company for episodes only. She looked forward to being with him at the play, but although he acted the perfect gentleman while the actors were performing, as soon as the lights began to flicker on, he left to be with his cronies. She shared her observations about the show with Sarah instead while she scanned the latest fashions worn by the elite in their private boxes.

"Look over there," Sarah said in a scathing voice, indicating Luke in a box on the other side. "No, don't. I don't intend to. He'd take it as a compliment. The best way to treat him is to pretend you don't know who he is." She sounded satisfied.

"Why would I do that?"

"Oh… He has an ego that needs deflating," Sarah said in a light voice.

Charlotte nodded, remembering Luke's behavior toward Sarah at the regatta. He had treated her casually, and even now, Charlotte couldn't tell if he was a friend or enemy of her husband, which meant she was uncertain of her status with him, too.

Finally, Nick returned, a little more relaxed. In the dark of the theater, she surreptitiously inspected him, the curve of his mouth, the angle of his perfect jaw, and the tap of his fingers on his thighs. Again, her breath shortened, and she wished she could concentrate on the play rather than thinking about the hot, heavy hardness of his male part. He glanced at her, and so she eyed the stage, so conscious of his presence that when his sleeve touched her bare arm she gasped.

Through the last act of the show, she could think of little more than her embarrassing investigation of her husband's body the night before, so strangely pleasurable for her and so awkward for him. Should he seek her bed again, she would do no more than snuggle into his back. If she scrupulously behaved herself, he would grow accustomed to sleeping beside her.

Somehow, she would do as Alfred had suggested—wean Nick away from his disreputable companions.

* * * *

Nick needed a drink so badly that he'd taken one too many. Suffering from a rare bout of introspection, he opened the sitting room door for Charlotte. He had been much mistaken about her, and not only in her pregnancy and her affair. At the theater, her main aim had been to push Sarah forward. She did indeed care for her cousin.

His head pounding, he grabbed the brandy bottle waiting for him on the side table. Charlotte might as well become accustomed to him in his cups because drinking was his only release. He poured a generous measure into a glass, intending to fill the gap in his knowledge that Tony had exposed this morning.

"Just a question. I'm quite remiss not to know, but I don't. What were the full names of your parents?"

She hesitated by his bedroom door, stripping off her long white gloves, her every movement poised and understated. "My mother was Adeline Mary Dunbar. She was Sarah's mother's sister. My father was Joseph Adam Davies."

"And he was who?"

She shrugged. "A sea captain, as respectably born as my mother but with no high connections. You and your friends would say they were nobodies and that would be true. My mother was only a parson's daughter."

"I wouldn't say either of them were nobody. My father started as a furniture maker. Have you ever heard me be so crass?"

She shook her head, her eyes shaded by her incredible lashes. "Do you plan to sleep with me again tonight?"

He fingered his glass. "I hadn't planned that, no," he said, his body taking unexpected note of the idea. "Who knows what might happen if I did. I might want to fuck you."

Her eyes fixed on his face, and if she asked what the word meant... He would hate himself more than he already did, for he now believed he had the wife he didn't want, one who had no idea about him or about coupling.

Her left hand upswept her scrupulously coiffed head, showing the faultless shape of her arm and the graceful curve of her neck. She didn't appear to be wearing her wedding ring. "You have the right," she said, her voice perfectly modulated.

His blood rushed to his cock, and he turned aside, almost groaning. "But I don't want *the right*, my dear."

With almost undignified haste, he wavered into his celibate bedroom. Once seated on his bed, he lifted his glass in a toast to a woman he thought he had read from the start, a woman he had judged more harshly than anyone had ever judged him, a woman he wanted to plough the night long, not because she was beautiful and his, but in spite of those drawbacks.

Chapter 9

For Charlotte, the next week passed in a whirl. During the day, she barely had time to do a thing but pay social calls with Sarah. At night, she attended various functions with Nick among which were a musical evening, a soiree, and once without Sarah, a card party. Charlotte didn't dare win, but she enjoyed playing nonetheless.

After choosing her gown for this evening's entertainment at the home of Mr. Arnold Worthing, a politician cousin of Luke's, she stepped into her white evening gown to which she'd lately added a low black and white striped collar and a looped half-skirt of the same reclaimed fabric, blessing her mother for keeping so many old gowns. She turned her back so that Vera could hook her latest re-creation.

Vera studied her with a satisfied expression. "Want me to do your hair, ma'am?"

"Not tonight. I can manage, and I'm sure Miss Sarah would like your help."

The maid left. Charlotte gathered her dark hair into a thick bunch at her nape, pulling out a few strands and letting the curls trickle around her neck. She examined her reflection critically, noting the pale face and darkened areas under her eyes brought about by restless nights racked with guilt.

Although she'd managed her first step of moving Sarah into her circles, she'd been too successful in keeping Nick away from his, not because of her womanly charms, but because he had fettered himself with her needs. If she had beguiled him into changing his preferences, she would have seen that as fair, but him making a sacrifice for her when she had done nothing at all for him wasn't. She would rather not have a real husband than one brittle enough to snap.

As if she'd conjured him by thinking, his reflection appeared behind her. The man looked magnificent. Under his black eveningwear sat an embroidered waistcoat of red, highlighting the snowy laundering of his shirt and the elegant bow of his tie. To be worn as his accessory could only be flattering to a woman as shallow as she.

"I have a small gift for you," he said as she turned. He handed her a square, green sharkskin box.

Inside she found a gold bracelet inset with onyx and pearls, the perfect match for her gown. Her delighted smile wavered under his expression of courteous interest, and she confined herself to briefly touching his hand in appreciation of his thoughtful gesture. With her smile rivaling his for emptiness, she presented her wrist around which he fastened the piece.

Sarah knocked on her door. She looked pert and pretty in her light blue gown. "Look," she said, lifting the soft curls in front of her ears to reveal pearl earrings. "Oh, there you are, Nick. I don't know how you knew I wanted these, but they're perfect. I'll have to knit you a waistcoat in appreciation."

Nick laughed. "Spare me. Let's hope they impress whichever gentleman you have decided to impress tonight."

"I'd like to impress James Hawthorn." Sarah turned her mouth down. "But I have the idea Daphne plans to keep him for herself. I don't care. At least I'll have the chance to meet some of his friends."

"They're a ramshackle lot. You'd best stick to someone older, like Luke."

"He's far too smart for me," Sarah said in an airy voice.

Charlotte cleared her throat. "Nick gave me this lovely bracelet." She held up her arm to show Sarah.

"He must be the best husband in the world." Sarah aimed an open smile at Nick. "Let's hope I can find one half as good in my desperate hunt."

"You will find one just as good." Charlotte pulled on her gloves. "You look so lovely now."

"Lovely?" Sarah raised her eyebrows. "It's how you are inside that counts."

Charlotte knew how *she* was on the inside—conscientious, parsimonious, careful, and wracked with guilt. Why? She'd maintained her bargain with Nick. She'd covered his absentness, she'd shown the world a real marriage, and she'd not interfered with his pleasures. Smoothing on her gloves, she left for the carriage with Sarah and Nick.

In the main hall of the mansion in North Adelaide, she met Luke's second cousin, Arnold Worthing, short and stout, and his tall, slender wife who presided over the reception line. Inside the ballroom graced with a polished dark-wood floor and faux black marble columns, guests milled, glancing over each new arrival. The din covered the sound of the small orchestra tuning up for a cotillion.

Nick moved Charlotte and Sarah toward a group of welcoming faces and plucked out James Hawthorn. "Dance with Sarah," he said, urging Charlotte's cousin forward. "So that I may dance with my wife."

Without a backward glance, he took Charlotte to the ballroom floor. During the formations, she saw Sarah happily entertaining her partner by tossing words at James each time they met in the complicated patterns of the dance.

While Charlotte's feet automatically took her through the movements, she imagined lying naked with Nick. She imagined his hands on her skin, on her buttocks, and lifting her against his hard body. Her cheeks flushed and the lower part of her body filled with a sudden erotic heaviness. She would never experience coupling, but she had begun to understand carnal desire.

Before the next set, Luke joined the group. "Good news. Not two hours ago Amelia delivered a red-haired son. And I," he lowered his voice, "stayed for a while to support Ivor."

"Ah." James nodded. "That explains your tie." He pulled one end to even Luke's bow and stepped back. "And your stupid grin. You've been supporting Ivor with brandy." He left with Daphne to form a set with Emily and Hubert, and Sarah moved off with another of James's friends.

Watching them leave, Luke made a wry face at Nick. "A redheaded son. Poor Ivor is not sure whether to be pleased or suspicious."

Nick raised his eyebrows. "Should he be suspicious?"

"You know Ivor. His bastard was fair like him, and so I think he expected the same again."

Nick stood motionless, his face stiff. "Are you being obscure?"

"Not deliberately." Luke rested his lips against his closed fist and coughed. "Brandy tends to loosen the tongue. I forgot you were still in New South Wales last year when Ivor was caught out by a house-maid."

Nick frowned. "You shouldn't be discussing this in front of Charlotte."

"I shouldn't. It's past history." Luke gave her a seedy smile.

"Last year?" Charlotte asked, seeing the situation from another side entirely. Ivor would have been married around that time. "Surely that is rather awkward for Amelia?"

Nick's eyes glittered. "Apparently she accepts his bastard," he said in a deadly tone. "Or do you belong to the school of thought that says a man should be punished throughout eternity for his mistakes?" He backed a step, turned, and strode toward the opened doors leading to the outside.

Eyes wide, she stared after him.

"Forgive him," Luke said, quietly. "Heaven knows he'll never forgive himself."

"Forgive him?"

"He would have married Clara in an instant had she not already been married."

She stared at Luke, lost. "Clara?"

"Not that any of us thought he should. The woman was old enough to know better than to throw herself at him."

"She threw herself at him?"

"From the very moment she met him. She wouldn't leave him alone. Nick has...had that effect on women." He shrugged, his gaze flittering away from her.

"But he wasn't interested in women."

"He could have his pick—click his fingers—done. Women followed him in the street."

"He might not have been as flattered as you suppose."

Two lines formed between his eyebrows. "He certainly never seemed to notice the stares. Or perhaps he didn't care, which made it all the more surprising that when Clara told him about his baby, he decided to run off with her."

"His baby." Her brain numbed. "Yes, of course he did the right thing."

"It's unfortunate she died after the boy or Nick wouldn't still be blaming himself. He was just twenty-three at the time, younger than James is now."

She concentrated on breathing. "Hush. You don't need to convince me. I understand." Her voice sounded perfectly normal.

God forgive me for my sins, Nick had said, his words slurred, the blood pouring from his head wound while she'd tried to stem the flow. *I wanted him.* Him. His son.

"And I hope to be forgiven, myself, for causing an upset."

Luke's flattened palms warmed her hands. "Nick doesn't have a temper. He'll be back."

She forced a smile. "Now, do you mean to dance with me or do you intend to continue chastising me?"

He tucked her arm under his and led her to the floor.

She performed the country-dance, her head whirling faster than her feet. Rather than wanting to be forgiven for desiring another man, Nick had been grieving the loss of his son, a far more likely event, given that she appeared to be the only person in the world who thought he was bent. Perhaps now she ought to be chastising herself, but when she saw Luke's boney face transformed by a wide smile, she realized he was merely returning hers.

He had done her a great favor. But for his thoughtless speech, she may well have spent months in ignorance of Nick's past. Her heart sang, and she whirled about on feet scarcely touching the floor. Perhaps she had based her marriage on a faulty premise, but at least she knew now her husband was no sodomite. He did not have *other interests* as he said.

She had a real husband. She didn't need to hope to be an aunt. One day she could be a mother herself, God willing. She didn't have to spend a lifetime of guilt condoning Nick's illegal practices, whatever they might have been. As the set finished, she saw Nick return to the sidelines. Isolated by the stark expression on his face, he propped his back against the wall and crossed his arms. His former illicit relationship must have taught him a very harsh lesson about ostracism from society.

Suddenly self-conscious, she let Luke deliver her to her husband, who was no longer the man she'd married. This new man stood square shouldered and lean hipped, the masculine strength of his face apparent. He couldn't be manlier if he tried, but of course he didn't try. A man with his natural elegance had no need.

"You must think me very narrow-minded," she said, unable to hold his penetrating gaze.

"Not at all," he said, his words clipped. "You must think me very petulant."

"Not at all. I don't want anyone's punishment for a mistake to be extended to eternity. Surely a month or two would suffice." She lifted her head.

His mouth relaxed. "As long as the punishment is harsh."

"Served with undercooked offal."

"Certainly with braised liver." He almost smiled, and she saw the truth of Luke's words. Nick didn't have a temper. Nor did he hold a grudge.

With virtually nothing more to say, she stared across to the dancers. "The orchestra is playing a waltz."

His eyes met hers. With a tilt of his eyebrows, he indicated the dance floor. She nodded, and, without a word, he took her into his arms and glided her into a waltz, her first with him. His clasp was firm with one palm in the middle of her spine and the other supporting her hand. Each step made her more aware of his thighs scraping against her skirts, forcing her to concentrate on not moving closer.

When she saw his smile of tolerant amusement, although her insides jumbled, she remembered her posture, unwilling to be the sort of woman who would follow him in the street or throw herself at him. For years he had protected the memory of a dead woman. A love like that was rare, not to be taken lightly by a woman who had married him for his social position.

As his wife, she had a duty. He had married her thinking she was bearing Tony's child. This gave her reason to believe he was not at all averse to being a father, but not only that. The episode in her bed last week seemed to indicate that however reluctant he might be, he would like his own babies. She would not have to spend the rest of her life childless. Perhaps he would love the other woman until the end of his days, but the fact that he had succumbed to kissing and caressing his wife showed that his guilt was abating. He more than attracted her, always had, and the bargain was now null and void. Surely.

Her pulse flickering in her throat, she edged her fingers onto his shoulder and higher, and brushed across his chin with her thumb.

He tensed. "What are you doing, my sweet salvation?"

"Flirting." She smiled.

"It's against the rules." His expression turned watchful.

Her breath shortened. "Whose rules?"

"Mine." His step became longer, and he whirled her into and out of the corner.

"Is that fair? To stop me flirting with you? I'm your wife."

His mouth firmed. "In name only. Do you want to talk or dance?" He stopped in the center of the room, his head tilted, awaiting her answer.

"Talk."

Taking her hand, he led her off the floor, guiding her to a secluded area backed by two of the faux marble pillars. "So, you want to talk about flirting, do you?" He faced her.

"I want to talk about having children."

He folded his arms. "I don't want children, which is why you married me. You saw me for what I am, and you knew we would never reproduce. If you want to try out your womanly wiles, find someone else."

"You mean as a replacement for Tony?" She waited.

"I misunderstood." He rubbed the side of his neck. "He and I have cleared that up, and I don't mind if you ride with him. However, I do mind if you flirt with him. He's a happily married man."

"So, with whom should I flirt? Luke?" She smiled inside. For the first time she had him on the defensive. Confidence and independence seemed to be serving her well. Nick didn't know that Luke had told her about Clara. He thought he had to keep up his pretence of being uninterested in females. Instead of being the pursued, she could be the pursuer. "I want to practice with you."

Firm faced, he glared at her.

"You have such nice eyes," she said, threading her fingers with his. "And your hand is warm and large."

"You really want to flirt with me? I warn you, Charlotte, I know how to win *this* game."

She glanced up at him. "Perhaps you'll teach me how to play."

His eyes glittering with amusement, he slid his fingers into the opening of her glove and caressed her pulse. Her breath sped up, her heartbeat fluttered, but her body relaxed. She didn't doubt that he'd noticed her reaction, for he rested his mouth where his fingers had left a tingle of sensation.

"What are you two doing, away in a corner by yourselves?"

Charlotte reared back, pulling her arm away.

"Sarah, have some tact," Luke said from behind her. "That's not a question you ask of newlyweds."

"Nick bit a hanging thread from my glove," Charlotte said without thinking.

"See." Sarah lifted her nose at Luke. "You don't need to remind me of my manners. Dance with Daphne. I'm sure she'd enjoy your version of the waltz, slow and precise. I've promised this one to James."

"Yes, change partners." James brought Daphne to the group of four. "Daphne and I have known each other too long to find any excitement in dancing together."

Charlotte's glance met Sarah's.

"There, Lolly. What did I tell you?" With a wicked smile on her face, Sarah took James's arm. With the same noise that had attended the interruption, the four departed.

"And what did she tell you?" Nick asked with a narrowing of his eyes. "Lolly."

"She thinks James is nowhere near as interested as Daphne supposes."

"Nor is he interested in Sarah. He's interested in amenable females, *Lolly.*"

"She promised never to call me that in front of anyone else."

"Sweetness on a stick. It suits you. I'm sure you'd be very nice to lick."

She turned her head away as a hot blush overcame her. Many things he had said that she had ignored were blatantly suggestive. *You play my games, and I'll play yours. Undress and get into bed with me.* Whether he liked the idea or not, he would eventually accept his conjugal rights.

"Lolly." He picked up her arm and pressed his lips between the buttons of her glove. The tips of his teeth flickered over the sensitive skin of her wrist. "How am I managing? Am I as good as a real man?"

Her insides shivered, and she longed to bury her fingers in his hair and hold him close. "You could fool me," she said, her voice husky. "But I don't think that's at all difficult."

"I don't want to fool you. I'm not all bad. Where you're concerned, I've been exceptionally good."

"It's easy to be good when you're not tempted."

He scrutinized her face. "True."

"Nevertheless." She faced him. "Should you ever be tempted, I'm your wife."

Folding his arms, he leaned back against the wall and crossed one ankle with the other. "I know."

"I won't mind." She tried to breathe normally.

"Won't you now?"

She gave him a smile that wouldn't in a thousand years show her thoughts. Never once had she considered another man. She'd certainly not ever presented herself to one, and this one had just rejected her, again. He didn't care that she was beautiful. He was more beautiful. He didn't care that she was attracted to him. Every woman was attracted to him. Only one fact made her different from any other woman—he had married her. "Heavens, Nick. I know you're not tempted by me. I knew that when I married you."

"Oh, I find you very tempting." He stared at the dancers on the floor. "You're an enigma, a puzzle. You're young and inexperienced, but you're never at a loss. You've just offered yourself to me but only because you assume I won't take you up on your offer. That's almost enough to make me do so."

She pretended to be amused, but all she had on her mind was playing the role of seductress. "But you won't."

"Are you issuing me a challenge, Charlotte?"

"You couldn't rise to it."

He gave her the strangest smile. "I could make you feel desire."

Now that Nick had called her Charlotte, not Blossom or Petal or Lolly, she might well encourage him to do so.

Chapter 10

Charlotte walked with Nick into their sitting room. After all her hopeful anticipation, instead of hurrying her into his bedroom, he stopped by his door and took her hands. "Good night. You won. You completely out-bluffed me—no mean feat."

She laughed. "You're easy to bluff," she said, keeping her voice casual. "I know exactly what you're going to do."

"We're not playing a game of cards, you know."

"That's how you play cards, too. By bluffing." She ran her fingers along his jaw line. "A woman couldn't make you feel desire. I could do anything I liked to you, and you wouldn't react." She pretended her thumb found a scrap of something on his bottom lip. "Look what happened when we were in bed together. You took my hand off your...um."

"It seemed wise at the time." He sounded husky.

"You're afraid that if we do anything, you'll change your orientation."

"Trust me. I'm not about to do that."

"Bluffing again?" She moved right up against him, casually placing her hand onto his shoulder.

His expression changed to one of glittering cynicism. "You should have concentrated on the words in our wedding ceremony. Marriage was ordained as a remedy against sin and to avoid fornication."

"I think the minister meant us to avoid fornication with others." She concentrated on his smooth-skinned neck, tempted but was not quite brave enough to place a kiss there.

"He didn't sound specific."

"Nick." She rested her other hand on the flat of his hard chest. "A wife is not supposed to avoid fornication with her husband. Am I tempting you to try with me?"

He cleared his throat. "Are you standing close enough to feel my temptation?"

She breathed in. Despite the fullness of her petticoats, she could feel the growing size of the part she had fondled previously. She would have liked to touch him there again, but once rebuffed, she didn't have the courage to try again. "Yes." She brushed her lips against his. "It's my duty as a wife to reform you."

He gave a twisted smile, reached for the knob, and opened his bedroom door wide. "How very noble when you feel not a pinch of desire."

She moved into his room. His bed was cherub-topped like hers. A side table held books tilted in a precarious angle, a stack of opened letters, an empty bottle of spirits, and a tumbled set of shirt studs. "You said you could remedy that."

He slung off his jacket, dropping the garment on the plush chair beside him. Eyeing her, he unknotted his tie, and then he sat on his bed. After unbuttoning his shirt, he took off his shoes and silk socks. Although interested in every detail of his life, she knew she shouldn't stare.

"Not undressing?" He sounded bored. "I thought you were keen to copulate."

"I don't know what I should be doing."

"Getting this over with."

She gave an uneasy smile. "Should I change into my nightgown?"

"Just undress."

Her hands began to shake. "Easier said than done." With numb fingers, she worked at the buttons of her gown, made more clumsy by the speculative glint in his eyes.

He leaned back. "Don't go any farther. Truly, my pretty, you don't have the skills to gain my interest."

Her eyes closed briefly. "I have a lot to learn."

"Apparently. You seemed to have moved through life without living."

"Perhaps we're perfectly matched." She pulled at her buttons. "You avoid life, too. You fill your time, but you accomplish nothing productive."

He gave a harsh laugh. "Go away, Wife. I don't want you."

"You don't want involvement." She left her bodice and stood, hands clenched at her sides. "Nor did I. The difference between us is that I'm prepared to change."

"To change from a woman who married a man for his money to a woman who is prepared to whore for that money?" He gave a short laugh.

"To change from a woman who accepted she wasn't good enough to one who realizes that if she never asserts herself she'll never win the prize."

"And the prize is…?"

"Respect," she said in an undertone. "Equality."

"Do you imagine I'm going to respect you because you offered yourself to me?"

"No," she said through her teeth. "But I imagine you won't bother with me or try to know me if I didn't, and then of course we'll be nothing to each other. Nothing. And that's what I want to change."

He massaged the back of his neck. "You want us to be friends—confidantes? Because we fuck?" He shook his head. "That's not how it is between opposite genders. Best you continue to surround yourself with serene indifference. If I bedded you, I'd want to change you into a bed partner I could enjoy."

Her jaw firmed. Her hands relaxed, and she gazed at him. "What sort of bed partner could you enjoy? You couldn't possibly couple with a man."

He raised his eyebrows. "What makes you say that?" His eyes searched hers.

"Logic. It's not possible, physically," she said, voicing her true belief, which wasn't the reason why she had said that. She'd slipped and almost let him know she knew he wasn't a man lover.

He sighed, and for a brief moment, his lips quirked. "Then we will proceed. Come here."

Stiff-shouldered, she stepped over to him. He settled her knees between his. With a single hand, he undid the rest of her gown, and using both, he edged the garment off her shoulders. Yards of fabric slithered past her hoop onto the floor. As if talking to a child, he said, "Step."

She kicked her gown aside.

He stared into her eyes. "Last chance. You can leave now or put up with anything I might do."

She gave him her *serenely indifferent* smile as she blotted her palms on her chemise. He'd intimidated her and the act ahead frightened her. Her mother had told her that a woman's duty was to please a man. He'd implied he didn't particularly want her to do her duty, and yet she was almost sure he hid his true feelings. He'd ridiculed her more than once, but in the repelling, he managed to draw her closer.

He tugged the ties on her crinoline. "Step." He collected the yards of her petticoats and her cage and threw them both to the chair where they settled like a deflating balloon.

Her mouth dried. She focused on the top of his head, on his gleaming brown hair, on his wide shoulders, and her skin quivered. Despite his attitude and her apprehension, she wanted to know the pleasures of the flesh.

He bracketed each side of her head with his palms and brought her face down to his. His eyes changed from their amazing light blue-green to glinting, almost impossible silver. His lips took hers, demanding. Like the witless fool he assumed her to be, she tightened her fingers on his shoulders, impelled by a strange possessiveness. He tugged at her hair, sliding her clips from her shoulders to the floor.

His palm flattened against the side of her neck, and his thumb tilted her chin. Her mind emptied. She knew nothing but the tease of his tongue. He shifted forward, slightly off the bed, clamping her legs between his. One insistent hand worked at the ties of her chemise. He made a sound of appreciation and bared one of her breasts.

Her insides shivered, twisted, and tangled into wanton confusion, and her fingers grasped his hair. He lifted his lips from hers, stared at her, and said words she had never heard before, not words of love or passion but long, descriptive words she knew as self-disgusted swearing.

"Don't look at me like that." His gaze left hers.

"Like what?" Her voice trembled.

He laughed harshly. "The way I wanted you to look at me." Rising to his feet with a growl of suppressed tension, he dropped his hold to her waist, opening his hot mouth over her throat. The rub of his shaven chin abraded the skin of her chest. He gentled. She gazed at the fans of his thick lashes, sliding her fingers again into his crisp hair.

His mouth moved to her breast, licking and kissing. He took her moistened nipple into his mouth while skimming away the other strap of her chemise, leaving both breasts bared and both straps hanging to her elbows. She struggled to free herself, and he leaned back a little so that she could lift both arms out of her confinement. Her nipples had changed, standing out from the puckering around.

He stared at her, breathing through his mouth. His eyes looked hazy, desirous. Very slowly, he ran his palms down her upper arms and his thumbs along the outer sides of her breasts. Her skin heated with anticipation.

"You have a beautiful body," he said in a constricted voice. "Pray for my control." With that, he nuzzled into her other breast.

This time his fingers dug into her waist. His nuzzling became sucking, and the pit of her belly jolted with sensation. He dragged and nipped, and she tugged at his hair, not sure whether she urged or repelled.

She didn't understand herself. She knew the mechanics of coupling and still she craved him. In her imagining, his large part forced between her legs and tore her, and yet in that same place she throbbed, wanting the pain, craving the pressure inside. She'd enjoyed touching his male part, and her urge to do so again made her fingers clench.

He tugged the tie on her under-drawers and with her chemise both slid to the floor. She couldn't step for his knees held her legs together. His mouth left her breast, moved to her ribs, her stomach, and pressed there, nipping, licking, hungry, exciting. The muscles of his shoulders strained against the fabric of his shirt. She wanted to see his beautiful skin naked. She groaned softly, wondering if she loved him.

"You're a surprise," he murmured, his thumbs caressing her hipbones. He sat her onto the bed beside him. "I hadn't thought you'd be so responsive. Perhaps I *can* give you what you need."

Leaning back, he took her to the middle of the bed with him. She lay on top of him, but he rolled her over. Her underwear tangled with her shoes and stockings around her ankles, and with a gleeful laugh, he peeled off the lot.

"A bit constricting," he said, kissing the side of her mouth. "Though, a man likes the whorish look of a female who has nothing covered but her calves and ankles."

She acknowledged his words with a smile. A man as clever, handsome, and rich as he would never need to know a whore.

By lifting and arranging her bare body, he made her comfortable, her head on his pillows and her body in the center of his bed. The last time they'd shared a bed, he'd been semi-naked, and she had worn a nightgown. Apparently, this time they would change roles. Although unbuttoned, he remained clothed.

She laughed with the tickle when he kissed her neck, her face, and her ear. He smiled back and rolled her onto her stomach, leaving the places his mouth had pleasured to re-warm against the sheets. As his hand ran lightly down her back, she felt his lips on her ankles. She wriggled her toes with enjoyment and pressed her smiling mouth into the pillow. His lips progressed slowly up her legs, cooling and warming at the same time.

She appreciated his taking his time. Her mother had not told her that a man could be so wonderful with his teasing, so inventive with his kisses. When he reached her buttocks, he nipped gently. She almost lifted to beg for more, and she murmured with pleasure while he pressed soft kisses all the way up her spine to her armpit. He licked there, and she shivered with delight. He'd already made up for the pain he would inflict soon.

His kisses continued as he rolled her over to face him. He ran his lips over her shoulders and moved down to her breasts again. A faint whimper eased from the back of her throat when he drew one hardened nipple into his mouth. Her fingers pressed avidly across his shoulders. He breathed out, lifted, and buried his tongue in her navel. Her body pounded with excitement. He even sucked her toes.

She couldn't think where to put her hands, and so she clenched them, threshing her head on the pillow. His mouth moved up her legs again. His hands glided under her thighs. He moved them apart and dipped his head between them, licking at the aching wetness.

Her knees shook. "Don't, Nick. Stop."

His mouth breathed on her, heated her, and his tongue flattened, soothed. Somehow, he sent a bumping excitement through her.

"You'll love this, petal. Relax and let me pleasure you."

His tongue circled until she couldn't think.

"I'm supposed to be pleasuring you," she whispered.

"That comes later when you know how to."

Unable to restrain herself, she lifted, pressing the flats of her feet onto his waist. He gave more, with his lips, with his tongue, with his teeth, and she didn't care about being good, or bad, or expressing her emotions. She threshed, wanting more, wanting less, wanting Nick. The words "I love you," tore from her throat.

"What!" He stared into her eyes.

"I love you," she repeated softly.

He took his palms from her buttocks. "This is not love. This is lust."

His face firmed as he pushed himself to the full extent of his arms. She noticed the taut flexion of his shoulders and every muscle in his neck as he lifted.

"You're too inexperienced. I shouldn't have done this. Why didn't you go back to your room when I told you to?" He rolled over her leg to the side of the bed, lying face up with his elbow across his eyes, jaw tensed.

She lifted herself onto her elbows and stared at his tight face. "Why did you do this if you knew you shouldn't?"

"You're a temptation, my precious, and one I don't need." His lips firmed.

"So not all men have a need to couple?"

"I don't know about all men."

She dropped her gaze to his unbuttoned waistband where the large and rod-like shape she had touched before stood clearly delineated. He certainly wanted the pleasures of the flesh.

"Why do you deny yourself?"

"I can satisfy myself any time I like." He slid his hand into his trousers. "Like this, if I choose," he said, glancing at her as if testing her reaction.

She breathed in. The thought of him touching himself beneath his trousers made her embarrassingly warm. She lifted his sheet and pulled the linen over her shoulders to hide the quick puckering of her nipples. While knowing nothing about the married act, she wanted him inside her. He, experienced, didn't care to be there.

"You know I'd let you satisfy yourself with me."

"*In* you? No. I wouldn't have done that. I would have taught you to do what I'm doing now. No matter which method I choose, I don't spill my seed productively." His hand stroked slowly, and his head arched back.

She couldn't fail to see his enjoyment. His face looked stark with pleasure, his eyes half hooded.

"Teach me to do it now."

Almost with reluctance, he took his hand out of his trousers. "There's no point. We won't be together again."

"Why?"

"Because coupling with you would be a sin," he said tersely. "You'd want to get involved in emotions I lost years ago. You'd be thinking about love and babies and other impossible things."

"Is a baby impossible?"

"Of course. Why else do you think I won't take you? You can't imagine that I don't want you. You can see I'm rigid with wanting."

"I can't see anything," she said desperately. "We're married and being together is not a sin."

"Copulating causes babies," he said roughly. "And I won't give you one."

She stared into the corner of the room. Her clothing had tangled with his on the chair. Not too long ago, her body had tangled with his. "You're refusing me because you don't want a baby?"

He closed his eyes. "I gave you what you wanted."

"And now that you've amused yourself, you'd like to sleep."

He sighed, and with a lowered gaze, he separated a strand of her hair and pulled the curl through his fingers. "Scarcely that." He took her into his arms and snuggled her head under his chin.

He stroked her head and shoulders for some time. Baffled by his behavior, she remained silent. He'd seen her body, which he'd touched and licked everywhere, and she wanted him, physically. Yet, she had no sense of ownership of him or of knowing him.

Frustrated, but taking comfort in his warmth, she finally slept. A little before dawn, when she left his room with her clothing gathered in her arms, she saw he slept, still in his clothes. His dishevelment gave her lewd thoughts.

She'd changed from an impartial virgin bride to one completely seduced by her confusing husband.

* * * *

Nick awoke alone. He noted the imprint of Charlotte's head on his pillow and he stretched. He'd never taken a woman he loved, for he'd loved none. Lust had impelled him, never the finer feelings. He couldn't let himself love Charlotte, but he hadn't withheld her fulfillment because of that. Perhaps his new role as a tentative husband had caused a form of moral rectitude.

Scowling, he poured himself a glass of brandy. Too long without alcohol and he sweated. Best not to risk showing his need.

After he'd washed, breakfasted, and read the paper, he thrummed his heels. He was bored, bored, bored. A long day lay ahead with nothing to do but stretch out idle occupation. He might have sought Beth's company, but for realizing she wanted more from him than he was able to give while he could think only of his wife. Instead, he waited for Sarah, prepared to ride with her.

"I'm not riding today," she said when she arrived late in the breakfast room dressed in a morning gown. "Daphne and her sister are taking me to the museum for a day of sketching."

He nodded and watched her eat a normal breakfast, appreciating the fact that, when pre-occupied, she didn't need to be the center of attention.

"I thought I might do some sewing," Charlotte said after she came in from her ride. She didn't meet his gaze. "With a few other ladies at Nell's house. Unless there is something pressing for me to do at home."

He shook his head. "I wouldn't know. That's your province."

His father would spend his day with his business manager. His cronies would sleep late and wander off to various sporting or social events. He could do the same, always had. He had no need of money and no ambition but to drink his life away. He slammed his newspaper onto the table. A man who could sire no living child had no need of an existence!

"Bad news?" Alfred asked, entering the room.

"Do you want company today?"

"Yours? You'd be bored. Today I plan to sort out my new row of city cottages."

"You wanted me to occupy myself. I'm offering."

Alfred raised his eyebrows. "I accept. If you don't learn to manage our affairs before I'm gone, you'll be in a pretty pickle afterward."

"Lord. You're expecting to turn up your toes at any moment." Nick put his head in his hands. "Funds and trusts and properties and stock markets. I don't know if I'm up to it."

"Not if your head isn't clear." Alfred rang the bell. "Eventually, you will need a long discussion with my man. Today you can start smaller. Supervise the detailing of the new cottages. I want them sold and off my hands within the next six months."

Nick spent his first morning inspecting Alfred's houses, a row of four built for the average workingman in bluestone and sited in a city street. Each had space for a tiny garden in the front and a vegetable garden at the back. In his opinion, each needed to be slightly different from the others.

Taking his father's business manager, he went to a nearby inn for luncheon and later he visited his father's sawmill. He liked the smell of the hot machinery, the shavings, and the boiling glue. For a full six hours, he discussed and inspected fittings for the houses without once thinking about any of the women in his life.

Before he retired for the night, he wanted to tell his wife that for the first day in a year he had occupied his time productively as she had suggested. He wanted to relent and ask her to sleep with him. One more night of frustration would surely kill him.

However, he had gone without a woman for months while he'd lived with Clara. Beth would be available if abstinence became untenable, and so he took his old friend, the bottle, to bed instead.

He put in his next day with a plasterer and spent his night thinking of his inexperienced wife laughing and smiling while he had pleasured her. Had she touched him, thoughts of the pleasures ahead would have made his nightly tortures unbearable. Brandy put him to sleep.

He didn't resent changing from a dilettante to a worker. He worried that he'd start to listen to his wife, grow to enjoy her candid observations, respect her practicality, and crave the touch of her cool hands on his hot and needy body. If he wanted her too much, he would accede to all her desires. Married he might be, but a papa he could never be. He would see Beth again when he had settled his wife into society. Charlotte needed his attendance now, but he didn't know how much longer he could last working all day and drinking himself to sleep.

He swilled his nightly dose of brandy, remembering that Tony had begun to investigate her. Presumably, he hadn't continued. After all, Charlotte's antecedents didn't affect him. They certainly didn't affect Nick, for his respectability was based purely on his father's money. Nevertheless, the faintest niggle remained. Charlotte never mentioned any life she might have had before Miss Main's school.

Perhaps he needed further conversation with Tony.

Chapter 11

"Do you plan to be at the cottages today?" Charlotte asked Nick as he seated her at the breakfast table.

For him, the past four days had been tiring—by day making sure his father's cottages were readied for occupation and at night watching over Charlotte and Sarah at social events. By this means, he evaded private little chats with Charlotte before retiring with his bottle.

"We just started the roofing. In Port Adelaide, we used wooden shingles for the tenants' cottages, but in town we're using slate." He seated himself in front of his breakfast, realizing he'd said *we*.

He had shocked the tradesmen by his participation in the various building projects. As a lad, he had done his share of outdoor work on the property at Stirling. Roofing was new to him, but during his satisfyingly active boyhood when he'd still had a reason to care about his inheritance, he'd had some experience with fence posts and tree lopping. He had always enjoyed working with his hands.

"Slate? Why the change?" His father stared at him in surprise. "We can make the shingles in the factory."

"Mainly availability. Wood is too scarce, and your manager suggested trying a longer lasting product. They're quarrying slate in Mintaro now."

"You'll have to take us to see your new cottages," Sarah said, finishing her egg. "When they're done."

"Perhaps we could get Harvey to drive us over one day." Charlotte glanced at Nick, who completed his breakfast with a sustaining ale.

Finally, Charlotte stood, ending breakfast. He opened the door for her, and as she passed him into the hallway, her gaze met his long enough to cause his entire body to crave.

"You're making your father very happy by taking on so many of his tasks." She ran a light finger over his newly-shaven cheek.

His skin tingled. "Many? Not so. Just a few cottages," he said, his voice strangely gruff.

She dropped her palm to his lapel. "You are taking a great load from his shoulders, and now everyone is much happier, including Sarah and me."

His hands settled onto either side of her waist. As he stared into her frank blue eyes, his blood rushed to his groin. He wanted her. He could have her if he wished. She could have him if she wished. Instead of waiting to see how far she would go in her attempt to turn him into a quivering fool, he backed her against the wall and slid his hands to her bottom.

"Not here," she said, her voice low.

"Why not? I could take you quickly." He heard her intake of breath.

She glanced at him and back to the breakfast room door, clearly anxious.

"I prefer the prohibited." He saw in her eyes that he had raised the stakes too high, and he let her off, the competition being uneven. After adjusting himself, he stepped back. "Then again, hammering nails into slate will probably satisfy me as well as a few minutes with you."

Leaving her to see the connection, he shrugged, certain he had proved any attempts to seduce the daisy she assumed he was were doomed to failure. "I won't be home in time to attend whatever you have planned. I'm sure you and Sarah will manage without me."

Now and always, letting her undoubted charms to inveigle him into her bed was out of the question. Nodding curtly he left, the high card regrettably his.

* * * *

Charlotte awoke with a start. A hard thump echoed through the night and the crash of overturned furniture. A familiar voice swore repeatedly in the sitting room. She sped out of bed and arrived in the outer room in time to see her husband weave his way to his bedroom door. "Do you need help?"

"No." He kicked his door open and stumbled. This made him swear again even more loudly.

"Are you sure?" She stood in his doorway while he cast his jacket onto the moonlit floor.

"Yes." He sat on his bed and tried to pull off his shoes.

"Are you drunk?" She stepped into his room.

"Legless. Now you're here, help me with these shoes."

"You need a nursemaid," she said, annoyed.

"I've had one of those. I need a wife."

She turned on his lamp while he waited for her to grasp the heel of his shoe. He eased the shoe off. She helped with the next as well. "Oh, no you don't," she said in her firmest voice as he shut his eyes and rolled to the center of the bed, taking his spread to cover him. "Take your clothes off first."

"If you want them off, you take them off."

She suppressed the urge to shake him. "Why do you do this to yourself? How can you keep up this way of life?"

"Practice, my dear one, practice."

She narrowed her eyes and stood well back, her arms folded. "I doubt you need to keep practicing a task you manage so well." The cynical tone she used almost shocked her. If she didn't watch her tongue she'd be... She squared her shoulders. She'd be a wife, his wife, a woman who belonged, a woman who could confidently express her true opinions.

He mumbled some incomprehensible words and began to undo his shirtfront, but clearly couldn't coordinate his fingers. She gritted her teeth and helped. His hands dropped, and he watched her. She pulled his shirt over his shoulders while he struggled his hands through the cuffs. He lay back down again, closing his eyes. Drawing an irritable breath, she set her hands on her hips and her gaze on his creamy-skinned torso, so wide at the shoulders, and so unjustifiably muscled and ridged that she drew a breath of helpless admiration.

His eyelids flickered. "What about my trousers?" He rubbed a palm over the flat navel she could just see above his waistband. "Do you mind if I sleep in *these*?"

"You shouldn't. You should take them off."

His hands flopped to his sides, demonstrating he'd do nothing for himself. Firming her mouth, she undid his trousers. His belly moved with his breathing. The area under his fly had filled with the thickened part that reached to his waistband. She lifted the material off his protrusion to work at his buttons, but his hand clamped down over hers. He forced her palm onto the shape she so badly wanted to touch that she shook.

"Now, look at that," he said in a voice of mock surprise. "I'm hard for you. Perhaps I'm beginning to change my orientation." His fingers latched into the neckline of her nightgown, and she found her face on his bare shoulder.

He rolled slightly, and she fell across him onto the bed. His head lifted and his mouth took hers. Although he had heavy fumes on his breath, she didn't care. He had strong gentle hands, and while he worked his magic with his lips and his tongue, he pushed her hand under his trousers. Beneath, he was hot and heavy and hard.

"Straddle me," he whispered, "and put me inside you."

Her lower body rushed with heat, and her breath came in panting gasps. An all too easy conquest, she put her hands onto his shoulders, wondering how she ought to accomplish her mission. "I can't even get your trousers off without your help."

His look of sleepy satisfaction disappeared and a wary crease formed between his eyebrows. "Sweetheart." He flicked a lock of her hair back off her face. "Are you trying to take advantage of me while I'm drunk?"

"This morning you seemed quite willing to take advantage of me."

He took her hand out of his trousers and sat up. "Bluff. I can't perform now, my love. I've had my fill tonight."

For a moment Charlotte sat with an empty mind, and then the air in her chest expanded. With an explosion of white-hot rage, she shoved him onto his back. "Fill? You've been fornicating?"

He looked surprised, and when he laughed, she pummeled his shoulder with her fists. "Careful." He held her wrists. "You might hurt me."

"I want you to be hurt! I want you to feel the way I do!"

His expression blanked and he let her go. "You'll get over it." He pushed his hair out of his eyes. "I can't make you out. You never minded before."

"If you were fornicating, you wouldn't have been with a *man*. You can't make love to a man."

He began to laugh again. Rolling her beneath him, he kissed her face between gasps. "Is that what you thought? I thought you were being liberal."

"Well, you can't, can you?"

"That is the question. Whether 'tis nobler in the mind to suffer."

"Which depends on the affliction," she replied, taking her tone down a few decibels. "You've sobered, somewhat. Are you are being truthful with me?"

He glanced away, patently unable to continue with his ridiculous lie about fornicating.

"Well?"

"Go back to bed." He eased his leg from her, turned over onto his back, crossed his arms under his head, and stared at the ceiling.

She pulled her nightgown straight. "If you won't touch your wife, you certainly wouldn't touch another woman." Rubbing at her wrists, she sat up, positive she had bruised her hands on him for no reason and sure that her jealous reaction had been unjustified.

"You're right. I drank myself into a stupor so that I wouldn't want anyone," he said with weariness in his voice. "And that's the truth."

"That's the alcohol." She climbed off his bed. "You don't know what you're saying."

She left him to sober up, returning to her cold and empty room.

* * * *

Charlotte didn't expect Nick at breakfast, and she was prepared to make excuses for him. For at least a week he had been working at a job very unsuited to a gentleman, and last night's drinking would have taken a toll.

"Morning," he said in a disgruntled voice before she had taken her place.

She glanced from her perusal of the offerings on the sideboard and answered, "Morning," in approximately the same tone.

Sarah had not yet arrived, but Alfred smiled at Nick. "Big day today. The delivery of the slate. I expect you'll be glad to see the end of it."

Nick looked somewhat dour. Charlotte noted the dark depressions beneath his eyes. "It's the beginning of the end of an interesting exercise," he said as he served himself breakfast. He evaded her gaze, put his porridge at his place, and pulled out her chair.

She took porridge as well and sat.

"Good morning, all," Sarah said, entering and taking a plate of fruit. "The dinner last night was fun, Nick. You would have enjoyed it. Everyone was there and the table seated thirty. Thirty! I wouldn't think we could manage so many here."

"We've another three or four leaves for this table," Alfred said, glancing around as if the sections might be propped against the walls. "I think we could do thirty. Are we planning a dinner any time soon?"

"You wouldn't mind?" Charlotte asked, suddenly breathless.

"Of course not. We need to show family support of Sarah, after all. I didn't have a daughter, and so I hadn't thought of the little miss's position but... What do you think, Nick? Shouldn't we be hosts ourselves?"

"That would be Charlotte's province. If she is up to it, I don't see why we shouldn't." He poured himself a tall glass of water from the jug on the table.

"A dinner? Or a small dance?" Charlotte's head whirled with a thousand ideas. On paper, she knew exactly how to do this. "Which would you prefer, Sarah?"

"If it's for me…" Sarah's eyes widened. "Fancy. What would I need to do?"

"Possibly little more than you need to do when attending the dinners or dances of others," Nick said in a growly voice. He rubbed his forehead, which Charlotte hoped was aching. "The girls from Miss Main's school learn how to organize dinners and dances as well as household and husband management, and so I'm sure Charlotte can do everything required." His tone said otherwise.

She had no sympathy for him. None. If he wanted to drink himself surly so that he could continue on with his pretence of being effeminate, he could take the consequences.

"If we want to begin entertaining, we need to make a plan before the weather gets too hot." She drew a breath. "I would be pleased to manage a function of some sort here."

"What fun." Sarah took a sip of tea. "We've never done anything like this before, have we, Charlotte? Will you be at the cottages today, Nick, or will you be coming to the garden party with us?"

Nick rang the bell. "I'm needed at the cottages."

Charlotte didn't mind that he hadn't considered being her escort. For a few weeks she'd been a part of a couple. Although his presence validated her, the strain of keeping up his pretence was telling on him, hence his excessive drinking. Presumably, he wanted her to believe he was a deviant because he was afraid of the possibility of conceiving a child. He thought death in childbirth too great a risk, but even the queen had had nine children, and if the monarch of England could live through that, the wife of Nicholas Alden could live through one.

"Perhaps we could get Harvey to take us to see your cottages today?"

"You'll get dirty," he said tersely.

"We're not planning on building. Just looking." And with the proper questions, she might hear some useful tips on where to find the right materials for her own building program.

"We could come after the garden party." Sarah finished off her fruit.

The maid entered in answer to the bell.

"A tankard of ale," Nick said. "A large one."

Chapter 12

Nick *hadn't* seen Beth, and that was the problem. Hung-over and irritable, he presented at the cottages and helped load the first roof with slate. As the tradesmen began on the tiling, having worked off enough of his interminable restlessness, he sat on a window ledge, mulling the plan to host a large dinner with dancing afterward. By taking up this idea, Charlotte would be well launched into society, Sarah would be shown to her best advantage, and he would finally be off the hook and able to see his mistress again.

Satisfied with his head-aching ruminations, he began to pick through the stone for the fireplaces. No sooner had he laid a row of mortar than Luke appeared.

Nick straightened. "The garden party was challenging, was it?"

Luke shrugged, loosening his tie. "I'm not hanging out for a wife."

"Not your own, no."

"Give it a rest. Failing not having a wife of my own, I'm not wanting to get into any tangled or illicit relationships."

Nick gave him an incredulous look. "I doubt you'll find one at a garden party held by the Metcalfs and attended by the usual crowd."

"You would be surprised if you ever bothered to attend," Luke said casually. "When the conversation at the gathering got around to your latest doings, I decided to take myself off to see you soiling your hands. Here, let me at that." He picked up a stone and balanced the straightest edge atop Nick's lime mud. "Not bad, not bad."

"You'll need to finish a row before you can pass that sort of judgment. And watch your natty attire." Nick wore workman's garb, cheaply purchased a few weeks ago.

Luke removed his jacket and his tie and began to work with a will. Nick confined himself to chipping more stone. Between them, they completed the sides.

"If I am ever dissatisfied with the law, I could take up stonework for a living," Luke said, standing back to admire his work.

"The masons work ten hours a day, six days a week. You desk workers would never manage." Nick gave his friend a light punch on the shoulder, in accord with him for the first time since his marriage. "Do you know how much you would have earned if I had to pay you?"

"A penny or two," Luke said. "You could buy me a pie for tuppence. It's after noon. Come over to the tavern where I left my horse, and we'll have an ale."

Nick dusted himself off, but not before James and Hubert, the heir to Sir Patrick's properties, appeared. "Ah, two more likely apprentices."

Mild-mannered, Hubert pasted a look of horror on his cherubic face, but James offered his relaxed smile. "We heard word at the garden party that Luke might be here. No, we didn't come to get in your way. We're off to help Tony. One of his mines caved in yesterday. No casualties, fortunately, but a few injured, and he needs to get the shaft cleared. Want to come with us to Kadina, Luke?"

Luke indicated Nick. "We're about to wander over to the tavern for a bite to eat. Join us, and after I'll go home and grab a valise, as long as it's only for the next couple of days. I have a court appearance on Tuesday."

The four men spent a surprisingly convivial hour together while James's driver went to fetch clothing for Luke that might be suitable to wear during a few days heavy work in the country. Like the others, Nick was well content with a simple meat pie and tankard of ale.

The meal consumed, the four idled outside the cottages, waiting for the return of James's curricle. James was pushing the lighter, shorter Hubert in a wheelbarrow along a builder's plank when a brougham arrived bearing Charlotte and Sarah.

Nick stood, arms crossed, but one glance at his wife told him she bore no grudge for his drunken fumbling last night and his surly behavior this morning. He sighed. Desiring her didn't entitle him to lash her with his frustration.

A tiny frivolous hat sat on top of her dark curls. She wore a green trimmed, short-sleeved gown that made much of her graceful body. "Nick, do you have time to show us around the cottages? If you're otherwise engaged, we'll come back another day."

Luke pushed past him to the carriage. "He's not otherwise engaged with us," he said, opening the brougham door, apparently sure Nick would welcome another diversion. "We're all about to leave for Tony's house at Kadina." He handed her out.

Sarah followed, left to take the steps by herself. "Which would be a *gentleman's* residence and therefore perhaps not *quite* the right place for you."

Luke looked down his nose at her. "Ah. I see you're still pleased with me."

Sarah offered Luke a sweet smile. "You might need your eyes tested."

Fascinated, Nick stared at the couple while Charlotte, evading James's precipitate arrival with the entrapped Hubert, sidestepped to the nearest cottage's entrance with a laugh of alarm.

"Isn't that gown cut a little low for morning wear?" Luke glanced at Sarah's cleavage.

"Do you have a flair for fashion?" Sarah twirled her parasol. "Your jacket says otherwise." She turned her back, about to follow Charlotte.

Luke's bottom lip took his square chin forward. "You're fated to be a spinster, Sarah, unless you learn to guard that sharp tongue of yours. It would cut the insides of a man's mouth to pieces."

Sarah stopped.

"You'll have to forgive Luke," James said, discarding his wheelbarrow with a thump that shot Hubert to his feet. "He's been hefting stones, and the unaccustomed exercise has clearly affected his brain. We are about to take him away for a weekend in the country where he can keep working off his bad temper."

Luke stood as stiff as a maypole and nodded curtly at Sarah, perhaps his version of an apology.

With a sideways glint at him, she glided past him to James. "Thank you," she said, smiling up at the lad and taking his arm. "You have the chivalry Luke lacks."

Luke crossed his arms and leaned against the brougham.

"I didn't know you and he had such a volatile relationship," Nick said to her, torn between laughing and sympathizing with Luke.

"I just don't like rude people."

Nick eyed Luke. "He's a very eligible bachelor."

"I prefer polite eligible bachelors. Like James."

James grinned. "I'm not sure that being preferred to Luke is a compliment."

She laughed and the episode ended nicely, James taking her to join Charlotte in the first house into which she had disappeared. Hubert followed, and the four stood in the wood shavings, gazing around the main room, none but Charlotte appearing interested.

Nick left them inspecting the new fireplace, already bored by the sightseers. He wanted to get back to work, but instead he watched Harvey reposition the carriage to make room for James's recently arrived curricle, blocking the tiny street. The resulting ruckus brought James and Hubert outside to take their leave. Luke re-appeared mounted on his horse and joined the pair.

After the group left, Nick quickly showed the ladies the other cottages and delivered them to Harvey who was waiting with the steps down and the carriage door open.

Adjusting the perfect tie of her hat, Charlotte turned to Nick. "James told me that Tony is already in Kadina. That leaves Nell at home alone."

"Alone with twenty servants," Sarah said, climbing into the carriage. "Stop worrying, Charlotte. She'll be adequately cared for."

"I don't like to think of her being without anyone but servants when she is so close to her time." Charlotte's lips pressed together. "And so, I'm going to drop Sarah off at the Grace's and call on her."

"And you're asking my permission?" Nick stepped back, annoyed that Charlotte was keen to gossip about babies and forthcoming accouchements when she would never have a baby of her own—a good thing, too. A body as beautiful as hers should be preserved forevermore to tantalize her desperate husband.

"I'm letting you know that the brougham won't be collecting you later. You'll need to find your own way."

Harvey shut the door on her last word. Nick heaved a breath, his physical frustration deciding him to take the long way home.

* * * *

Charlotte followed a young maid into a room furnished with cushioned chairs and small tables littered with fabric, paper patterns, scissors, and button jars, among various other knickknacks.

"Mrs. Alden," the girl said, stepping back so that Charlotte could enter the sunlit area.

She had been in this room before with other ladies, making baby gowns for the residents of the Adelaide Maternity Hospital. "James said he was off to Kadina this afternoon and that Tony was already there."

Nell was sitting on a long couch, a book balanced on the limited space of her knee. "Forgive the informality," she said, holding out her hand to Charlotte. "Tony took the butler with him and half the servants. He'll need help with the injured men. We don't know yet what has happened. Since today is the normal day off for the servants, I let most of the others go, too. I'm making do for myself in here."

Charlotte crossed the brightly patterned carpet and shook Nell's hand. "I didn't like the thought of you being alone with the servants, but I had no idea you were alone *without* the servants."

"I have Millie." Nell indicated the departing maid. "My needs are few while I'm in this condition, but it's so kind of you to call. I think now that I'm at term I make people nervous. Either that or they can't bear to see me this size."

Charlotte smiled. "I doubt both, and I'm not being kind. Rather, self-serving. I want your advice."

"Ah, the words every woman loves to hear. Please sit. There is nothing more satisfying than giving advice. How can I help you, my dear?"

Charlotte made herself comfortable in a chair lined with soft velvet cushions. "Nick's father wants me to organize a dinner or a dance, or a combination, but I have never organized a social function other than as an exercise at Miss Main's. I was hoping you would help. You manage all your own functions with such flair, and I would love to succeed on my first try."

Nell's book slid off her knee. Bearing in mind her size, Charlotte picked up the novel and put the shut pages on the table.

"Thank you," Nell said in a forced voice. "I should be able to help as long as you don't plan to hold your function this week. I believe I will be otherwise occupied."

Charlotte examined the other woman's expression. Her words sounded unaccommodating but not her tone, which was a little breathy. She waited a moment, and then realization dawned. "The baby?"

"Yes." Nell made a wry face. "I've been having odd cramps all afternoon, but I seemed to have settled into a routine of pains about every ten minutes."

"Have you sent for the doctor?"

"Indeed, but I'm a healthy country girl. I don't expect complications."

"I should leave. My petty concerns are of no account compared to this momentous occasion." Charlotte gathered her gloves and reticule.

Nell gave her a pleading smile. "Although I'm trying to be very brave, I have to admit I'm relieved you came. I'm not quite sure Millie will be as much use to me as I had hoped. The other servants won't be back any time soon. Oh, no." She took a deep breath and paused, breathing hard. "I assumed I wouldn't need anyone until then, but I'm not so sure now." She glanced at the fob watch in the table beside the book. "That was under six minutes."

Charlotte absorbed the information with only a vague idea of her use here. "How long ago did you send for the doctor?" she asked, unable to suppress the quaver in her voice.

"About an hour ago, but he was away from home. I think I'll send Millie again."

"I'll send Harvey, my coachman. In the meantime, I suspect I ought to help you into bed."

"I believe I'm supposed to walk in these early stages," Nell said, sounding apologetic. "If you could assist me."

First Charlotte rang the bell and asked Millie to give Harvey a direction to the doctor's lodgings, and then she walked Nell to the far end of the passage and back. In that period, Nell had two more contractions. By the time Harvey came back with the message that the doctor was currently delivering twins, Nell was sitting on her bed wearing her commodious nightgown and having frequent long contractions.

"Have you ever delivered a baby?" she asked Charlotte in a shaky voice.

"I'm rather hoping they deliver themselves. But I don't know a thing about babies. Nick says the only thing I know is how to make them." Charlotte clamped her lips, horrified she had been so indiscreet.

"You're not...?" Nell doubled over, her eyes on Charlotte's face.

"Expecting? Of course not. It isn't possible." She glanced around the room, hoping to find a hole to swallow her up. First she had given Nell the impression she was more knowing than she was, and now she had blurted out the truth. "From bad to worse. I think I'm panicking. I'm so sorry, Nell. You must be wishing anyone but me was with you."

Nell gave a low laugh. "If anyone could take my mind off this, you could. I don't intend to be sticky-nosed, but I had a long conversation with Nick some months ago. I had the impression that he never intended to have children. And so I was very surprised when—" She doubled over again, rocking and panting.

Charlotte assumed Nell was about to say she was surprised that Nick had agreed to marry Charlotte, but she didn't want this conversation. "I think we'll need to send for another doctor." She rang the bell and Millie appeared in the doorway. "Tell Harvey to find a doctor. I'm sure he knows one. And tell him if he doesn't, to find my husband. He'll help." Wide-eyed, Millie left at a run.

Nell lifted her head and smiled at Charlotte. "I'm so glad you're here. I couldn't have asked for a better support. I'm sure you'll manage your supper dance well, judging by your current behavior. You haven't panicked despite what you say, and you're so very practical. What a good idea to call for Nick. May I have another sip of water?"

Charlotte half filled a glass from the jug on the bedside commode.

Nell gave her head a little shake. "After the tragedy with Clara Benbow, I could see by Nick's face that he thought I was also doomed."

Charlotte nodded, passing over the water. "He doesn't approve of women having babies."

Nell laughed and shrugged. "He believes he killed Mrs. Benbow by giving her his baby, but I suspect that having a stillborn birth killed her rather than the labor."

"Stillborn?" Charlotte's mouth dried.

"The baby was malformed Tony said. Nick blamed himself—shiver my *timmmmm-bers*. The next pain." Nell began panting, breathing, panting, and ended with a long groan. She leaned back on her pillows and closed her eyes. Her face looked red and hot.

Charlotte wiped the sweat from Nell's brow.

Nell's eyes opened. "How very unfortunate that we should be discussing a woman dying in childbirth."

"When do you expect Tony back?"

Nell raised her knees and massaged her abdomen. "Some time tomorrow. He'll be so cross with me. I told him I had days. Oh, dash, dash, dash," she said, her face creasing with pain. "Why did I think having a baby was a good idea?"

Charlotte took Nell's hand and had her fingers crushed. She hoped Nick would answer her plea for help. Without the only person she knew who had been present at a birth, she didn't know how she could manage if this baby came before the doctor.

* * * *

Nick settled at Beth's dining table with his accounts for the cottages, which he planned to total. A sulking mistress was preferable to a wife who would likely prose on about layettes and her rosy views of babies and childbirth, reminding him he couldn't have a full physical relationship with the only woman he desired to the point of sweating out his fantasies. He turned to the second page, noting the price of glass hadn't been included.

The front door shook with a thundering knock.

"What now?" Beth uncrossed her arms and pushed herself out of the chair in which she'd been muttering to herself. With a swing of her heavy skirts, she marched to the door.

A gruff voice loudly said, "I wonder if I might have a word with Mr. Nicholas Alden."

"Never heard of him."

Wood crashed against plaster, and Beth gave a squeal of alarm. Nick knocked over his chair in his leap into the hallway where he spotted Harvey. "What the devil are you doing here?" He planted his fists on his hips.

"Mrs. Alden asked me to get you," the man said, a wooden expression on his face. "Thought you would be able to help her find a doctor. Mrs. Hawthorn is in distress. The baby, you know."

Distress. Nick's chest thumped and his mouth dried. *The baby.* His brain numbed. In a dim haze, he collected his hat. The street was quiet and dark and still. Only a single echoing hackney trundled past.

"If you leave me for her again, I won't take you back," Beth said, her arms crossed.

Nick glanced at her and back to the coachman. "Harvey, did Mrs. Alden tell you where I was?"

"No, Mr. Nick. She asked me to find you." With a creak of wheels, Harvey settled on the driver's seat.

Nick moistened his lips. "You may as well go home now."

"She might want me, Mr. Nick. I'll go back to her."

"You will retrieve my accounts' books from Mrs. Blocker and return home with them. If I need you again tonight, I'll send for you." Nick crossed to the mews where he'd stabled his horse. He couldn't imagine what might have happened to make Charlotte send the coachman for him, except the very worst of events. In which case… The muscles in his face froze. At least this time he wasn't the direct cause of the disaster.

* * * *

A parlor maid knocked on Nell's bedroom door. Nick attributed the girl's reluctance to bring him this far to his working garb. He held his breath until the door opened a crack.

Charlotte appeared, her face so white that the color of her huge eyes reflected on the dark circles beneath. She sidled out and shut the door behind her, further eroding his confidence in a promising outcome of Nell's pregnancy.

Another step and she reached out to him, landing against the wall of his chest. "I don't know what to do," she said, her voice muffled in his jacket.

Nor did he. He kept his arms by his sides and closed his eyes. After Clara had died, he'd watched the women clean up the bed. The baby had been taken away long since.

"If the doctor won't come, who else can we call? There is not a single servant in this house who knows." She turned her face up to him, resting her hands on his shoulders.

"I know who you can call," said the maid, a pretty young creature who couldn't manage to keep eye contact. "Not that I should say, but Mrs. Adams has delivered many a baby."

Charlotte dropped her hold on him. She turned to the maid, frowning. "Who is Mrs. Adams? And why did you not tell me about her before?"

"Mistress wanted the doctor, according to Millie. Mrs. Adams is a midwife."

Charlotte glanced at Nick as if asking his opinion. He shook his head, trying to clear his foggy mind. "The baby isn't here yet?"

"I'm sure it won't be long if we can find someone who knows what to do."

"Are you telling me you've been here all this time alone?"

"Alone with Nell, yes."

"And all you want is a doctor or a midwife? Perhaps you should have sent Harvey for aid. He appears to know everyone's business."

"I sent him for the doctor or you." Her shoulders drooped. "I didn't think of a midwife."

He took a deep breath in an attempt to collect his wits, and then he looked the maid in the eye. "You go off and find this Mrs. Adams."

"Yes sir," she said, her eyes lowered. She backed to the staircase and fled down the steps.

"Please stay, Nick." Although Charlotte's eyes pled, her posture stiffened. "Just be here. I can't do this alone."

He opened Nell's door, strode to the bell-rope by the bed, and yanked. "I expect someone can boil water and provide clean sheets and a newspaper."

"Newspaper?" Nell echoed faintly from the bed. "I'm too busy to read. Good evening, Nick. How kind of you to call."

"I can't stay," he said, with a polite inclination of his head. "But at least I can help you women get organized. You'll want newspaper padding if you don't intend to ruin your mattress."

"Ah, the practical details. I see we are in safe hands, Charlotte."

Charlotte sat beside Nell, staring hopefully at Nick.

Wishing he were anywhere else, he sat on a chair in the hallway, contemplating deserting Charlotte and invading the kitchen to give his orders. When the baby was born, someone would want to wash the creature. They'd need warm water. And they'd want to wash Nell, be she alive or dead. Fortunately, the bell was answered by a manservant who looked harried. He explained he'd had an afternoon off, apologized for the wait, and hurried off to attend to the water.

Nell moaned. After some time, the maid returned with a message from Mrs. Adams that she would arrive as soon as possible.

"Mrs. Hawthorn's personal maid has just arrived back from her day off, too," she said, hesitating. "She'll be here as soon as she has changed into her uniform."

When the woman arrived with an alarmed expression on her face, he ordered Nell to be made comfortable.

The maid entered Nell's room, and Charlotte came out. "Do you think she is nearing the finish?"

Vainly hoping to see the midwife sprint up the passage, he said, "I doubt it. She's not making half enough noise."

Charlotte smiled wearily. "She wouldn't, no matter how much it hurts. She's incredibly brave. Could you come inside with me now?"

"Tony would have my head if I did."

"Will he come in, Charlotte?" called a voice from the depths.

"He thinks Tony wouldn't approve."

"Tony is a pragmatist," Nell called. "He knows the end justifies the means. I think the baby's almost here. I'd be happier with an adviser. I've had the urge to push during the last few contractions, and I'm about to give in to it."

With reluctance, Nick moved into the room. Nell lay on her side covered from toes to shoulders with a sheet. She smiled, though she looked strained and blotchy. The maid was bathing her face.

"I expect if you want to push, you ought to. Whatever is natural can't be wrong."

Charlotte glanced at Nick and nodded in agreement. He noted her worried expression before she turned back to Nell. After two deep breaths, Nell closed her mouth and made a mighty effort. Nick could see every vein on her neck. He suppressed his urge to find a bottle of brandy. Charlotte would collapse if he left, and Nell would die alone.

Brave Nell. She deserved better than him watching her breathe her last. She reached out to him. He took her hand in his. As she stared into his eyes, her earnest gaze held him.

"The pain is worth the prize, Nick," she said, squeezing his hand as the next contraction overcame her.

"What's all this then, Mrs. Hawthorn? Can't you wait till I get here?" A very loud voice came from a surprisingly small woman. "This should be my easiest job today. You've almost finished. Now, roll onto your back and hold on to your ankles when you get your next pain, and give an almighty heave. You there, hold her head up for her. Can't you see she's tired?"

The note of authority in the woman's voice rallied Nick. Reprimanded and on edge, he sat behind Nell to support her head and shoulders as ordered. The small, noisy woman piled more newspapers under a sheet beneath Nell. "I'll want water to wash my hands."

Charlotte nodded at the maid who left. Nick stayed, sick with apprehension.

The woman aimed a piercing glance at Nick, indicating Charlotte. "Tell that girl there if she faints, she'll have to stay where she is. I've no time to be stepping over people."

"I think she heard you," he said, finding a husky murmur.

As pale as paper, Charlotte nodded and breathed deeply. When the next contraction came, Charlotte murmured encouragement to Nell. The midwife started to busy herself. Nick closed his eyes. He concentrated on Nell's pain, not his, knowing he'd lost all emotion. He stayed, too tense to move.

"Here's what we want," said the midwife finally.

A brief cry spluttered and stopped. His chest a lead weight, Nick stared at the tiny blue form held by the midwife. Unwilling to hope, he watched the blood-streaked creature begin to struggle, slipping around in her grip. Each breath transformed the dead blue skin into a live pink and, finally, a healthy red.

When the dawning realization hit him that this child lived, he eked out a long sigh. Nell struggled to sit, but her tired body refused to obey her will. Nick lifted her, his reactions automatic, and the length of his smile making his face ache.

"What is it?" Nell asked, clutching at his hand.

"A baby," Charlotte replied in a droll voice.

Both Nell and Nick laughed, Nell in delight and Nick with sheer release as the midwife cut the cord and put the baby into Nell's arms.

"A great, big, black-headed boy," Nell said, nuzzling her face into the bloody bundle.

"Big?" Nick murmured. "Surely he's small."

"Bless you, Mr. Hawthorn. He'd be a nine pounder at least."

"Mr. Alden," Nick said. "I'm Nick Alden and this is my wife, Charlotte."

"What are you doing in here then?" The midwife pressed her fists on her hips, her eyes wide with outrage. "I've never heard of such a thing. Calling in your friends to help you have a baby! Out you go."

"Come to see me tomorrow," Nell said, counting the baby's fingers and toes as Nick and Charlotte fled the room.

"Next week," said the midwife.

Chapter 13

Outside, her hat looped by the ribbons over her arm, Charlotte leaned against the Hawthorn's front door. A gas lamp lit the semicircular front drive.

"I can't believe I'm so tired." She took Nick's arm into her hands and rested her forehead against his shoulder. The birthing had been exhilarating and somewhat frightening, but Nick had shown that she could rely on him, which had been a hope rather than an expectation when she sent for him. "I don't know what I would have done without your support."

"You would have managed. You're tougher than you think. I sent for the brougham." He indicated the burgundy and gold conveyance held steady by Harvey who showed only a careful profile. "I'll leave you to take yourself home. I have some unfinished business to attend."

She smiled. "Let your business wait. We should be celebrating tonight. It's not too often you have a chance to attend the birth of a baby."

His mouth tilted wryly. "Be that as it may, I shouldn't have been there. Nell is another man's wife."

She took a deep breath. "And yet you have been with another man's wife at a birth before."

He reared back, his face hard.

"I'm not absolutely sure I chose the right place for this." She indicated Harvey, who still hadn't turned his head. "Would it suffice to say that I know about Clara?"

He opened the brougham's door, waited for her to enter, and followed. The vehicle moved off as the door clicked. "And what do you think you know?" His voice sounded icy, and he folded his arms, his expression masked by the hooded interior.

"No more than anyone else." She glanced out the window. Only one or two vehicles traveled along the dark streets. "You're not the sort of man I thought I married, one who prefers male company." She repositioned her hat in her lap. "You were carnally involved with a married woman, that is, another man's wife, and she had your baby who died." She waited, her spine tense.

"It was only a matter of time before you discovered that." He massaged his forehead. "And so, now you know why I won't go through fatherhood again."

She faced him, not unsympathetic. "I wouldn't have hoped you might help me with Nell if I hadn't known you'd had the courage to stay with Clara."

"Courage? I had no choice," he said in a voice of disgust. "We were hardly the respectable couple. I couldn't afford a doctor, and I had no faith in the midwife—she kept shaking her head every time she felt the baby, and I thought she didn't want to help. No matter. It's done and gone and buried, literally. Fortunately, tonight's outcome was very different."

She put her hand on his knee. "Because of you. You gave us both confidence."

His laugh sounded like a mixture of surprise and outrage. "You both?" He shook his head. "If I had known you knew the truth, I could suspect a conspiracy—some sort of attempt to show me that my ever-present fears were groundless."

She considered. "You either hold women in too low esteem or perhaps too high. I hadn't thought of trying to influence you." Yet, she remembered Nell saying Charlotte had been clever to have asked Nick to help. Perhaps Nell had a plan. If so, she had been very generous and given Charlotte a great opportunity, which she must not waste. She inhaled a breath. "I was scared. I didn't know what would happen, and of course my first thought was that Nell might die."

He took her hand and turned over her gloved palm. "Yet you didn't leave her or stop supporting her for one moment despite your qualms and your lack of experience. I would call that courage."

"Or merely stupidly hopeful."

The hackney passed under a light, and Nick turned to examine her face. He didn't seem to be admiring her but simply trying to read her. Her breath stopped. For the first time, a man was trying to see through her façade.

"Not stupid," he said. "No, not stupid."

She thought he might kiss her, but instead he put her hand back in her lap and stared straight ahead.

"Nell is the real heroine." She wound her hat ribbons around her wrist. "I can't imagine how she went through that pain for that length of time, and I can't imagine managing with such dignity myself."

"Ah, my rambling rose. But you won't have to go through childbirth." He stretched out his legs, back to his usual mocking self.

"So you said." Testing herself, or him, she leaned her head against his broad shoulder.

He re-crossed his ankles, his hand again moving to hers and picking up two fingers idly. "Nell's baby can't be nine pounds. Clara's was that size, and he came two months before his time. The midwife must have made a mistake."

"She sees newborns every day." Charlotte entwined her fingers with his, trying to keep her breaths even. "It's easy to forget how babies look, newly born."

"Perhaps."

"Couldn't your unfinished business wait until tomorrow?" Her chest tight, she turned into him, slowly sliding her palm across his upper thigh. "I might want to seduce you tonight."

His hand clamped over hers. "So, I should let you have your wicked way?" He sounded cynically amused. "That would be an interesting experience."

"I expect so. You like me touching you."

"I like anyone touching me."

She put her hand between his legs and found he was hard. For her. "My. So you do." Ignoring the thundering of her heart, she measured her palm along his shape, but again he stayed her hand.

"Don't encourage me. We won't be coupling tonight."

"Because you don't want a baby?"

"My father has a saying—you must pay for the goods you spoil. I don't need to take an unnecessary risk."

Ignoring the second part of his statement, she said, "But I need to have my wicked way. Let me, Nick. I like touching you, and you like being touched. You like touching me and—why can't we please each other? Surely every coupling doesn't produce a baby?"

He rubbed his chin on her hair. She listened to the steady tap of the horse's hooves and the jingle of the tack. On either side, lit houses stood silhouetted against the silvery sky. The silence expanded, and the brougham turned through the stone gateway of Alden House. The graveled driveway crunched under the wheels.

"There are ways and means of preventing pregnancies," he said, finally.

"Well, then," she said with faked confidence. "That's settled."

The brougham stopped with a jolt. As if reprieved, he straightened, opened the door, and sprang out to await her.

She took the narrow steps and landed on her feet and against the flat of his chest. "Kiss me," she said, offering her lips, determined not to let him evade her this time.

"One moment." He signaled Harvey to drive on.

She held him around the waist with both arms, even now scared that he might decide to complete his unfinished business.

When the brougham reached the carriage house, he placed a kiss on her lips, one she easily prolonged by sliding her hands to the back of his neck and tickling her tongue across his mouth. She heard his breathing speed up, and she tingled with her success.

"And now, wife, to bed," he said into her neck.

Over his shoulder, she saw Harvey stroll from the carriage house, glance at them, and stop. The man slid his hand into his pocket and lifted out an envelope which he mimed he would like to give to Nick. Charlotte shook her head.

"What?" Nick said to her.

"Harvey is behind you."

"It would be wiser for him to stay there. I don't want to see his face again tonight, which he knows." With that, he changed his hold on her and hurried her into the house.

She clung to his arm, determined to bed him this time. If, after doing no more than insisting on her wicked way she became a real wife, then she would never regret being herself.

After reaching their night-lit rooms, he guided her into his bedroom and settled her onto his down-filled coverlet. A bottle and a glass sat on a tray with his bedside lamp. He hesitated for a moment before he began to undress. The light flickered over his smooth skin. From behind, his back was muscle-corded.

He stepped out of his rough working trousers, baring his tight buttocks and long, muscled legs. Fighting the unprecedented lack of coordination in her body, she swiped off her shoes. She'd wanted this, he had granted her wish, but the man was large, experienced, and quick to reject her when she annoyed him. Her hands trembled.

After stacking his clothes onto his bedroom chair, he faced her. Her eyes focused between his legs and stayed there. His naked part was much larger than she thought.

With a glinting questioning smile, he inclined his head. "Need help?" He sat on the bed beside her. Kissing her neck, he unbuttoned her gown, unhooked her corset, and eased her bodice past her shoulders.

Where his lips touched, her skin burned. Collecting her shaky limbs and faking self-possession, she slid off the bed and let her corset, gown, and petticoats drop. She peeled off her stockings. Wishing for half his confidence, she wriggled out of her under-drawers and her chemise.

Desire hazed his eyes, and he held out his hand to her, his gaze sweeping her body. "You are amazingly beautiful," he said in a thick voice. He pulled her onto the bed, encircling her arm around his neck. "But you know that."

He didn't require an answer, and although he was also amazingly beautiful, she knew that was the least of all attributes. In her nervousness, she clung to him like a vine. Fortunately, this disguised the tremors in her exposed skin.

"I've never been with a virgin," he said, his voice reverent. "I'll be as gentle as I can." A careful hand caressed her shoulders, and where he touched, she dissolved. His lips teased across hers.

He set the pace with gentle kisses, and when she had almost forgotten she lay naked in his arms, he lifted her onto the center of the bed. While flattening her palm on his smooth warm chest, he brushed his lips over hers, rolled, and she lay atop his perfect body. His protrusion pressed against her belly. As she prayed he wouldn't move, he rocked, settling his male part between her thighs. She found she could concentrate on nothing else.

He smiled. Disarmed, she smiled back and tried to appear as unconcerned as he. Taking heart from the easy expression in his eyes, she leaned down and took his bottom lip between hers. His hand covered her breast, and he groaned into her mouth.

Her belly contracted with pleasure, and she moved her hand between them. He hardened even more under her fingers and glided back and forth in her palm, devouring her mouth, demonstrating his approval of her avid grip. Back arched, she lifted, realizing her body needed no instruction to guide him. As she eased her hips to take him into her, he tensed.

"Not yet." He rolled. "I can't have you unless I'm wearing a French letter, our protection against pregnancy." Raising his head, he reached to the cupboard beside his bed and removed a white box.

He took out a flexible object and, without a flicker of embarrassment, stretched the casing over his male part. Although interested, she pressed her hands on her cheeks to cool her sudden blush.

Steadying her voice, she said, "You always meant this to happen. And you let me beg you."

He gave her a strange look. "Because I have protection available? You can't assume that. I was a single man for many years. Don't worry about this," he said, watching her expression. "You won't notice a thing. Touch me, sweetheart. You can't tell, can you?"

"No. You're still there, beneath."

"Ah, that's good." He leaned down and kissed her belly, and she quaked involuntarily.

Twisting a smile across his mouth, he said, "I have the idea that we'll have to start again. That's the curse of these things. They break the mood. You'll have to get used to me using protection. It's the only way we can be together."

"So we will be together another time?"

His gaze caught and held hers. "That depends on many factors, not the least of which would be your feelings in the matter." He took her mouth lightly, and she slid her arms around his neck and began kissing him again. He reciprocated with enthusiasm, caressing her and murmuring enticing words. Need built inside her. When he teased his hand between her legs, he again made her jolt with excitement. She threshed her head from side to side, and when he caught her mouth with his, her passion culminated. She seemed to explode in wave after wave of intense pleasure.

Carefully lifting his body over hers, he guided his male part into her. She eased the slight discomfort by settling her calves on his buttocks. He murmured encouragement, and she lifted to take him. Without warning, a scream of pain burst through her throat.

He stilled. His heart pounded against hers.

"You hurt me. Take it out." She squirmed under him, breathing in panicked gasps.

"Relax for a moment."

"I am relaxed."

"Your fingers are gouging into my back. I won't hurt you again, sweetheart." Taking a deep breath, he withdrew slightly and slid back. "If that hurt, I'll stop."

She breathed out, calming herself. "It didn't hurt. I'm just scared."

"Don't be. You had a momentary problem, a hymen, and I think we've dealt with that."

So she discovered as he recommenced his rhythmic sliding. Her body responded again, urging fiercer thrusts. He drove deeper and deeper, adding the tease of his fingers, an exquisite torment. With a sudden contraction, she shattered, and at about the same time he withdrew from her.

She lay back, her mind emptied of all but him and her awe of the act he'd encouraged her to perform. He lifted himself away and removed his French letter. With a long questioning smile, he glanced at her over his shoulder.

His bronze hair fell limply over one eye, and he brushed back a gold-flecked lock with one hand. "I think you liked that."

"I think I did."

He covered them both with the sheet from the foot of the bed and took her into his arms. Gathering her onto his chest, he stroked her back until she drifted into sleep.

* * * *

Charlotte opened her eyes to the bright morning light. Nick lay on his back with his palms behind his head, staring at the ceiling. Catlike, she stretched, watching him. He turned his head. "How do you feel this morning?"

"Content."

A knowing gaze traversed her body.

She blushed. "Sinful."

Brows raised, his eyes met hers.

"Slightly sore." She evaded his gaze.

He ran his thumbnail over his bottom lip, considering. "Too sore?"

Without knowing how she could, she prickled with excitement. "I usually go for a ride before the morning meal."

"Well, then," he said. "We won't make an exception of today."

For the first time, they both missed breakfast.

* * * *

Nick finally dressed around midday. He had contemplated the brandy bottle for some time, inspecting the amber fluid and sniffing the aroma. His mouth dried with need, but as he hadn't had a brandy since the tavern about twenty-four hours ago and could still control his tremors, he thought he might confine himself to ale today.

Charlotte appeared in the doorway of his bedroom. She had left his bed long since. "Nell said to see her today."

"The midwife said next week." He grinned.

"Who takes precedence? A midwife or a mother?"

She looked utterly lovely today. Most women looked haggard after a night such as she'd had, but her beauty was as much a part of her as her serenity. Even now, he had no idea why she wasn't furious that he'd let her think he was a daisy for so long.

"In this situation I think you can choose," he said.

"Might you accompany me?"

"I'm not needed at the cottages today, though I could drop in later to check progress. Yes, I will come with you," he said, not only evading the lure of the brandy bottle but indulging himself with the company of his newest amusement a little longer. "If only to make sure you don't stay too long." With luck, she mightn't pall on him for a month.

"I would have asked Sarah, but it seems she has gone to a picnic."

Strangely, being second choice prickled. Last night he'd been first.

They arrived in the hallway of the bluestone and redbrick built Hawthorn House in the middle of an event that looked like a cleaning spree. The hallway floor was marble-tiled in black and white, the walls painted red and mirrored, and the various entrances pillared. A maid from last night turned, hid a duster behind her back, and curtseyed to Nick and Sarah.

"The master's home," she said in a significantly dire tone.

Nick smiled. He could imagine how annoyed Tony would have been to miss all the excitement. This now made the visit worthwhile.

"Announce Mr. and Mrs. Alden," he said to the manservant who had to restrain himself from sweeping under Nick's feet.

The manservant came back with Tony hard on his heels. Far from being in the towering temper Nick expected, Tony was the proud papa to his fingertips. Nick almost couldn't look at him, such was his momentary jealousy, his second galling experience in less than an hour.

Tony took Charlotte by the shoulders and kissed her on each cheek, while Nick stood dumbfounded.

"Kiss me and you're mincemeat," he said, folding his arms.

"Thank you for the warning." Tony laughed. "I owe you both. Lord, what a time for me to be away from home." He glanced at Charlotte as if he was about to say something. Instead, he stepped back and ushered Nick and Charlotte up the long curved staircase to Nell's bedroom where she sat in a chair by the tall window. The light made her pale hair gleam silver.

"Not abed?" Nick asked, and she shot a glowering look at Tony.

"My lord and master has ordered that I rest today."

Tony spread his hands. "One day. Fortunately, my love is tired and can't fight back other than in words. One thing we haven't fought about is the name of our son. Charles Nicholas. And we want you both to be Godparents."

Nick stood, immeasurably touched. "We are honored." He put his arm around Charlotte's waist.

"We are lucky," she responded. "Charles is an exceptional baby. He didn't cry when he was born, nor while we were here. He seemed to be lord of all he surveyed."

"A true Hawthorn," Nell said drily. "Nick, I hope you know what an amazing wife you have. I will be forever grateful to you, Charlotte, and I consider you to be one of the family."

Tony looked at Nell. "That means you get Nick, too, you know."

She smiled, the door opened, and Charles Nicholas entered in the arms of his nursemaid.

Nick edged Charlotte to the door. "We shouldn't leave the horses standing any longer."

She stared at the baby longingly, but after saying all that was polite to his hosts, he ushered her out of the room. He drove his sporty gig to the cottages first—all was well—and craving a drink, he took Charlotte back home.

Sarah came out of the library. "Where on earth have you been? Nell had her baby yesterday. I heard the news at the picnic."

"We've just come from Hawthorn House." Charlotte put her hand on Sarah's arm. "We were there yesterday for the birth."

Sarah shuddered. "Ghastly. I don't want to know."

"It wasn't ghastly, was it?" Charlotte glanced at Nick.

"The outcome was successful." He walked up the stairs toward the brandy bottle. However, again he merely sniffed the aroma before he left for Dixon's gym, strangely resigned.

Chapter 14

Nick brought Charlotte to another shattering release. He couldn't believe his luck. By chance, he'd married a woman who appreciated the pleasures of the flesh and performed with starry-eyed enthusiasm. Rarely had he coupled with a woman who made no fuss over having her hair messed or her clothing tossed aside, who didn't insist on being feted in payment for sex, who didn't insist on anything.

Charlotte looked as exquisite naked as she did dressed, and she was the best card-cheat he'd ever met. He'd rediscovered that last night during a rare evening at home.

She smiled at him sleepily, her eyes already closing.

He tugged on one of her dark, springing curls. "I'm rather enamored of the idea of sleeping with my wife."

"It's done in the best of families," she said, snuggling into his chest. "Especially when couples want babies." She rested her lips against his chest.

He grasped her shoulder and made certain she looked into his eyes. "No babies," he said, jolted out of his complacency. "Not mine. Never mine. I can only make monsters."

She blinked at him. "Why on earth would you say that?"

"Previous experience," he said tightly.

"How many previous babies have you had?"

"Just the one. That was enough." He moved out of her hold and sat up.

She frowned. "You don't know you can only make monsters."

"I do." He swung his legs over the side of the bed. "I won't risk another child of mine being born dead or even worse, crippled."

"But why was that your fault? Couldn't the problem have been pure bad luck?"

He stood. "No."

"I want to know how you know that." She lifted her shining hair and wound the dark mass over one shoulder.

"My father was an only child, and my grandfather was an only child. My mother came from a prolific family, and she had five babies after me," he said, emphasizing each word, "but not one lived. The fault is clearly in my family, and I've proved it once. Once is enough. When you're a little older and know how to behave with discretion, perhaps you could find another to sire a child on you. I'll accept it as mine."

"As you would the child you thought I carried." She glanced at him, her head slightly tilted in query.

"Yes."

"You would like me to commit adultery."

"Not immediately." His insides lurched with a momentary panic. He was well on the way to being in love with her, but he couldn't let himself grow emotionally involved—not with a woman who would end up despising him. "If you have issues with my decisions, I'll go back to my former way of life."

She dropped her hair and gave a sudden laugh. "Not easy in your case when you so clearly love women."

"You wretch," he said, angling toward her. He'd thought they were having words, and they were, but not heated words. Words more of an exploratory kind.

She knelt behind him and circled her arms around his neck. He leaned back and lost himself in a deep kiss.

In the aftermath, she said, "Do I know everything I ought to know as your wife? I found out about the rowing and Clara from the others."

Meshing his fingers with hers, he gave a wry smile. "There was another woman when I married you. Others know of her, too." He waited, his chest tense.

She lifted his hand to her cheek.

He evaded her gaze. "And before Beth, there were others. Have I made myself clear? I don't want you to have any misconceptions about me or the sanctity of my relationship with Clara."

"Beth," she said, mulling the name. "She must have been very upset when you married."

His relationship with his mistress had ended, and a longer explanation would benefit no one. Unwilling to show himself in a bad light to his wife, he shrugged.

During the next week, he discovered why married men looked so self-satisfied. Mistresses kept a man waiting to hold his interest. Wives used other tactics, already having a husband's interest. His own wife, cool, elegant Charlotte, might have done her best to shock him in the carriage on the way home from a soiree but, instead, she seduced him so thoroughly that he didn't notice they'd arrived home. She just had time to wriggle out from under him and rearrange her skirts as Harvey opened the carriage door.

The coachman shot Nick a glance of dislike, but his gaze softened on Charlotte. Without a doubt, the old grouch knew what had taken place moments before, but he handed Charlotte out as if she were the queen about to visit dignitaries, and he let the door bang on Nick's knee.

Nick laughed to himself on the way into the house. The coachman had developed a protective instinct for Charlotte, who, without stirring a single hair on her immaculately coiffed head, had turned a large household of lackadaisical servants into devoted slaves. Her quiet presence made a house into a home and a difference of opinion into an irrelevance. He put on his own smug face as she went into her bedroom to undress.

Hesitating in the connecting room, he noticed his mail had multiplied in the past three days and needed inspection. He skimmed through; his attention caught by an unmarked envelope, which curiosity tempted him to open. Hearing a board creak, he looked up and saw Charlotte coming toward him wearing nothing but a knowing smile.

With no preliminaries and pausing only to toss the envelope toward his tray, he took her against his bedroom door. Unprepared for the immediacy of the moment and appalled by his lack of control, he managed to withdraw before his final thrust, spilling his seed onto her belly.

He cleaned her up with his shirttails, realizing that his hands were shaking. "No more little surprises, my love. I don't want to make any accidental babies."

She cupped his face with her hand. "I'm sorry. This is new to me. I suppose I was testing my attraction."

Although he didn't want to, he laughed. "You don't need to test a young, healthy male. He tests himself at least ten times a day. Which in my case is much safer."

She gave him a considering look and sashayed into his room. He followed and undressed while she watched from his bed. Just a glance from her could harden him, which he could see pleased her. He'd thought he wouldn't be interested in a woman so young, but somehow his self-contained wife was helping him see life from a different perspective. For some time, he hadn't wanted or thought about drinking.

"Sarah ate two slices of bread today. I've never seen her happier."

"She has a social life par to none." He slid into bed beside her. "She's never at home. I expect you'll have her married off this season."

"Do you think she has a chance with James?"

He knew she wanted to talk, but at this moment, he didn't care about Sarah's prospects. "I doubt it. His family is the wealthiest in the colony. Who did you say her father was?"

"A country doctor."

"Not quite the sea captain yours was. A sea captain can become an admiral, but a country doctor is always a country doctor."

She turned down the lamp. "I thought she was aiming too high. The Hawthorns are a very old, landed family, not just rich. I don't doubt my birth made me an ineligible wife for James, not that I had ever considered James. Though I don't think Tony knew that."

He smiled. "I suspect you and Sarah received Nell's invitation for the ball so that he could closely inspect you. You both were also honored by an invitation to the dinner beforehand. You must have had him really worried."

She snuggled down under the covers. "Nevertheless, it was a good opportunity."

"Of which you took full advantage," he said smoothly.

"I can't take all the credit." She gave a mischievous smile. "You were drunk."

He laughed, despite her unrepentant expression. "Then it serves me right."

"It's a shame Sarah doesn't like Luke."

He blinked at the tangent. "I don't think he's hanging out for a wife."

"Nor do I," she said, surprising him, for he had assumed she didn't know Luke was still in love with her.

The fool had lost her because he had taken so much time to make up his mind to propose. Nick hadn't saved one friend from an undesirable marriage and the other from a scandal. As the cards fell, he'd saved neither friend in the seeking of his family's salvation, but had instead found himself a very suitable wife. She may have disrupted his life, but she had also made his family house into a comfortable and welcoming home—and her husband into a doting fool.

Nevertheless, hers and Sarah's invitation to the Hawthorn's exclusive pre-ball dinner did seem a heavy-handed way to inspect a flirt of James's, not typical of Tony, who could have used the ball alone for the same purpose. The pre-ball dinner was tantamount to approving Charlotte and Sarah's acceptance into society.

Tony was normally subtle rather than obliging. Something about his attitude toward Charlotte before and after the birth of his baby simply didn't fit.

Nick rubbed the back of his neck. He and Tony really did need to talk.

* * * *

Charlotte, a sated but still uneasy wife, picked up the letter opener. Lately, she'd had not a qualm about raising her face for her husband's kiss, hugging him, teasing him, laughing with him, and sliding into his bed at night. Her mother had been the same, obsessed by one man only. Adeline saw the man, whom Charlotte recalled as very tall and dark, only a few times in her distant memory.

She was lucky, far luckier than her mother. In time, Nick would come to accept that few women died in childbirth and even less babies were born deformed. Then her life would be complete. She could wait. Most people didn't change overnight.

She glanced at the unmarked envelope on the top of her pile, assuming the note had been hand-delivered and needed quick attention.

My darling Nicky,

You know I am insane about you…

Charlotte frowned. She had opened correspondence to Nick. She shouldn't read on. She refolded the paper and replaced the letter in the blank envelope. Staring at the silver tray that held the rest of her correspondence, she stood, slapping the note repeatedly against her skirts, her mind churning. Finally, she pulled the bell-rope. Vera answered almost immediately.

"Vera, I found this letter on my tray. Do you know how I came to have it?"

Vera blinked. "Good morning, ma'am. I found it on the floor this morning. Did I put it on *your* tray? It was meant for Mr. Nick."

"You found it on the floor?"

"It must have dropped there. I brought it up with some other letters two or three days ago, I think. Harvey give it to me—said it was for Mr. Nick. He doesn't take much interest in his mail, does he?" Vera glanced at Nick's overflowing tray.

"Most of his letters are bills." Charlotte shrugged. "Mine are mainly invitations, and so I deal with them daily. How did Harvey come by the note?"

"I expect he wrote it." Vera laughed. "He's been in the black books lately, and so he's likely passing on tips about the horses. Good at that, he is, and many's the time he's put Mr. Nick in the way of a sure bet."

"Oh." Charlotte assumed her scatter-brained expression. "Is that what it was? I opened it by mistake and, heavens, I thought it was for me." She waved the letter like a fan. "Thank you, Vera. No harm done. My husband will never know I've discovered his dastardly secret."

Vera left, grinning. Charlotte sat with the note that a woman in love with Nick had given to Harvey to deliver surreptitiously. Finally, she left for the drawing room. When she had finished discussing the weekly menus with the housekeeper, she sat for some minutes with her hands clasped. Better the devil she knew. She sprang to her feet, hurried up the stairs, and opened the blank envelope again.

With shaking hands and her heart in her stomach, she read:

You know I am insane about you. Would I put up with your behavior were I not? My jealousy was unfounded and unreasonable. I know you have to be seen with your wife occasionally and, in future, I'll not say a word.

Believe me, repenting my temper, I am ready to make amends any way you so choose. Unless I hear otherwise, I'll expect to see you as usual tomorrow.

Your Beth.

P.S. The dressmaker's bill arrived. You'll be pleased to know that the red gown only cost five pounds.

With icy hands, Charlotte lowered herself into Nick's brown velvet chair, grasping the worn pile on the arms. He'd told her he had finished with Beth when he had married. Judging by the letter, they'd merely had a recent spat. She shivered, swaying forward over crossed arms.

Although she didn't want to say the words to herself, and especially not to him, she loved Nick, possibly had from the day he'd been struck unconscious and feverishly calling for forgiveness, or possibly she'd loved him the night, proud and lonely, he had agreed to marry her to keep his secret, the secret that didn't exist. Instead, he'd married her to get her baby, which ironically also didn't exist.

She put her head in her hands and squeezed her eyes tight. She'd been so foolish. She didn't know a thing about men. She'd been trapped by Nick's kindness to her cousin, by his unthinking generosity, by his cynical amusement, and his gradual changes of heart. She had hoped that one day he would care for her, too. But he'd lied to her. He only used her for his own ends.

Perhaps she was being too quick to judge. He lied rarely, he said.

She stood and examined her face in the mirror, the face that others praised so highly without seeing the woman behind the features, the woman who disliked putting herself forward and detested being judged by how she looked. Somehow Nick had learned to accept his looks, though he wasn't any more above using them than she was. He had also given her an opportunity to be someone other than a decoration, a caring and efficient wife.

She had to be fair; she had to give Nick a chance to explain. Although her eyes ached, she put the note back into the envelope and placed Nick's letter back onto his mail tray.

* * * *

Nick wanted to renovate the workers' cottages on the property in the hills where these days his father ran an apple orchard. Originally, the place had been built for respite during the summer heat, but his father was a natural businessman. In recent years, the orchard had expanded to a commercial size. Better accommodation would keep the itinerate workers longer. For the past week, Nick hadn't had an alcoholic drink, and he'd spent the day in his father's offices on Rundle Street putting the costs together. He pounded up the stairs to his sitting room.

Charlotte's bedroom door stood open. Pleased with himself, he strode over, greeted by the sight of his exquisite wife standing in front of her mirror brushing her thick hair. She wore a corset and petticoats, and she looked delectable. "If this is the outfit you plan to wear for dinner, I think we should have dinner in the bedroom." He raised his eyebrows.

She turned, twisting her hair into the long roll that with a few more turns made a frame for the back of her lovely neck. "We're engaged for an evening at the Hendersons'. Cards and dancing for the younger set." Soft tendrils caressed her lovely face.

"I'll need to change."

She stabbed a few lethal-looking pins through the knot and turned to the dull red gown laid out on her bed. With a sensuous wriggle, she pulled the draped confection up over her hips. The color of her gown enhanced the perfect white of her skin. She arranged herself into her bodice and settled her heavy skirts. Nick automatically moved over to hook the back. When he finished, he brushed a kiss over her delicate nape, noticing her light rose scent.

After a glance at her face in the mirror, he pressed another kiss to the lobe of her ear.

"What do you do at your club?" she asked, wriggling away.

"These days I mainly use the gymnasium." He pushed his hands into his pockets. "I enjoy the exercise. Why?"

"Four hours is a long time to spend exercising."

He shrugged. "I socialize as well."

She leaned closer to the mirror and primped the low shoulders of her gown. "Thomas put out your evening suit."

Reluctantly, he backed to her doorway. Like most women when bent on a plan, she could be single-minded. "Right. Time for me to change."

"I put your mail in your room, too."

"You spoil me, my pretty peony."

"I wonder if perhaps I do." She angled her head sideways and screwed on a jet earring, concentrating deeply on her already faultless appearance.

Dismissed, he left. Ten or more letters sat on his bedside table. He opened the first, tossed the envelope into his waste bin, and left the bill flattened on the table. The second had not been addressed. He read Beth's epistle, sighed, and glanced at his waste bin. However, self-preservation made him tuck her note and a wad of money into his evening jacket pocket. He'd been remiss. Although he'd ended his association with Beth, he still needed to settle her bills, as per her reminder.

Squaring his shoulders, he presented himself back in Charlotte's doorway. "It seems I have a previous engagement. Make my apologies to the Hendersons, would you? I'll arrange for Harvey to bring me along later."

"Of course," she answered, choosing a black-beaded evening bag from her drawer. "You're not needed. This is mainly a function Sarah wanted to attend."

Noting her disinterest, he stood, hesitant. She turned, smiling gloriously at him, and with a lighter heart, he buttoned his jacket and departed.

* * * *

Two hours later, Nick arrived in the stately, over-decorated, dark green drawing room of his hostess, Laura Henderson. Mrs. Henderson had presented her youngest daughter last year, at which time Nick had only recently returned to the family fold. She had not invited him to her function then, very wise, for he didn't enjoy innocents.

"I thought this might be a trifle tame for you." Mrs. Henderson, an experienced sophisticate, indicated the room filled with the usual respectable set, gossiping, balancing plates of food, or sipping delicately at sherry. The youngsters would be dancing in the adjoining room as indicated by the sound of feet pounding to the dirge of a piano and a few strings.

"Marriage has reformed me," he said, smiling lightly.

Her expression politely disbelieving, she indicated a room to the right. "You'll find your wife in the card room."

An alarm bell rang in his head. Alerted, he strode into a comfortable room set up with five or six small tables where Charlotte sat enthroned at a table for four, attended by three fawning courtiers.

"Nick." She lifted her head, and the flickering gaslight made mysterious shadows on the stark purity of her face.

He moved behind her and kissed her cheek, glancing at her cards. She had a good hand.

"No room here," said one of the gentlemen, Delemore, barely moving his gaze from his cards. "Find another table. Oh, it's you, Alden."

"I'm not playing. I'm here to bear my wife off."

"I can't leave now," Charlotte said, with a charmingly innocent smile. "I'm restoring your fortune."

He started to sweat. "No need, my precious. I haven't lost a penny."

"Nor has she. The damndest luck," said a good-looking male in his early twenties.

She glanced at Nick. "Have you met Mr. Eglinton?"

The man nodded at Nick. "The lucky husband, I presume. Not only is your wife beautiful, she's an expert card player. I expect I'll leave tonight with empty pockets." He aimed a long intimate glance at Charlotte.

"Oh, dear. You're begging for mercy," she said with a great fluttering of eyelashes. "Now what shall I do?"

She gave a smile that exposed two dimples Nick had never noticed before. "I suggest you turn in that appalling hand of yours before anyone asks to see it," he said, hooding his gaze. "I have an urgent desire to dance with you."

She turned to stare at him. "I'll finish this hand first. Do sit, Nick. Your face is making everyone nervous."

He moved back, wishing he'd given her pause by describing her good hand as appalling. Though perhaps because she always beat him, she thought he didn't know a good hand from a bad one. With her lips in a pretty pout, she not only made fast work of the game but also managed to lose most of the money stacked in front of her. Relieved, he bore her off to the ballroom.

"You're open game, you know," he said as he took her into a waltz.

"And *you* know I play quite well." She gazed around the room as she danced with him, smiling and nodding at almost everyone.

"That's not quite my meaning," he said slowly. "You're a married woman, and you were flirting with those three gentlemen. Each would have let you win."

"I don't allow people to let me win. I win only on my merits." Her perfect jaw firmed.

"Again, we're talking at cross purposes. Each of those gentlemen was more interested in tossing you onto your back than tossing in their hand."

At last, her gaze met his. "As your wife I need to know how to entertain myself and so I began tonight."

His head ached. Not only had he needed to sort out Beth's overdue accounts, he'd also had a raging argument with her as he'd tried to leave. To say the least, he'd experienced an unpleasant end to a successful day. "I see. I was late, and I'm being punished."

She sighed. "Nick, I've been to more functions without you than with you. I'm simply telling you that I meet very pleasant people whose company I enjoy."

"Mr. Eglinton being one."

"He's also very handsome. I like flirting with handsome men."

"Perhaps, but I don't share my women."

"How strange. I expect they don't want to share you either. And now, if you don't mind, I promised this next dance to Luke." She stopped with the music and was swung back onto the floor by Luke, who had apparently been waiting behind him with Sarah.

"How lovely to see you here, Nick." Sarah looked anything but pleased as she watched Luke leave. "There he goes again, pattering after Charlotte like a good little lap dog. I don't know why she bothers to pat him occasionally. It only brings him back for more."

"Perhaps you would honor me?" He held out an arm to Sarah, who accepted and proceeded to comment on Luke's pathetic behavior.

"Are all the functions I miss as boring as this one?" he asked, now completely annoyed.

"This one is particularly dull. I don't have any objection to leaving early. Though, Charlotte looks as though she could dance all night."

He waited with her for the set to finish, and then he took the two ladies home. The conversation in the carriage was desultory, and Charlotte said not a word to him after they entered their sitting room. Smiling politely, she walked to her bedroom and shut her door.

Eyes narrowed, he strode to his own room and *slammed* his door. Like too many women, his wife assumed sexual intimacy with him meant she could govern his every move. He tossed his jacket into the corner. Perhaps she intended to manipulate him by withholding her favors, but a man couldn't chase after a woman who wanted complete control over him. Strange. She hadn't seemed like the controlling type, which was possibly why their marriage had been strengthening day by day. And, reminded, he couldn't say he knew her character at all.

Tony had been investigating her. The time had come to ask his findings.

Chapter 15

Charlotte put off her early ride, washed, and dressed for breakfast. Gossip had always been perfunctory while the gentlemen read their papers, but this day Nick kept his beside his plate. He and she greeted each other politely, and she served herself a coddled egg. She wouldn't be her mother, waiting until all hope was lost. Sarah kept up a running commentary on world affairs and the doings of her set, one and the same in her opinion.

Automatically, Nick bent to kiss Charlotte before leaving for wherever he had decided to go. She turned her face slightly, leaving his mouth to brush her ear. She saw impatience on his face, and she hardened her heart. A conjugal relationship based on convenient lies and physical attraction was not enough for her.

After completing her meal, she returned to her room and dressed in her newly tailored burgundy riding habit, adding a firmly planted citrus pillbox hat with a burgundy net bow. Pulling on chamois gloves, she went to Sarah's door. "Would you like to join me for a ride?"

"You know I can't keep up with you."

"It's too late in the day for me to take a gallop. I'll be riding sedately in the park and greeting every other rider."

"That sounds desperately boring."

"It's as boring as you want to make it. I've been trying to show myself off as a respectable young matron, which I need to do if I want to advance you in society."

Sarah scrutinized her expression. "You *are* in a bad mood. You only needed to ask if you wanted me to go with you."

Within five minutes, dressed neatly in a dark brown outfit and a hat comprising curling blue flowers, she joined Charlotte, who instead of collecting her own horse, asked the stable boy to bring their mounts to the front door. She and Sarah rode off to the park.

Those with social pretensions rode by, greeting others and stopping to gossip. After they'd smiled their heads off in every direction and spoken to those few who Charlotte knew, Sarah said in a dire tone, "Oh, no. What bad luck. How do you do, Mr. Worthing? Shouldn't you be occupying yourself in court?"

"I'm a solicitor, not a barrister, Miss Page, and my office opens at ten." He pulled a fob watch from his pocket and checked the time. "I will be there in half an hour or so. Good morning, Charlotte."

"Good morning, Luke. I'm sure you have Sarah's permission to call her by her first name."

"Not any longer," Sarah said with a jut of her bottom lip.

He ignored her and glanced at Charlotte. "Why do you look put out today?"

"Perhaps because I missed my early morning exercise." She patted Red Robin's neck.

"Perhaps you merely look more married."

"Which you would see as a reason to be disgruntled." She gave him a happily married smile, bright and wide.

"Except you're married to Nick, which would be pure bliss," Sarah said. "You're the luckiest woman in the world."

Luke shrugged. "I suspect being married to him is about as blissful as being one of his friends."

Charlotte held his gaze. "So you must feel very lucky, too."

"Not quite. He was the man who won you," he said with a shrug.

With no answer to that, Charlotte readjusted her reins, preparing to move off.

"Quite the spurned suitor, aren't you?" Sarah said to him, tight-lipped. "Let's say the better man won. Nick adores Charlotte, and he is a wonderful husband."

"I'm sure he is a very indulgent husband. He loves women, *all women,* young, old, smart, silly, pretty, or plain."

A warm flush of shame colored Charlotte's cheeks. Men stuck together. Luke knew about Nick's infidelity. "I'm sure I feature somewhere on your long list."

His shoulders lifted. "You're the woman he married. Of course you do. I never thought he would be interested in you, which is why I didn't see what was going on under my nose."

"Why wouldn't he be interested in me?"

Luke raised his brows. "You're beautiful, not simply pretty, and Nick doesn't worry about looks. He has enough of his own."

"Jealousy, jealousy," Sarah said in an acid voice. "You are saying he's vain."

Luke raised his square hand as if for peace. "He doesn't care how he looks. That's easy when nature has endowed him not only with the looks of a Greek god, but with brains and charm. If only the good Lord would endow him with red hair for one day of his life."

Sarah gave him a rap on the knuckles with her crop. "How ungallant. You might not like your hair, and with good reason, but mine is my crowning glory."

He stared at Sarah as if he had never noticed she, too, had reddish hair. "Beautiful people are greatly advantaged and don't understand that the less beautiful have to strive harder, behave more nobly, and *watch their tongues*."

Sarah gasped.

"You say I'm beautiful," Charlotte said, carefully. "Do you think I don't try hard or behave nobly?"

Luke hesitated. "I think you accept your advantages, yes, and I also think you should open your eyes and deal with the realities." He tipped his hat and rode off.

"I said he was a brute." Sarah gave a smug smile. "He as good as told you, his perfect woman, that you're shallow."

"I certainly haven't proved I'm anything else." Charlotte blinked and swallowed hard. Luke's advice, although unwelcome, bolstered her belief that Nick would never have the same feelings for her as she had for him. "I can't change the way I look, and I wouldn't want to, but I can try harder."

"To do what?" Sarah sent her a quick, suspicious glance.

"To deal with the realities." Charlotte moved her horse to a clipping walk. "Mama spent her whole life preparing me to marry well, and she died. I've achieved her dream, but I have my own dreams. Life doesn't end with marriage." Not wanting Sarah to see how hard Luke's knowledge of Nick had hit her, she took Red Robin into a controlled canter and, with Sarah following, she left the riding track.

A very long time ago, she'd expected to have her own children. After marriage, she'd thought she might dote on Sarah's, but now both were pointless objectives. Although she could run a house invisibly and plan a menu for a month without wasting an item of food, her management skills were as yet untapped.

Yes, she would deal with the realities. Despite how she acted, she was no fool. She was perfectly competent and more than willing to work hard, and yet she'd left her renovation project to others. The time had come to take an active part. The sooner she completed outfitting her building, the sooner her unmarried mothers would be secure.

She had more to think about than a hopeless, loveless marriage.

* * * *

Nick followed Tony into his study. "Good of you to spare the time to see me. This shouldn't take long."

Nick had been in this room last on the night of the ball. That night, he'd been the one interviewed, which in his drunken state he'd found hilarious. This time, he kept his face serious and glanced around the cedar-paneled room, wondering if he would enjoy having a space like this to call his own. His father had one.

"A friend who made sure my wife survived childbirth may be sure of my attention." Tony took a seat behind a desk large enough to sleep two.

"I was in your debt in the first place. That business with Clara—but for you and Luke helping me through the burials, I would have topped myself."

"I doubt it, and since the drink hasn't killed you since, you are certainly a survivor. Now, how can I help you?"

Nick settled himself into a comfortable chair and crossed his legs. "I want to know what you haven't told me about Charlotte."

"Why would you assume I know more than you?"

"Because you investigated her and because the last time we had a conversation about this, you hedged your words. You didn't need to do that if you didn't know a fact or two you thought you should hold back."

Tony shifted his gaze. "I'm not sure if I should tell you or her or neither. It's a damned awkward situation."

"Which will be resolved by telling me what you know."

"Do you have feelings for Charlotte?" Tony stared directly at Nick.

Nick hesitated. "I have a great regard for her. She is everything a man could want in a wife."

Tony rubbed the back of his neck. "I don't want her hurt, and amazingly enough I believe you don't either. And so I'll begin by telling you that almost a year ago my solicitor told me that a woman to whom my father had granted a life pension had died." He meshed his fingers, leaning forward. "Naturally, I stopped our payments, and naturally I looked up the recipient, a woman named Mrs. Adelina Davies."

Nick frowned.

"Yes, Charlotte's mother. I discovered that twenty years previously, my father had signed over a house in Kensington to her."

"Very generous of him," Nick said slowly.

"Bear in mind that Charlotte owned a house in Kensington. Also bear in mind that the first time I saw Charlotte she was with James, and they both turned to me at the same time with the same querying expression on each of their faces. I swear I took a step back. Their likeness is astounding."

Nick paused, examining the backs of his hands. "Are you implying what I think?"

"When I asked about her parents, she told me both had died. Further pressed, she said her father was a naval captain who died before she was born. If I'd pushed harder, she'd have avoided me, I thought. So I told Nell of my suspicions and together we tried to ease her into friendship."

"The income and the house don't prove she's a...related to you. Or the fact that she has a resemblance to James."

"I don't have proof, no. I found her father's death certificate. He did, indeed, manage to die before Charlotte was born, in fact only three weeks after his marriage and four weeks before the birth of his only child. The British navy's records show him to be a fine, upstanding officer who exceeded his orders at the battle of Waterloo."

"Making him a little older than the normal newlywed."

"He was seventy-six at the time."

"Ah, a deathbed romance."

Tony rose and turned his back to gaze out the window at the garden below. "Miss Page said their grandfather was a man of the cloth. I have distant memories of my father and a rector having some sort of ruckus in our hall. This was during my first years at school. I couldn't say exactly when." He turned back and faced Nick. "I surmise the man was insisting my father oblige him by finding a husband for his daughter. I really have nothing with which to confront Charlotte, and I hate to destroy any illusions she might have about her mother."

"Does her paternity matter?" Nick used the tips of his fingers to knead his forehead.

"Perhaps not to you, but naturally, when Mrs. Davies died, I stopped her income. Had I reinstated the money when I found out about Charlotte, she would have been in just as much of a pickle. She would have known my father was keeping her mother. If she didn't know, and since she has never confronted me, I have to assume she didn't, she would surely wonder why. Since I can only surmise why, I decided with Nell's cooperation to keep quiet and bring her out, so to speak."

"You stopped her income?" Nick asked, beginning to see, perhaps, why Charlotte had told him she *had to marry and soon*. "And since she had no other means of support, she wanted a husband, any husband, instantly."

"Apparently, she wanted you." Tony shrugged. "And why not if you had previously, ah, dallied with her?"

Ignoring Tony's reasonable logic, Nick shook his head, almost in admiration. "I can't imagine how she managed to get noticed without any connections in society."

"Of course you can."

Nick nodded slowly. Of course he could. He knew very well that people were judged by their looks. Even he, despite his drinking and his past, was happily accepted into society, though his father's money helped. "Why didn't you tell me of your suspicions on the night of the ball?"

"Had I, you would have left her to me. Then what chance would she have had of a respectable marriage, acknowledged as my father's by-blow and compromised by you? Do you think Luke would have snapped her up?"

"Oh, he assumed I had compromised her."

"You were drunk."

"He was mighty easy to put off." Nick smiled sourly.

Tony gazed across the desk. "Now you are married and the gossip has no teeth."

"And if you find she is your sister?"

"James and I had every advantage. If a sister of mine had to live without knowing who her father was, or in low circumstances, I would like to even the score, somewhat."

Nick rose to his feet. "Do you plan to tell her?"

"Wouldn't you want to know who your father was?"

Nick let his face express his cynicism. "This takes us into a discussion about whether he's the man who plants the seed or the one who wants the child. I think Charlotte would like more family, but I know she has social aspirations. I see no reason to dash them. Let's not make a decision yet."

He left, not certain how he should have reacted or if he should care that Charlotte's mother had been Tony's father's mistress. In all, he didn't, but he was quite sure she would.

After an afternoon with a surveyor and a bout at the gymnasium, he arrived home, changed for dinner, and presented himself downstairs.

"Apparently, Charlotte has a previous engagement," Alfred said, querying Nick with his eyes.

Nick shrugged.

"She said she could be a little late," Sarah said, helping herself to asparagus.

Nick suspected his wife might be giving him a lesson in punctuality. By the time the fruit and cheese had been removed from the dinner table, he began to fidget. Sarah maintained an animated conversation with Alfred and neither looked the least worried about Charlotte's tardiness.

Interrupting Sarah's lofty assessment of Luke, Nick said with a frown, "Does anyone know where Charlotte went?"

"She didn't say, but stop worrying. I see you've scarcely eaten a bite." Sarah gave a significant nod, emphasizing, no doubt, the times her intake caused comment.

"We had a slight disagreement last night, and I thought she might be in a mood."

Sarah stared at him. "Charlotte doesn't have moods."

Nick put his napkin onto the table. "I'll stroll over to the stables and see if her plans were known." With burgeoning apprehension, he left the room.

After noting Red Robin in her stall, he called to Rob. "What time did Mrs. Alden leave?"

"Mr. Harvey took her out in the afternoon, but she sent him home a small time later, Mr. Nick."

"And she didn't ask to be collected?" Nick tightened his jaw. "Does anyone here have a thought for her safety?"

"Mr. Harvey said maybe he needed orders afore he went ferretin' around in her business," said Rob in a hurt voice.

Nick planted two loose fists on his hips. "So, he's learned his lesson." He confined himself to forcibly shutting the yard gate before returning to the dining room. "As I thought. She's playing a childish game."

Frowning, Sarah said, "I'm sure she wouldn't be putting herself in danger. More likely she's with friends."

He gave a casual nod and left the room, certain if he went chasing around after his wife she would use the same childish tactics each time she wanted to teach him a lesson. How him being a couple of hours late for a boring soiree could have so annoyed her was beyond his comprehension. Upstairs, pacing the floor, he decided to wring her neck if she'd not been involved in a fatal accident.

A little before ten he heard a carriage in the driveway. A few minutes later, the sitting room door opened.

"Where have you been?" he asked, his face iced, looking pointedly at the clock on the mantle.

"Do I ask where you've been when you come home late?" She removed her cherry-colored hat and stripped off her gloves.

He folded his arms. "A man doesn't marry to wait up for his wife."

"Oh. I assumed you had other options," she said, heading for her bedroom.

He scowled, staring at her closed door. Roiling with irrational anger, he went to his room and undressed, then lay in bed with his hands behind his head, breathing flames. If she'd had a reason to be jealous, he would understand, but she didn't.

By breakfast the next morning, he'd decided to forgive her—if she apologized, if she told him where she'd been, but she didn't appear for breakfast.

"I heard Charlotte come in last night," Alfred said gruffly after Sarah left. "You must tell her she should take the carriage for her visiting. It's not right for her to be hiring hackneys."

Nick heaved a breath. "Perhaps I should have told her that instead of being justifiably righteous."

"She had you worried."

"At least I didn't threaten to withhold her allowance."

"Waste of time, my boy. I gave her an allowance when she married you, and she has already spent this quarter's."

Nick frowned. "You gave her an allowance?"

His father lifted his chin. "I wasn't sure you could afford her."

"Let me get this straight. You gave Charlotte an allowance, but when I couldn't support Clara you withheld mine." Nick leaned back in his chair, his voice tight.

His father remained silent.

"Charlotte married me for security. Clara lost hers, and her life, because she couldn't marry me."

Alfred cleared his throat. "I didn't want to repeat my mistake."

Nick dropped his gaze and momentarily concentrated on the rose pattern adorning his teacup. Teacup! When did he stop drinking ale? And why? He closed his eyes briefly. "It was my mistake, not yours," he said in a low voice. After a short silence, he faced his father and leaned back in his chair. "The worst being that I didn't love Clara. Oh, I know I've let you think she was the love of my life, but that's not so. My interest in her lasted no longer than the act that tied us together. I wouldn't have seen her again but…" He shook his head, reliving his helplessness. "What choice did I have? She was bearing my child. Her husband had thrown her out, and she had nowhere else to turn." His fingers cramped in his tight hold, and he rubbed them, watching the color return.

"Nick, my boy, I'm not about to pass judgment."

"My baby killed her, and I've made enough mistakes I'm not intending to repeat." He squared his shoulders, pushed out his chair, and left for a meeting with his father's business manager, well aware that one of those mistakes was blaming his father for an event that was none of his responsibility. For too long Nick had indulged himself over the episode that had changed the course of his life.

Now, because of his marriage to Charlotte, he seemed to be on the path to redemption. He drank tea instead of ale, he kept reasonable hours, and he preferred his wife to his mistress. However, he needed to take control of his tongue.

His wife was currently displeased with him, and she had mentioned some man or other as a flirt.

At this stage, he certainly didn't intend to share her.

* * * *

Charlotte had mulled over her mother's predicament too many times to count. A discussion a month ago with Lady Grace had led to an agent who found her a dwelling large enough to house up to ten needy women. Half her quarterly allowance had been spent on renting the building for a year. Another fifty pounds was currently being spent on renovations.

Determined not to care that Nick was only amusing himself with her, she'd pushed her plans forward, despite lacking the funds to progress until next quarter. Therefore, her next task would be to speak to Alfred about an advance. She plotted all his favorite meals as she opened her invitations.

Nick entered the sitting room after breakfast and settled into his favorite chair. "Do you have plans for today?" He meshed his fingers across his lean belly, offering her a somewhat winsome smile.

"Yes." She skimmed an envelope and opened the flap after noting the return address.

"Not to be shared with me?"

"You would be welcome to join us if you can knit. With others, Sarah and I will be at Nell's house most of the day sewing squares for blankets." She put the invitation in the pile to be answered later. After taking up the next, she read the return address and placed the envelope on Nick's tray.

"What was that you placed with my mail?"

"I don't know. It was addressed to you."

"Why wasn't it on my tray?"

"For any number of reasons, including a simple mistake. Mrs. N. Alden is easily enough confused with Mr. N. Alden. I'm careful, these days." Her cheeks warmed and she glanced at him, a mistake because she could read his expression, one of dawning awareness.

"So, that's what happened." A frown line formed between his brows. "You read the letter from Beth?"

"It wasn't addressed," she said, her cheeks warm. "I discovered she gave her correspondence to Harvey, who apparently assumed it would be delivered to your room. However, I found it with the other letters."

"And I failed your resulting test when I read her letter. Rather harsh I'd say, when you must have read she was short of money," he said, keeping his tone deliberately casual. "I had a responsibility to her. Had. I've seen her for the last time."

"You let me believe you saw her for the last time before we married."

He rose to his feet. "I used her so that I wouldn't want you. And it didn't work. I wanted you."

She nodded, her cheeks cold. "I'm more convenient." Pretty words and false embraces would no longer influence her.

"Can I redeem myself?" Holding her gaze, he stepped closer to her.

She stepped back. "Not with empty promises."

Despite a chest full of loneliness, and an urge to take comfort in her husband's treacherous embrace, for the first time in her life she walked out on a conversation.

Chapter 16

Charlotte settled a bowl of large pink roses onto a side table in the drawing room. The social season, which started in late spring, petered out during the summer heat at which time many families retired for a few weeks to the cooler weather in the hills or along the coast. And so, while she was free of social engagements, she could now prepare for Sarah's supper dance, which she planned to hold soon after the hordes returned, bored, and therefore more likely to accept an invitation from an obscure newlywed.

Before they left, Daphne and Emily and their mamas had been invited to call on Charlotte, who wanted to practice her skill as a hostess. Cook had made a pink-iced sponge cake and a plate of tiny sandwiches for the ladies.

"Are you and Nick fighting?" Sarah settled her full skirts artfully around her chair.

Charlotte heard the note of annoyance in her cousin's voice and she balked, perhaps for the first time. "I don't care if I never speak to him again."

"I care," said Sarah, grimly. "I live in this house, too. I don't have a place anywhere, and I will have even less a place here if you estrange yourself from your husband."

"So, am I supposed to abase myself so that you can feel comfortable in the home Nick so generously provided for us?" Charlotte prinked at the lace edging of her sleeve.

"For us?"

"He agreed to that from the start. I don't doubt he cares for you as much as he cares for me, so don't worry about your place here. And don't expect me to fix something I didn't break. I am an obedient wife, and that's all my husband wants of me."

"Are you being obedient when you ignore him?"

Charlotte folded her arms. "That's his choice. Don't interfere, Sarah. You know nothing of the matter."

Sarah clamped her lips. "It seems not. Just remember, Nick is very handsome and very charming. If you don't want him, someone else will snap him up without a blink. And then what will you do?"

Charlotte couldn't remember closing off her mind to Sarah previously. She stared out of the window, seeing no sign yet of her visitors. How strange that she and Sarah contended over a man who'd been "snapped up" when he married Charlotte, and who had made certain she'd agreed, on marriage, not to interfere with his pleasures.

She would avoid him until her heart stopped pounding at the mention of his name, until her body didn't throb in an unseemly place when she thought of him, until she could sleep at night without imagining his clever, knowing hands on her body. Only then she could take back control of her life.

She heard carriage wheels in the driveway as a shadow loomed in the doorway. "Ah, we're at home today, are we?" Nick asked with a casual smile. "I expect that carriage outside is my signal to leave." He flicked a glance through the window.

Sarah laughed. "Though, you are coming with us tonight, aren't you?"

"Remind me what is happening tonight."

"An informal arrangement at Hawthorn House with Nell and Tony." Charlotte couldn't meet Nick's eyes. If she did, he would see she couldn't yet maintain her indifference to him, and he would take the same advantage of her he had previously. "Your father is escorting us."

"As will I. I am invariably available to attend informal arrangements held by my friends." He buttoned his jacket and smoothed a lapel.

Charlotte nodded, and the female voices in the hall signaled Nick's departure.

"The only functions we attend are held by his friends," Sarah said, glancing at Charlotte. "The least you could do is take him, too."

"Every invitation I open is left on his tray. He can make his own decision."

* * * *

Now that Charlotte's familial relationship with Tony had been revealed to Nick, he saw the Hawthorns as family. Two days ago, he had discussed with Tony the timing to reveal the information to Charlotte. They'd agreed that first she should have her chance to present Sarah as her protégé, an extraordinary event, given the ladies' respective ages. Later, she could decide whether to be a Hawthorn distant *cousin* or simply ignore the connection. Whichever way she decided, Tony intended to reinstate her lost income as her natural right and her dowry.

With a tickling of déjà vu, Nick escorted his immediate family along paths lined with formal clipped hedges angling toward a central lantern-hung tree, only too aware of the last time he had been in Tony's lush garden. That night he'd been called into Tony's study to be told he would marry Charlotte. He'd agreed, though the girl didn't interest him then. She did now.

Although she was as much a mystery, he knew now that her lovely face hadn't been expressionless. More likely, regretful. She had a great ability to mask her thoughts, and even now, married to her for almost three months, he had no more idea of her feelings today than then. All he had learned in that time was that she was far from foolish. She'd known, even on that night that being ostensibly protective of the drunken sot in the garden would do her more good than shrieking and bemoaning her loss of reputation.

"Serve your ladies a glass of punch, Nick," Nell said, breaking into his thoughts. "We're being very modern tonight."

"I wonder where Daphne is." Sarah glanced toward James, who had with him a sleek, dark-haired young lady.

"You can lead a horse to water without letting him drink only so often before he slakes his thirst elsewhere," Nick said, and he had James introduce his friend, Miss Armitage, to Sarah and Charlotte.

Ivor and Amelia arrived and, shortly after, Luke and Emily and Hubert, and later Tony with a couple of older men, cronies of Alfred. Despite their great wealth, the Hawthorns had an easy way about them that allowed their guests to relax. Nick, ignored by his wife, let the apparently very available Miss Armitage take her choice of two admirers.

Charlotte, dressed in a low shouldered, sleeveless, blue gown trimmed with green ribbon was snapped up by Luke, led to a seat, and plied with pastries and oysters. Luke stared at Nick, who told James to take himself off, all the while keeping his wife and Luke in view, wishing he could lip-read. Luke's body language was casually unconcerned. Charlotte's was a replica, both of which Nick saw as dangerous. Eventually, Charlotte dropped her head as if convinced and thinking. About what, Nick couldn't tell.

Luke took her hand, brought her fingers to his mouth, and kissed the tips gently.

She let him.

Steaming, Nick saw her focus on Sarah, who was standing alone and watching the byplay as well. She beckoned Sarah, who joined the two.

Nick, who appeared to have won Miss Armitage, had to gracefully concede her back to James, who would doubtless be well rewarded for his forbearance.

In the carriage on the way home, Nick remembered saying to Tony that he had a great regard for Charlotte. At the time, he'd meant his words, but now, only a week later, he re-examined his meaning. He'd misled himself about her. She was neither inarticulate nor shallow, and she certainly had more on her mind than her next new gown. He could see her as admirable, but he could also see some small cracks in her shell, namely a high-minded intolerance of mistakes and an inability to budget. In which case she needed to be reminded that she herself wasn't perfect. And so he snidely said to Sarah, "I believe you might have lost your beau to Charlotte."

"To Miss Armitage, more like, though it's hard to tell who James favors. I was sure Daphne was a forerunner until tonight."

"Ah, the oldest Grace girl," said Alfred. "She won't land him. Sometimes I wonder if he's not hanging about the Grace family because he's waiting for the next one to grow up. Either that or he has a passion for Frances for which I don't blame him. Interesting woman, that."

Sarah hooted. "More likely Lady Grace than Chrysanthe. She's a brat."

"Not James. I meant Luke," Nick said, glancing at his wife. "He seemed mighty intent on Charlotte tonight and not a week ago I had to peel him off you."

Sarah smiled tightly. "Some of your friends really aren't suitable company for respectable women, Nick, and I class Luke as one of those."

"He's never been known to take up *less* than respectable women. He's very conventional, you know," Nick said, hoping Charlotte could hear his warning, but she gazed out of the carriage window. "I doubt he would consider scandalizing society, no matter what he might say."

The carriage stopped and Nick alighted, helping out Alfred, Sarah, and last, Charlotte, whose cheek he touched with a casual finger. She flinched.

He wondered what on earth Luke had said to her.

* * * *

"If you force Nick to compete for you, he might discover what he has to lose. Don't worry about her," Luke had said, indicating Miss Armitage. "Nick can't be in a room more than five minutes before the most available woman accosts him. True. Long ago, Tony and I timed a few."

And Charlotte had glanced at Miss Armitage, smiling prettily, trying to angle so that Nick could note the fullness of her breasts.

"The thing about Nick is that there has never been a woman he can't have," he'd continued. "I'm guessing your apparent ignore of him means that you've finally found out about his nocturnal interests."

"His mistress? Yes."

"Your best move is tit for tat. If I just pick up your hand, like this... Ha, he's staring over here with suspicion in his eyes. If you ever want to wake him up, I'm willing to be your...ah, decoy."

Charlotte tried reading in her lamp-lit bed, but this conversation kept repeating in her head. She stared at the printed pages, wishing for the right to insist on her husband's faithfulness. Teeth clenched, she put her book face down and swung out of bed. In her dressing robe and slippers, she pattered down the stairs, through the conservatory, and out into the garden where she found a seat by the still pond.

Nothing but a ripple disturbed the peace. Not a leaf stirred in the hot night air. She willed her mind to empty and wondered if she was merely as perverse as Nick, wanting only that which she couldn't have. Love. Her mother had been so obsessed by her own mistakes that she was determined her daughter would be accepted anywhere, and she constantly sidelined Sarah in the push for Charlotte's achievement. If her mother had acted out of love for her, Charlotte wouldn't have minded so much, but her mother had plotted her success purely as revenge on her father who was an important man in the colony, or so Adelina had said. Charlotte saw little to admire in a married man who seduced an innocent young woman and left her to bear his child alone.

Charlotte, reluctantly, had been educated with the daughters of the wealthiest settlers, perhaps not the role most suited to a penniless female who had no interest in being a rich man's trophy but merely wanted to be loved, to be unique to one special person. Had her mother not died and had her income not been cut off, Charlotte might have had a choice other than to get herself a husband quickly. Since she had Sarah to support, too, she had chosen to trap a man who might benefit from her presence, one to whom no woman was special, though not in the way she'd presumed. Instead, he loved them all while she grew to realize that marrying a man she couldn't hurt didn't protect *her* from hurt.

Footsteps crunched on the gravel path. She turned, hand to her throat as a shadow loomed and a figure cut in front of her. Nick, dressed in trousers and a loose unbuttoned shirt, stood before her, hands on his hips.

"Not sleepy yet?" Blocking off the night, he reached down and scooped her into his arms. "I have the cure."

"No," she said, leaning back, her heart still thumping and her fists in front of her, squashed against his chest.

Ignoring her protest, he kissed her forehead, her ear, her throat, one cheek again, and then he sought her mouth. "You can't know how much I want you."

"I don't care," she said, thrumming her curled hands against his shoulders. "I won't be used for your amusement."

"And what about your own?" His mouth covered hers.

Her body sprang to life stimulated by his lips and his hard frame against her. Heat and need filled her veins. By stepping into her, he moved her onto the mown lawn by the rose garden, and she found herself on her back with him on top. Again he kissed her face before angling his mouth across hers and pinning her arms above her head. He imprisoned her ankles with his feet. The grass prickled beneath her. She *didn't* care.

His tongue tipped her lips, teasing her with the parody while his hands slid to her breasts, cupping and caressing as if he had to relearn her shape. He untied the high neckline of her nightgown, pulled aside the fabric, and rubbed her hardened nipples against his bare chest while he unbuttoned his trousers.

She could hear nothing but breathing and heart pounding, his or hers. Her nightgown settled around her waist, and she could feel his hard part between her legs. His mouth lipped at her breasts and nipples. Lost, she lifted her knees and arched into him. Tearing at his back with her fingers, she wriggled closer as he thrust inside her. She had never known him—or herself—so desperate to couple. She said not a word.

He plunged deep into her. Her heels tightened over his back. He surged and drove harder, and she responded with uncontrolled passion, hearing the slap of flesh against flesh. As her excitement expanded, she heard him whisper, "Stop me, stop me," but she clung tighter. He called on God, shoved high one last time, and stilled. As she tried to catch her breath, she experienced the most marvelous sensation she had ever known, the endless pulsating pleasure of him bursting inside her.

His head dropped onto the juncture between her shoulder and her chin. He pressed his face into her flesh. "No," he said in a shuddery voice.

She smoothed at the skin of his back, amazed at the need she had to keep him inside her.

Her fingers spread but he lifted, withdrew, and rolled onto his back, elbow over his eyes. She ran her gaze over his body. In the aftermath, his arousal looked swollen, but had lost the upright thickness. Previously, she'd only seen him naked in his hardened state. She appreciated the look of him, sated. Sitting up, she pulled her gown over her knees, resting her chin there, smiling.

"Damnation! How could I do that?"

"We did it."

In the moonlight, he looked pale and strained. He brushed his elbow over his wet face, and she realized he'd wiped away tears, not sweat. Her chest ached with the knowledge that giving her his seed had caused him such needless distress.

She clasped her knees to her chest. From the start, she'd wanted to save him from himself, seeing how heavily he relied on drink. When he was hurt by the hard ball smacking into his head, and stunned, though possibly by the alcohol, she'd been given her chance to see him close and hold him in her arms. He was even more beautiful up close than in passing, so much more real while semi conscious, too real, for she'd thought she'd heard he lived his life as a sham.

Foolish creature that she was. Nick's main attraction after his looks was the way he made a woman feel necessary and special. He appeared to care, not by saying so but by listening. Luke said Nick loved women, and she believed that. She also believed that her initial feelings for him only made her one of many. Other women wanted to save him, too, and to be special and necessary. She could hardly believe she had contemplated living her own life and leaving him to take his pleasure elsewhere.

Tonight his breath was fresh. He still had the minty taste but not the underlying alcohol. She hadn't even seen him with a glass of punch at the Hawthorns' garden supper. Therefore, her hope of changing him was not entirely unfounded. She shouldn't punish herself for succumbing to him when she'd sworn she wouldn't. "Are you quite determined not to have a baby?"

He closed his eyes. "You know I am."

"And what had you planned to do when you followed me here?"

"I had no plan. I saw you bathed in moonlight, and I wanted you."

"Despite the fact that you don't want a baby?"

"Sometimes lust overrides all."

She dropped her gaze. Sanity intruded. Despite knowing that he would use her as the most available option for as long as she let him, she also hadn't fought her desire. Perhaps she had changed him slightly, but to hope for a happy outcome with a man whose overriding aim was not to father a child was pointless.

"I see." Defeat softened her voice.

"You surprised me by looking so utterly desirable."

"And now I'm *really* going to surprise you."

She stood and shook her night-robe down. After collecting the bulk of the skirts in one hand, she ran toward the house. Nick sprang to his feet and chased after her. Speedier, he grabbed her gown. She kicked out at him and, while evading her foot, he let go. She reached the conservatory door, now certain that the passion that had transpired tonight was simply him asserting his ownership.

She didn't doubt that she would love him until she died, but she wasn't about to be used by a man who could never really love her.

* * * *

Nick sat in the breakfast room with the paper. Charlotte had locked her door against him last night. He decided he should reason with her after she'd had time to reflect and he had worked out how they could resolve their problem. No matter how much she wanted a child, he would not give her one, but his future with her was a foregone conclusion. Last night he had confirmed that she was everything he wanted and needed in a wife, an inherently good person, frighteningly likeable, and a passionate lover.

Sarah sighed and sat at the table. "It's impossible to pack for two weeks when one can't forecast the weather. Usually January is hot, but we often have cool changes at this time of year. If I pack everything I own, I'll fill the carriage."

"Where are you going?"

"To Stirling. You can't have forgotten."

"I wouldn't have forgotten if I'd known."

"Glory, Nick, you've known for more than two weeks I was invited by the Graces to stay in their country residence, just the way Charlotte used to do."

"Perhaps I didn't concentrate when you told me."

"You might have guessed, even if I hadn't said a word. Everyone who is *anyone* goes to the country during the warm weather, and I'm *almost* anyone." She laughed.

"So, you'll be staying with the Graces," he said, even now not concentrating. Having Sarah out of the house for a week or two would give him a chance to romance his wife, the plan he'd decided on last night.

"The Graces live one paddock's distance from the Hawthorns, and so they'll all be there, too." She reached for the teapot.

"Everyone goes out of town, recuperating. As for the social whirl there, it's simply more of the same, with the same people looking for connections for their sons and daughters before the next round of city amusements."

"Luke has a house there, too, I believe."

Nick lifted his eyebrows.

She dropped her gaze. "Even the Downings have a property in Stirling. That's how you all know each other. You and Hubert and Luke and the Hawthorns had the same schooling, too."

He shrugged. "As you said, we only live paddocks away from each other, but you'll find the place is more urban than you expect. And Luke's too set in his ways for you."

She pressed her finger to the center of her chin, and her cat's eyes gleamed. "He's eligible. I'm no more averse to having multiple dancing partners than any other woman."

He buttered his toast. "I rather enjoy the way you keep him trailing you by challenging him, but I'm not sure of your ultimate plan. If you are using him to make another step up to the mark, he's experienced enough to make you sorry. If it's him you want…" He shook his head. "At this stage, he has another lady on his mind."

Her face stiffened. "I'm teasing you. I'm not as giddy as you think."

"Sarah is far from giddy." Charlotte entered the room with Alfred. She looked calm and cool and unutterably beautiful in emerald green and blue. "I'll be seeing you in Stirling, Sarah. I've just dashed off a note to Nell telling her I changed my mind and will join her and Tony."

Sarah put down her fork. "I wish you'd decided this sooner. I would rather have stayed with the Hawthorns, too. Will they pick you up this afternoon? Perhaps I could—No, that would be rude."

Nick concentrated on the silver epergne in the center of the table. A harsh beam of light hit the middle crystal bowl, monetarily blinding him. "Neither of you need to stay with others. Our house is there. I'm sure my father wouldn't object to opening the place up. This is the time of year he usually goes away." He queried his father with his eyes.

"And I would have if I thought the rest of you were leaving. As it is, I put my plan back a couple of weeks, for when the peaches ripen. I suppose I could go now instead."

Charlotte put her hand over Alfred's. "We don't intend to change your plans. Sarah is happy with the young ladies, and I will very much enjoy being with Nell and the baby. Please don't let us disrupt you."

"It would be a different matter if Nick were coming, too." Sarah began eating with appetite. "Though I must say I'm not sure of the need to cobble together new plans for a mere two weeks."

"Nor I." Nick continued eating breakfast while Charlotte described the Stirling countryside to Sarah. In his belly lurked a yawing pit of regret for Charlotte's original mistake about him. As a small boy, he had chased small girls who wanted to be chased, but his advice to Sarah about Luke held true for himself, too. Now older and more experienced, he no longer chased females who hoped to be caught. If his wife wanted him, she could have him, but he wouldn't be manipulated into ruining her life with a monster child.

He stood when he had finished his last mouthful, said his good-byes to the ladies, and headed off to Dixon's, where he planned not to drink himself into oblivion, but to punch a bag until he had accepted that he couldn't change his past.

Charlotte wanted him to reverse his decision about a baby, but his decision was irrevocable. If their relationship had any hope of surviving, it could only be on his terms.

Chapter 17

"The house sounds empty," Alfred said, peering at his roast beef. "You get used to the ladies, don't you—the way they talk all the time and the way they fill a room? The house doesn't even look the same."

Nick, sitting in the sweltering dining room, noted the same furniture, the same curtains, and the unusual emptiness. "Flowers. That's what's missing. I'll tell Mrs. Wishart we want flowers in the house, as usual."

"Did we have flowers in the house before we had the ladies?"

Nick rubbed his chin. "I think so." He hadn't spent a lot of time in the house before they *had the ladies*. "And while I'm about it, I'll tell her I like starch in my collars. I'm sure I had starch in my collars until two days ago."

"It's a plot," his father said dourly. He put his knife and fork on his plate. "This meat's tough enough to sole my boots. I've a good mind to eat at my club. And breakfast—not worth getting out of bed for."

"I suspect Cook is just as uncomfortable in this blistering heat as we are."

His father lifted a sweating, miserable face, but didn't speak.

"Are you staying for me? Don't. I can survive without Cook. Like you, I can eat at my club."

"When I go up to Stirling in a couple of weeks, as planned, I'll leave Cook with you and the ladies. Mrs. Potter will do for me alone in the country house."

Nick shook his head. "As it happens, a brief sojourn to the hills now and Mrs. Potter's cooking would suit me well enough. You're worrying about your peach crop, and I wouldn't mind inspecting the workers' cottages. You'll give me a free hand there, I hope?"

Alfred nodded and sat taller, taking up his knife and fork. "I'm too hungry to go to my club. This meat doesn't taste so bad after all. Ring the bell and tell Mrs. Wishart you and I are moving to the hills tomorrow. We should have gone days ago with our ladies."

* * * *

The journey to Alden View twisted up the hill for miles along a steep dirt road. In Nick's younger days the journey had been plagued by the gulley-men, robbers who relieved travelers of their money or goods, but these days none lurked behind the scrubby growth. The area had settled into small towns now, and most of the wealthy built summer retreats in the cool valleys to avoid the worst of the summer heat. Even the governor had a residence in Belair.

Five red brick chimneys identified Alden View from the distance. The closer view revealed rows of grape vines, apples trees, and the new peaches, Alfred's pride and joy. The warm sweetness of ripening fruit hung in the air. The carriage bumped down a long gravel drive to a coach house settled at the side of the two story main house built of natural stone. Nick hadn't been here since the cricket match last year although this place of his boyhood happiness had always been his retreat.

"Seems strange to be here knowing our ladies are staying elsewhere. They've never seen this house, have they?" Alfred stepped down from the carriage and stared at the rows of tall proud windows, arched at the top. "We have all the fruit growing here that the little miss could want. Best place for her. She'd regain her condition here better than she would gallivanting around the city."

Nick gave his father a light punch on the shoulder, and his father went into a defensive pose with a grin. Clearly, the cooler air invigorated his spirits, too. When Nick had last been here eight months ago, he hadn't spent the night. Instead, he'd been sent back to Adelaide with a bruised head. Almost cheerfully, he took his valise up the stairs to the suite he had used since childhood, and left the sparsely packed bag in his dressing room. His old clothes from before he had left for Cambridge had never been moved, and he chose favorites, slightly unfashionable light trousers and a utilitarian jacket. The trousers were a comfortable fit. The jacket pulled across his shoulders.

Four years ago, before he had deserted Adelaide with Clara, he would have whistled for a dog outside, but he doubted any would remember him. Harvey was, as usual, lurking around the stables. He had driven the traveling coach up and now appeared to have nothing to do.

"Get me a horse," Nick said, rectifying the problem. He waited amid the sounds of horses snorting and stirring and in the stalls. The clatter of shod hooves on stone preceded Harvey who appeared with a tall, well-fed bay.

Nick tested the animal's pace along the pot-holed and rutted track lined by native pines that separated the Alden lands from Luke's family holdings, an estate currently owned by the lawyer's older brother. For some time, Nick's horse, which clearly hadn't been exercised for some time, occupied him by shying at shadows.

In the distance, he spotted a stationary wagon. As he approached, he saw the driver crouched by the back left wheel. He pulled up his bay. "A problem, driver?" he asked the shirt-sleeved laborer who looked defeated.

"The road," the man said dourly, wiping trails of sweat from his face with his neck scarf. "I shoulda' taken the front way, but 'come around the back,' Mr. Worthing said, and I do come around the back like he ordered. Knowed this road was bad. Told him so. Now I'm stuck in this here hole."

"What's your load?"

"Bricks. Wouldn't you know? If I'da had feathers, wouldn't be no problem, but he didn't order no feathers."

"I suspect you'll have to unload."

"Sent the lad up to the house." The man's bristled chin pointed toward a narrow path that led to Luke's rough stone outbuildings. "I'll want help."

"I'll help you make a start." Nick dismounted, tethered his skittish horse to a fence post, and removed his tight jacket. Glancing at the load, he took off his tie and waistcoat, too.

With the driver, he hefted bricks onto the road. Every now and again, the driver went to his horse's head, trying to move him along. Nick suspected that almost the full load would need to be shifted, and he didn't mind a bit. These days, healthy exercise seemed to clear his brain. He saw no reason why he shouldn't call on the Hawthorns tomorrow or even wait until the next day just to show Charlotte that he was used to the manipulative ways of females and didn't mind her absence one bit. The road being entirely private, he removed his shirt as well.

"Now, there's a fine horse for a laborer," said a familiar voice.

He glanced up at Luke who accompanied a lad no more than fourteen years old who, by the look of his overlarge nose and dirty shirt, was related to the driver.

"The bay? He's not bad. This road is, though. When did it get this way? Years ago, I would say."

Luke shrugged. "Your workers use it. Mine travel across the fields. I suspect your father lost heart when you left. What are you doing here?"

"Just jaunting around the property."

"I mean in the hills," Luke said, hands on his hips and his gaze a challenge. "You don't want to be here. You'll be bored to death. Other than the same social life you scorn in the city, there's nothing to do if you're not interested in orchards."

Nick shrugged. "I don't need to be entertained. I'm here merely to watch over Sarah. I don't want you misleading her."

"Strangling her comes more easily to mind."

Nick raised his eyebrows. "You have no interest in her?"

"I've done my best to warn her off."

"Ah, so, I haven't been imagining anything."

"And I haven't been misleading her."

"If you do, you're going to be dealing with me."

"You've appointed yourself to be the guardian of *my* morals?" Luke lifted an eyebrow. "That's like leaving the devil in charge of putting out the fire. Your back's marked. Did you know?"

Nick straightened. "Every now and again I get lucky," he said in his most casual tone. Nevertheless, he walked to the fence and struggled his sweaty body into his shirt. Charlotte must have been more passionately involved during their moonlight encounter than he had realized.

Luke watched father and son unload the bricks. "You haven't changed your tastes in women, have you?"

"Probably not. I still tend to choose those who respond eagerly." More than putout, Nick snatched up his waistcoat, too. "I'll get this road seen to."

He dressed in silence, not too tidily, amazed that an insult to his wife could anger him, and he left Luke to unload his own damned bricks.

* * * *

Charlotte sat with Nell, Sir Patrick, and Lady Grace in the Graces' over decorated drawing room, cozy in the absence of the youngsters. Sarah, Daphne, and Chrysanthe had decided to inspect the new plantings of camellias, azaleas, and soft English trees. The Graces grew fruit and vegetables but only for household consumption.

"It's such a shame Nick couldn't come up, too," Lady Grace said to Charlotte. "But so kind of Luke to take his place as your escort."

"He's been a good friend." Charlotte, well aware of the talk about Nick being absent and Luke being far too present during the past four days, didn't let her smile waver. If Nick heard that the wife he had let go didn't care, all to the good. And Luke *was* a good friend. He'd told her that Nick had arrived in Stirling yesterday.

"I find that easy to believe," Sir Patrick said, crossing his legs. "He was always a good friend to Nick, and he ought to be the same to you."

"He is far more severe than my husband." Charlotte clasped her hands primly in her lap. "He told me the hat I wore yesterday was silly."

"How disgraceful. I can't see anything silly about wearing a box tied with ribbons." Nell kept her expression hooded.

"It wasn't a real box," Charlotte said, apologetically. "I just arranged the fabric to make it look that way. In which case, I find his comment very harsh."

The assembled company laughed and a housemaid entered the room, followed by Nick.

"Mr. Alden, ma'am," she said to Lady Grace, who smiled at Nick.

"How nice that you could come," the lady said as Nick kissed her cheek.

He inclined his head at Nell and his gaze met Charlotte's.

Just a simple meeting of his eyes caused her heart to thud and her chest to ache. Her fingers tightening, she managed her "pleasantly surprised" smile.

"It's taken half the day to track you down." He turned his back on the other ladies and focused entirely on her.

"Today?" She found a space on the side table to place the tiny cake she now couldn't finish.

"I had it on the highest authority that your calendar was full yesterday. As it happens mine was, too."

"Who on earth would be the highest authority?" Nell stood, collecting her reticule.

"I had a border dispute with Luke yesterday."

"You're staying at your place, are you? Well, if you saw Luke, he could have told you where we would be today. However, we'll be home in another fifteen minutes," Nell said, shaking out her layered skirts. "We must go. It's been delightful, Lady Grace, as always." She took her hostess's hands in hers, kissing the older woman on the cheek.

Charlotte, too, her manners intact, rose to her feet. "Perhaps we'll see you tomorrow, Nick. We have to go back to the Hawthorn's now for an early dinner. Then we're off to a harp recital at the town hall."

Lady Grace detained Nick with her hand. "You must stay and catch us up on the town gossip. Charlotte, as you can imagine, is very busy with old friends. She used to spend quite a bit of time with us here before she married, and she not only knows anyone who is anyone, but everyone who isn't, though I oughtn't say anyone *isn't* anyone. So snobbish of me. Still, you understand, I am sure."

Charlotte couldn't stop her wry smile outside the door. Her determinedly loyal friends seemed only too glad to help her evade Nick.

As she pulled on her gloves, she heard him saying that he would be very sorry to miss seeing Sarah and the three Grace daughters, whom he had known since their various births, but he had urgent matters awaiting him on the estate and a father who needed his presence.

"Why do you think he was trying to track me down?" she asked Nell in the carriage.

Nell shrugged. "If it was anything other than possessiveness, he would have made sure of explaining."

Charlotte nodded. In all likelihood, Cook had been taking advice from the housekeeper as to the menus, which would be biased more toward Alfred's tastes than Nick's. Or his manservant had gone back to his old ways, or the housemaids were spending more time with the grooms than in the rooms. Charlotte knew she made the house more comfortable for the gentlemen, but she doubted they did.

And she wouldn't go home to be a silly little flower arranger again. If she wasn't appreciated for herself, she refused to be appreciated for her unobtrusive skills.

* * * *

Nick wouldn't dream of asking to go with his wife to one of her dull entertainments. Harp music, when property matters occupied his mind! He'd tried to find her out of mere politeness. Had he not, the gossips would have wondered about their marriage.

He left the Graces as soon as manners permitted, deciding to set the orchard workers to the task of grading the access road, and consequently discovered that gravel was running short. Since the day was beginning to end, he would order more from the Stirling village tomorrow.

The next day, dressed like a laborer himself, he took the rangy bay and a dog to Stirling, where a wave from the saddler stopped him. "We all want to congratulate you on your recent marriage." Lachy's shop smelled of leather and oil, and Nick as a lad had been allowed to punch holes in belts for the man he had known forever. "Lovely lady. A real beauty. Nice, too. Has a word for all of us. Mr. Worthing has been taking good care of her for you, all right. Bedazzled a bit himself, I'd say, with respect." He let go of the stirrup strap.

"I'm a lucky man, there's no doubt, and lucky in my friends, too," Nick added, his expression careful. "Mumbles Hogan is still around, I take it?"

"You'll be wantin' to fix the road."

Nick frowned. "I expect the whole place knows what I'm about to do before I do."

Lachy grinned. "We talk some, among ourselves. I won't keep you. Looks like rain."

As Nick moved the bay into the yard where Mumbles Hogan presided, the first big splat of warm summer rain hit him on the nose. He dismounted as Mumbles approached.

"You're wantin' stone." Mumbles kept little more in his yard than second-hand marble headstones, adorned with names he could chisel off when needed, rolls of trodden wire, tins of all sizes and types, wheels—none new—and terracotta pots, also in all sizes. His use was in being able to obtain, through contacts, almost anything needed, legally or illegally. "Should have a load on your place by tomorrow, ordered as it was by me yesterday." He wiped his sleeve across his wet face.

Nick turned up the collar of his jacket against the downpour and angled his hat lower on his forehead. "I would have saved myself a wetting by leaving you to organize the whole thing."

Mumbles chortled. "Me and Harvey keeps in contact. Do you want shelter until the rain stops? Shouldn't be long. It's too heavy to last." He indicated a dilapidated shed to one side of the leaning front gates.

"I'll go somewhere more convivial." Nick swung up onto his horse and headed toward the local tavern, where he realized he didn't wish to be. The thought of ale was too appealing and not something he wanted to experiment with during this time of his sobriety.

Instead, he tethered the horse outside the old chandler's shop and stood under the shelter, watching the locals scuttle to various locations out of the rain. The stream of people ceased as, with an angry clap of thunder, the clouds burst, flooding the road with quick flowing rivulets. Thunder rumbled irritably and lightning peaked in the distance.

Across the road stood the town hall, a barnlike structure built of redbrick and native stone, with double wooden front doors and a tin sheltered side access. A face, Luke's, peered up out of the side door possibly to check the weather and disappeared again. Interested to see what dealings Luke might have in the local chambers, Nick leaned back against the wall of the shop waiting for the rain to stop, as Luke apparently was.

The rain ceased as fast as it had begun, the sky showing a clear blue, as if blown in for a fete. Luke again opened the door, and as Nick uncrossed his legs, he noticed a lady's blue skirt appear followed by the lady, Charlotte, beautifully dressed with one of her pretty little hats highlighting her perfect features. His joy at this glimpse of her astounded him. She looked even lovelier, standing in the shelter, than she had yesterday, although yesterday that would have seemed an impossible task. Charlotte's beauty comprised more than her perfect features. Her character showed on her face, her humor and her innate thoughtfulness. As a match for Nick, he was very much outclassed.

He straightened from the wall where he leaned, preparing to go to her when Luke reached out and circled one arm around her. She touched a palm against his chest, and he raised her face to his with a finger beneath her chin.

Nick's self-absorbed world shattered.

The couple didn't kiss, barely touched, yet tenderness never seen before showed clearly on Luke's face. Charlotte, as usual, disguised her expression, but not well enough. She held his gaze just a moment too long, and she lingered within his embrace.

If they kissed in public, Nick would knock Luke sideways. For a moment, trying to bundle his confused emotions, he stared at the toes of his boots. When, his face frozen, he glanced up again, Luke was hurrying Charlotte along the side path to the street where his tethered gig, not noticed previously by Nick, awaited.

Icy cold, Nick stayed out of sight, barely breathing. Five days ago he had shown Charlotte how much he desired her, and for days he had agonized over his commitment to the future. Now he didn't know if he had a future with her, nor even a present. Insanely, not long ago, he told her he would countenance being the father of another man's child. Not Luke's. Never Luke's. Luke would insist on keeping his own.

For a single moment, Nick experienced the first violent urge of his blighted life. Without a doubt, he could beat Luke senseless. He gave a savage laugh, staring after the gig as the couple drove away. Neither had spotted Nick who untied the bay's reins and lurched into his wet saddle, retribution the only thought in his head. Just as he had decided to be the man he ought to be and settle into married life, Luke made good his promise to serve Nick a backhanded turn and had stolen Nick's wife.

Not for one moment had he credited Luke's threat. He had known Luke for more than twenty years and knew Luke was only talk, without a mean bone in his body, or so he had thought.

Although the day had not cooled with the rain, an icy fear passed down Nick's spine. He slowed his horse to a walk and finally noticed his dog loping behind, tongue out, exhausted by trying to keep up. The faithful hound was ready to do as Nick pleased, which Nick expected of everyone.

He snapped his fingers indicating to the dog that he could spring up on the saddle in front, which the dog did with a burst of delighted energy.

Nick stopped the horse and sat, the dog's soft ears in his hand. The dog tried to lick his fingers. "Damn! No, not you. Me. I did this, not Luke."

No, Luke had held back, but his very restraint showed how much he wanted Charlotte. He had said so, but Nick didn't believe his friend had been more than infatuated with a beautiful woman who would infuriate him with her superficiality when he knew her better.

Nick's head ached with regret. Charlotte didn't have a shallow bone in her glorious body, yet Nick had continued to misjudge her, deciding to think little of a woman who had offered to protect him in exchange for a home and an income. Charlotte was no lying sneak who had crept off to be with her lover in the country. She'd married Nick for exactly the reasons she'd said, likely realizing that she was not a suitable wife for a man with Luke's rigid standards of respectable breeding. However, if Luke hadn't found out about Charlotte's birth until *after* he had married her, he would have had no trouble in hiding the truth, as Nick had, with Tony's cooperation.

Luke was the man for her, steadfast and strong. Only the Lord knew what Nick would have done without his and Tony's support after Clara had died. They'd not only arranged the funeral, they'd stayed with Nick during his days of darkest despair. They'd waited out his grief and borne his drunken escapades, forgiving him his many weaknesses and his excesses. And to repay Luke, Nick had taken the woman Luke loved, not out of spite but because he was a fuddled drunk. Inexcusable!

He reined his horse into a slow walk, knowing that vengeance wasn't his. Retribution was, and to his wife. Until the party where Sarah would be presented, Charlotte would need to put her relationship with Luke on hold. Then, if she couldn't stop loving him and Luke was willing to bear the scandal, Nick would let go.

In the meantime, he'd take his chance at redemption.

Chapter 18

Stiff with humiliation, Charlotte watched the passing scenery through the window while the brougham jolted downhill. Even now, she didn't know what she'd done or why Nick had collected her from the Hawthorns' country house an hour ago.

I'm taking my wife home, he'd said to Nell, and Nell hadn't argued. Even she'd recognized his uncompromising expression.

The tall, thin trunks of the gum trees and the scant undergrowth slowly shifted past. Desperate not to be crushed, Charlotte cleared her throat. "I assume we haven't had some sort of family tragedy? You would surely say so before now."

Nick sat in his heavily weighted silence, his long legs outstretched and his face resigned. He examined one palm for a very long time until he spoke. "I didn't guess," he said without looking at her. "I saw."

"Saw what?"

"You and Luke. He's in love with you."

She stared at him. "What do you mean, you saw us? Where?"

He raised his head. His thick lashed glance flickered. "Coming out of the town hall this morning."

"We were looking for my fan, the one painted with cornflowers that I mislaid somewhere last night." Noting the closed expression on Nick's face, she drew an extra breath. "I use it quite often. Luke offered to see if I'd left it in the town hall, but I wanted a trip to the village, regardless, to buy a toy for Charles Nicholas."

She paused, unsure of her ground, wondering what he had seen that caused him a problem. Outside the town hall, Luke had complimented her on wearing a real hat and not a box on her head, and she had taken his teasing in the same spirit. They had returned to the Hawthorns'. Nothing more except... When Luke had taken her outside the hall, his eyes held a strange gleam, and he had laughed and tipped her chin with his finger. If he had done that because he noticed Nick, she didn't care. "She doesn't like to leave Charles with his nursemaid unless she has to," she said, straightening her spine.

"Luke is the most conventional of my friends. Are you contemplating cuckolding me with him or have you already done so?"

She gasped.

He inclined his head to one side. "I may be mistaken, but I don't think you've done the deed yet. Although you're possibly a better actress than I suspect, you don't appear to be secretly elated."

"A reaction you would naturally expect in an unfaithful wife." Her lips pressed together.

He nodded. "One I would recognize. Also, I'm quite sure that if Luke had fucked you, he would honorably insist on telling me."

"Surely not. Such a thing would be foolhardy."

"Noble," he contradicted, "and up to the standard Luke expects of himself. He wouldn't marry a *bastard* for instance." He scrutinized her face.

She stilled, pounded by the pulse in her neck. He couldn't know about her. "He is certainly the most conventional of your friends," she said, controlling her panic.

"He's not a match for you. Surely you can see that? You must know that if you continue to fascinate him, letting him be your knight in shining armor, you will ruin his life as mine was ruined with, of course, my wholehearted complicity."

"So, you're saving *him* from me rather than saving *me* from him?" She forced each word to sound cool and calm, using only a pitch lower than usual.

"You seemed to have proved quite adequate in saving yourself."

She nodded, pride wrapping her in an invisible shield. "In my world that has been important. The lack of money makes us all beggars of a sort. You wouldn't understand."

"Perhaps it's time you put others ahead of yourself," he said, his voice hard.

His harsh assessment rang in her ears, and she sucked in a breath. He was right, but not about Luke being in love with her. Luke had been her constant escort for the past few days in a misguided effort to show Nick that he might lose a woman he didn't value. Instead, Nick was more worried about losing his friend to a misbegotten deceiver who had done little more than act out her jealousy and, in his view, finally fake an affair in a bid to make her husband notice her, neither action considering anyone but herself.

She faced his contempt for her ridiculous behavior in letting him think she cared for anyone but him. "You can't believe I had an affair with Luke. He would be mortified when he has only ever been your good friend."

"I'm tired of all this, Charlotte. Coming from a position of imperfection myself as I do, I can hardly cast aspersions. I want you out of Luke's life, forthwith."

"It's not possible," she said, squeezing her fingers together. "We will see him everywhere."

"You will not see him *alone*, anywhere."

"Please take my word that nothing of a physical nature has ever passed between us."

"Just what is his attraction?" he said in a tone of pure irritation.

"He was your friend before he was mine." She rocked forward, desperate to heal the breach she had caused between the two men. "You already know his character. He wouldn't steal the wife of another man."

"As I did?" His mouth twisted cynically, and he crossed his arms. "The thought is worthy of the deed and it's done. We will now discuss your new priorities as my wife. First, you will wear your wedding ring." His eyes shimmered. "It was pointless not to when in our circles, everyone knows you are married."

She blinked. "My wedding ring doesn't fit."

"You've had months to get it resized. Instead, you chose not to wear it."

Her cheeks warmed. "I will have that attended to as soon as possible."

He stared at her for some seconds. "I also want to live as my married friends do, entertaining at home on occasion. How can you expect to launch Sarah when all we do is flitter about everywhere?"

"I'll attend to that matter, too," she said, her head throbbing. "But I'm puzzled. Before you married me, you told me quite clearly that I wasn't to change your lifestyle. Are you sure you want me to organize the running of your home?"

"I want you fully occupied, sweetheart," he answered grimly. "Because your reputation and Sarah's success depends solely on how you handle yourself from now on. You don't have a respectable background to support you."

"How so?" She didn't look at him. The carriage trundled along, taking her to a respected home in which she could never have belonged without compromising Nick.

"Your birth certificate gives you two married parents. Their wedding certificate is more interesting. You were fathered by a septuagenarian who married your mother a week or two before your birth."

"And who can cast aspersions?"

He shrugged.

A small amount of elation diluted Charlotte's fear. Challenging his perception of her legitimacy had been frightening but her only option, and she seemed to have silenced him for now. He could not profit by ruining her, and so she couldn't allow his unspoken threat. "Why would you investigate me?"

"You're a mystery, my love. I wouldn't be the first to wonder who you really are, given that you say so little about your antecedents."

"Sarah shouldn't suffer over this silliness, too," she said, her voice forced. "Her birth is certainly respectable."

"I don't mean her to suffer, and I hope you don't either. And she certainly will if you continue to dazzle Luke." He reached across the carriage and touched her clasped hands. "I'll agree that you haven't tempted him to forget his morals if you'll agree to behave circumspectly around him. Let him think you love me. Trust me, this is for the best." He leaned back, an expression of sympathy momentarily visible on his face.

Her eyes prickled. She wanted to despise him for his misplaced understanding. She couldn't love Luke. Months ago, she had given her heart to a man who justified his affairs by his determination not to impregnate his wife, who tempered his indifference with kindness and his cynicism with hope. She loved him and only him.

She could only pray he would never expose her birth, for if he did, he would ruin Sarah, too, and he seemed not to want that. How strange that the day had finally come when Charlotte's wellbeing depended on her cousin when the reverse had been the pattern throughout so many years. Perhaps now she would have a chance to see life through Sarah's eyes and finally understand why she had a need to be so competitive.

"My father plans to stay in Stirling for the summer." Nick reverted to his former lounging position with his legs outstretched. "Since Sarah won't be back until the rest of them leave next week, we have the town house to ourselves for a while. That should give you time to see sense."

She, the woman who had lived her whole life with sense and decorum until very recently, nodded. Being sensible, rather than his brainless acolyte would please her. "Presumably you will fund our entertaining?"

"Who else?"

"Do I have a budget?"

"You will report your expenditure to me for sanction. You have a tendency to overspend, my pet."

"I've spent nothing but my own money," she said, too quickly.

"Your own money has gone. You are now attempting to spend your yearly allowance, too, and when you run out, you will be asking me for extra. Perhaps you could begin budgeting with your hats."

She didn't answer. If he couldn't see each hat was a mere refurbishing of her last, he hadn't looked closely. Tonight, she would begin working on Sarah's hats, too, and brook no objections from her cousin. In the meantime, she had a whole house to reorganize, beginning in the kitchen and with the battle between the housekeeper and the cook.

She made her plans as she contemplated the scenery only once making the mistake of glancing at Nick, who appeared to be sleeping. With his elegant, wide-shouldered body relaxed and his fallen angel face at peace, he caused her to ache with love. Having to live the rest of her life without his regard would be devastating.

The time had come to start earning his respect.

* * * *

"Let the kitchen staff know we have arrived home," Charlotte said to Harvey as he let down the steps of the brougham.

The coachman grinned, and she let him help her out. Nick followed as she entered the house, and he trailed her up the stairs to their sitting room, parting ways at their respective bedroom doors. Vera arrived as Charlotte removed her hat.

"We weren't expecting you," she said, puffing, apparently having run up the stairs.

"Only Mr. Nick and I returned. Mr. Alden plans to stay in Stirling for the summer. Do you remember the conversation we had a month ago about starch in my husband's collars?"

Red-faced, Vera nodded. "I had a slight misunderstanding with Mrs. Wishart. She told the laundry-maid to use lavender oil in the starch."

"That's not for Mrs. Wishart to decide. We know Mr. Nicholas likes lemon juice. See to it, please."

Vera left, a surprising smile on her face. Charlotte took a long, deep breath, buttoned her cuffs, patted her hair smooth, and went down the back stairs to the housekeeper's door, on which she knocked.

Mrs. Wishart invited her into the room, dark and over-furnished with mementos, and sat her on a straight-backed chair. "May I offer you a cup of tea?" The woman clasped her hands in front of the house keys dangling from her belt.

"Yes, please."

And Charlotte waited for the formal ceremony to begin, the handover of the house to her running. She familiarized herself with the laundry arrangements, the storage of the linen, the safety of the silver, and the uniforms for the staff. She checked invoices and prices for food, regular payments, and the accommodation of the maids. Two hours later, after she requested that the drawing and dining rooms be fully cleaned top to bottom, she said, "Now, will you call Cook in here?"

Tight-lipped, Mrs. Wishart sought out Cook and ushered her into the room.

Charlotte waited until both women had seated themselves before taking a long, deep breath. "I'm changing the routine in this house, and I hope you both approve. Cook, as the oldest, although not in years, of the household retainers, you know the foods Mr. Alden and Mr. Nicholas prefer. I would like you to prepare a weekly menu for me, which we will go over in my rooms. There is no need for Mrs. Wishart to approve the changes I might make from time to time. Further, we will be doing extra entertaining in the next few weeks. Perhaps Mrs. Wishart could see about hiring another kitchen maid, with your approval, of course."

Cook left, pleased, and even Mrs. Wishart smiled. "We could do with another housemaid, too, now we've got extras living in the house. Mr. Alden didn't give it a thought, and it's been hard, no doubt of it."

"When you have problems with staffing, see me. Mr. Alden won't be back for a few months, and Mr. Nicholas wants me to take over where his mother left off." Charlotte vacated the room taller than she had been two hours previously.

After a light evening meal with Nick, which she'd had set out in the conservatory, a cooler room in the hot weather with the greenery in front of the glass, she sat at Nick's desk in her suite, listing names of the various people she had met since her marriage. Time passed quickly, and she didn't realize how long she'd taken until Nick came up to his bedroom.

"Avoiding me?" he asked.

"How well do you know Mrs. Grayson?"

"She was a friend of my mother's. We're still on speaking terms, I hope."

"In that case, I will include her on the guest list for tomorrow night— just a few people for a companionable evening of whist, I've said on my invitations. I want the older group, but I don't know too many of Lady Grace's generation who have influence in society."

"An evening of whist?" His eyebrows lifted. "Initially that sounds dull, but I presume this is preparing us somehow for our function?"

"The problem is asking people on such short notice. I have a list of people I want at our supper dance, but when I don't know them, it seems a cheek. If I have some of them here first and broach the subject of a cousin's informal presentation, I think they'll spread the word and ease our way."

He didn't comment and went into his room. She packed up soon after. Tomorrow, she would be very busy. She needed her ring resized.

* * * *

Charlotte combined her morning ride with a visit to the goldsmith and came home ready to conquer the new arrangement of the drawing room and hall.

First, she went to the back of the house where the maids slept and the out-of-use furniture was stored. She noted her choices and found two male outdoor servants who she asked to move three small tables to the drawing room. Also, while there, she had them shift the two large, heavily carved credenzas to either side of the marble fireplace.

Even that simple change made a world of difference, and so she had them set the furniture back against the walls so that they could roll and stand the smaller Persian rugs in the hall. She stood in the doorway, directing the placement of the biggest dark red rug near the fireplace. The men stumbled around, mistaking one carved piece for another. They stopped and started and finally looked at her in puzzlement.

Containing her impatience, she had them set down the longest couch while she paced to the edge of the carpet, indicating how she would like the seating. After they had managed that simple task, they floundered with the next, the placement of the small tables, while she moved to the doorway again.

A hand settled to the back of her neck and pulled a curl on her nape. She glanced up at Nick, her whole body alert to the gently caressing motion of his fingers. While his action calmed her, the sensation set her body tingling, and she closed her eyes, wondering if she should pretend his touch didn't affect her.

"You're flustering them, my love."

"How so?" she asked, not sure if she should stop his distraction or simply enjoy the moment.

He grinned. "The same way you fluster all young men. You are making them too conscious of themselves."

"I'm being a martinet. I want the furniture just so, and I don't seem to be able to explain what I mean."

His hand continued the caressing. "I'll intervene, if I may."

Though she had trouble concentrating on anything but his hand on her nape, she tried to look composed. "I'm sure your mother didn't need her orders to go through your father."

"My mother, although attractive, didn't have a face that would stop a man in his tracks."

She caught his gaze, grabbed at his hand, and did her best to frown. "You are distracting me, which I think is the point. You've been showing me that certain things distract certain people. And all the time I thought you were being nice."

He smiled. "I'm glad I have the power to distract you. Now, if I might help?"

She nodded, and without raising his voice, he said, "Put down that table, please," to the men who instantly did so. "My wife will explain to you her idea for the room, and she will then leave you to do as she expects."

He waited while Charlotte told the men she wanted two areas made in the room, one facing the fireplace with seating and side tables precisely placed, and the other furnished with small tables dotted there and there and there for whist. While she spoke, Nick slid his hand from her neck to her waist and, idly, took her left hand in his. For the first time in her life, she didn't plan not to react. Instead, she smiled at him with gratitude, and she squeezed his fingers in thanks.

He nodded courteously, half smiled back, and left her to finish the room.

* * * *

Nick noted the rolled carpets in the hall, the boxes of ornaments, the empty vases, and the pictures waiting to be hanged. He could see Charlotte had already changed the main room for the better and was interested to see the result. As he had said, he was pleased his touch distracted his wife as much as her appearance distracted him and the male servants.

He would never know if Luke had made love to her. If she had conceived, he would only know he was the father if the child died or if it was a monster and not a baby as perfect as Nell's or Amelia's. He had come to terms with childbirth not killing every woman because the proof lay all around him. Very few, these days, were so unlucky.

He strolled to his sitting room and sat at his desk. Charlotte's pile of invitations had been taken for posting, and he indolently checked her lists of names. Nothing out of the ordinary there, and so he attended to the business matters his father needed addressed, taking longer than he expected. The opening door sent his gaze in that direction.

"Luncheon," Charlotte said, a smile on her lovely face. Something inside his chest lifted and warmed. "I'm having the dining room revised. Do you mind eating in the conservatory again?"

He rose to his feet. "Not at all, but I won't put you or the servants to the trouble. I'm sure Cook is already preparing food for tomorrow night and that you have more important matters to attend. I'll eat at my club today." She looked disappointed, and his heart lurched at the unexpected sight. Her expression so rarely deviated from serenity. He reached out and took her left hand, touching her wedding band as he had before. "The sign of ownership," he said, wryly. "A manacle, a warning to other men. I find I like knowing that they can see you belong to me."

"Do you mean that?"

"Would I lie?" Surprised, he waited.

"You have before, and you have to know that it's not fair that I belong to you, but you don't belong to me."

"Are you so sure about that?"

"Do you still keep your mistress?" she asked, her fingers so ready to leave his that he tightened his grip.

"No. There's only one woman I want, but other than with a ring, I'm not sure how to keep *her*."

She stared at his fingers. "I'm sure you could think of a way if you tried."

He took her into his arms and saw her expression deaden slightly. "Wrong way?"

She evaded his gaze. "I'm not ready to be cajoled."

His lips twisted. "Not before luncheon?"

Placing her hands on his chest, she pushed out of his hold. "You don't know who I am. And sometimes, nor do I. I need time."

His jaw tightened. "How much time?"

She held his gaze for some seconds before finally drawing a deep breath. "I don't know, but I'm currently indisposed. You feared a certain event?"

He held his breath, his chest thudding. "You can't possibly know if you are pregnant so soon."

"But I can know I'm not." She backed out of the room and closed the door firmly behind her.

Chapter 19

Arriving home in good time for the whist party the next evening, Nick strolled through the front door. Persian rugs had been spread across the polished wooden floor, muffling the sound of his shoes as he passed through a main hall he scarcely recognized. Paintings of rural England hung along the two side walls. The table no longer held a silver tray for cards but an enormous arrangement of flowers.

Approving, he checked the newly refurbished sitting and dining rooms, and blew out an admiring breath. Charlotte had style. The rooms no longer looked overcrowded, and instead seemed to be filled with light. He was hard to see how she had managed this change, bearing in mind that she had used the same furniture. The marble topped credenzas placed on either side of the marble fireplace balanced the room. The patterned carpet in front somehow made the area friendlier and more inviting with the seating grouped in a three-sided arrangement, sectioning this area from the more expansive space set behind with whist tables and the dining room chairs. The dining table on the other side of the hall had been shortened by the removal of a couple of leaves, making this room look more spacious. The ornamentation he'd known his whole life had been used in another way entirely.

His mother's precious ivory carvings were now grouped in a glass-fronted cabinet, and the porcelain maidens no longer cluttered every available surface. He suspected many had been packed away. Now only fruit or flower paintings hung on the walls. The stuffed birds had disappeared.

He bounded up the stairs and changed into his evening clothes. "This collar sits well," he said to Vera as he passed her in the main hall. "The starching recently has been, at best, variable."

Vera grinned. "The mistress has dealt with the matter."

"My wife?"

"She had a word with Mrs. Wishart."

Dressed in spotless black and white, Nick presented himself in the drawing room, wondering where dinner would be served. He'd barely backed in front of the empty fireplace to survey the renovated room again when Charlotte appeared, dressed elegantly in a white evening gown overlaid with a bodice of red lace.

"And yet another new gown, although this one was worth every penny," he said without a tinge of irony.

"Look closer."

Noting the expectant tilt of her eyebrows, he glanced at the gown again, reminded of the night he had met her and the white gown she'd ripped. He rubbed at his jaw. "Familiar, or not? Presumably I'm not mistaken in thinking this might be the fantastical gown that fell to pieces some three months ago in front of my eyes. The red lace is a repair?"

"The red lace is another remodeling. You have seen this same gown with a blue bodice, with a blue overdress, with a green overdress, and more. I have two evening gowns and this is one."

He moistened his lips. "Clearly I noticed you far more than the details of your gowns."

"Beautifully said. You're not alone. I doubt anyone other than Sarah knows the limitations of my wardrobe."

"However, you can afford more than a few gowns on the allowance from my father," he said slowly, scrutinizing her face.

She nodded. "I prefer to use the money for other purposes. We will have dinner in the dining room tonight as usual and I think—" She glanced across the hall to the dining area where Thomas, the manservant stood, waiting. "Yes, we are ready."

Nick seated her and himself at the table and was instantly served consommé by Thomas and not a maid. That finished, Thomas announced a course of asparagus and artichokes and crayfish, followed by roasted beef. Nick ate each, puzzled. "Is Cook afraid we might starve?"

Charlotte smiled. "In alphabetical order this week, we're experimenting with a few new recipes for Sarah's come-out. We will likely be feeding more than one hundred people, and we want to know which dishes we can manage here and which will need to be prepared elsewhere."

"If we've managed these without outside help, we've done well. Please tell Cook," he said to the manservant who left with the empty plates. "Thomas managed well, too. We haven't used him to serve at the table for quite a while. I don't know why."

"You had a skeleton staff because you rarely ate at home. Alfred didn't see the need for too much formality for himself. I was hoping that for the supper dance we could have some of the extra staff sent from Stirling. Mrs. Wishart assures me no one was put off."

He nodded. When he had told Charlotte she wasn't to change his lifestyle, he had meant his visits to his mistress, although Charlotte didn't know about Beth then.

Interested in the experimentation, he tasted apricots and cherries separately cooked in syrup. "And presumably, we will be serving supper tonight?"

"Of course, but it's only for twenty, and we're presenting quite simple dishes."

He shook his head, but in wonder. Clearly, he had married an exceptional woman, if at twenty years of age she could run a household while organizing large events without stirring a single hair on her perfectly groomed head.

The dining table was cleared and reset with stacked plates and regimented silver for the guests, none of whom had taken offense at their late invitations. Each arrival expressed delight, more than likely because each was a member of the older generation and flattered to be singled out by a younger couple. Nick, an inveterate gambler, found himself outclassed in whist and embroiled in delightfully wicked gossip about families he had forgotten in his stupor of alcohol and grief.

After a light supper, he approached the long, pink couch enlivened by tasseled cushions in red and Mrs. Grayson's welcoming smile.

"I'm glad to see you found time to be with us tonight, although I wasn't so sure while you were teaching me lessons in whist." He sat beside the fragile elderly lady.

"You're very good, you know, but youth doesn't have the patience of age."

"Nor, I see, the elegance." He picked up her hand and kissed her wrist. "You are looking very beautiful tonight."

She tapped him on the shoulder with her fan. "Your wife is a beauty with the sort of elegance that lasts, an elegance of mind. She also has a natural skill at whist, which gives one to believe she is a very clever young lady."

He hoped Charlotte hadn't been too clever. "I'm a lucky man."

"It wasn't always so." A wry smile crossed her fine-boned face. "Nor was my third cousin, Barrington Benbow. But his luck changed, too. His second wife, young Louisa, has finally presented him with a living son and heir. He's delighted, as you would suppose."

Nick nodded stiffly. He didn't know Benbow had married again. Clearly, his loss of Clara to Nick hadn't disturbed him too greatly.

"As you know, Clara lost her first by him. Louisa also lost her first with the same problem. Every now and again, one of the Benbows produces a child malformed in the womb, and with the frequency his were, Barrington thought he had no hope. This third child has put new heart into him." She stared at Nick for a moment and reached out to pat his hand. "Did I shock you by speaking of Clara? If so, I apologize, dear boy, but to me, more said, soonest mended. Was I wrong?"

He held Mrs. Grayson's frail hand, his thoughts shifting through the thick fog of his memories. Had *he* been wrong? Could Clara have been carrying Barrington Benbow's child? *She'd had a previous baby with the same problem. Her husband's next child had the same deformity.* Nick didn't need to be a genius to assume that the likelihood of Benbow being the father of all three babies was great.

He moistened his suddenly dry mouth. "No," he said, his voice husky. "No. Thank you."

That night, he lay in his bed, staring at the ceiling, still thanking Mrs. Grayson. Clara had also blamed him for the premature labor. However, he no longer believed the labor had begun preterm. The rounding of her belly when she had come to him expecting his help indicated she had been more than three months pregnant. Her labor had begun full term, not two months early as she had said.

In these past four years, he had been trapped by a lie that had directed him to be last of his line. Even now, he couldn't grasp the concept of having a normal marriage and possibly a few children. He sat up, tangled in his sheets, knowing that to begin again he had to make peace with the past.

Clara's first child had died, and she feared her second would have the same inherited problem. Perhaps she preferred to believe that Nick had fathered her child even to the day she came into labor, knowing as she must have by then, that she was having her husband's child and not Nick's. This explained her inability to bear her pain without damaging him, too, and her willingness to slip into death without a fight.

He covered his face with his hands, ashamed he hadn't understood Clara's fears, hadn't tried, and hadn't loved her enough to try. He had been too ready to lapse into despair, but for himself rather than her. Years of his life had been lost while he believed he had no future, but while he remained bitter, he would find no future to believe in.

He took a deep breath and sat on the edge of his bed. He had a chance to start again. No one had forsaken him, yet he had done his best to alienate his father and his friends, embarrassing them with his self-pity and his drinking. No more. He stood and paced his room, his thoughts shifting to his wife.

Not for a moment had Charlotte insisted on having a baby. The most she'd asked was that he considered one in the future, and this he'd refused to do. He'd wanted his way with her but on his terms only. He had decided long ago to have no feelings, but during his marriage he'd begun to experience various emotions like empathy for awkward, jealous Sarah, and antipathy for the unshakeable Charlotte. Initially he had wanted to spark opposition in the wife he saw as a pretty decoration, but no more.

He had undervalued her. From the moment he had met her, she'd handled every difficult situation with a delicate touch, from her original ripped bodice, to his accusations about Tony, and now his jealousy of Luke. If he'd had half her grace, he wouldn't be in this predicament now, in love with a woman he had driven into the arms of another. He laughed bitterly.

He loved her. How could he not?

Her humorous observations entertained him, her steadiness calmed him, and she hadn't once judged him. He could only admit his love for her now that his chance of fathering a malformed child was the same as the average man.

Given her excuse for refusing his advances, he had time to change his ways, convince her that his love was true, and not simply expedient. He didn't deserve, after the way he had behaved throughout his marriage, to have the love of his life fall into his arms the moment he held them out.

He finally hauled back his bed cover and slid into his bed, determined to proceed with patience.

* * * *

Charlotte wallowed all the next day in the success of her whist party. Nick hadn't shamed her, nor had he alluded to her birth. He had clearly enjoyed the company and had behaved like a proud new husband. Of course, not a single of his flirts had been present, though even the most elderly lady in the room had managed to hold his rapt attention for some time.

Charlotte had to face the fact that women of any age would fall for his casual, cynical flattery because the female gender enjoyed being so deliciously uncertain. And he had served his purpose expertly by fostering interest in the presentation of his wife's cousin. She couldn't ask for more.

Now almost certain of Sarah's success, she sealed her hundred invitations and bundled them for posting before ordering the carriage to take her to Stepney, where she inspected the newly refurbished premises she had hired for the next year. The flooring had been polished and the walls whitened, and when she had found twenty beds at a reasonable price, she would be ready to interview her prospective tenants.

Harvey drove her home without making a single comment, and she enjoyed having her thoughts to herself throughout the journey. She arrived at the gates of Alden House just as a smart gig pulled out of the driveway, bearing James and Chrysanthe. Each waved, but James didn't stop because he appeared to be arguing with the very much younger Zanthe, an occurrence only unusual in that James found baiting the seventeen-year-old amusing. Pondering an odd comment she'd heard from Alfred, she opened the front door and saw Sarah's bags in the hall.

Sarah stood, watching her approach. "Ah, from the life of the idle rich, back to the life of the idle rich." She planted a kiss on Charlotte's cheek. "The only life I want. Come with me while I unpack. I want to catch you up on all the news. James offered to drive me back to Adelaide," she said as she took the stairs, "but Lady Grace thought I needed a chaperone and so I was landed with Zanthe. Unmerciful child. She regaled me with stories of James's every foolish escapade from the moment she was born."

"They've known each other all their lives." Charlotte followed Sarah up the stairs. "They're almost brother and sister."

"Don't let Daphne hear you say that." Sarah entered her room, removing her hat and gloves. "She's absolutely positive she will be marrying James, and she says she doesn't mind if he sews his oats first. I'm not sure if she was warning me off or simply being boring."

"She does have a tendency toward the everyday." Charlotte shut her mouth guiltily. After living with Nick, she had learned to prefer the subtleties of conversation. "But the well off tend to marry among themselves. It's hard these days to force one's way into society without a rending of a gown."

"A subject I have given a small amount of thought to lately."

"Don't. If it becomes too fashionable to be compromised, everyone will want to try, and then we will be thought impossibly dull. For you, we'll simply do the right thing. I held a whist party last night and invited the doyens. I wanted to be approved as a hostess, and I think I was. Just today I sent off the invitations for your supper dance."

"You decided on the date? When?"

"Two weeks from today."

Sarah clapped her hands to her cheeks. "That doesn't give me much time."

"I've redone all your hats and chosen fabric for your gown."

"You might have asked me what I want."

Charlotte wrinkled her nose. "Nick said you have to have white, which is a problem I think I might have solved. I chose a very creamy white. If you don't like it, then it's just another gown and you can choose whatever you want, as long as it's white."

"I'm fussing needlessly. White is white and you would have chosen the right one. You always do. Do I look any different?" Sarah stood, hands by her sides waiting for an answer.

Charlotte narrowed her eyes and walked around Sarah. "Indefinably, yes. You're somehow…glossier. Perhaps it's the clean country air?"

"Hm." Sarah laughed. "I have an admirer."

"Who?"

"A gentleman well known in society. The only problem is that his intentions don't appear to be honorable."

"Are you interested in him?"

"Desperately. I have been from the moment I met him."

"But you won't tell me who he is?"

"Not by name, but I'm sure you can guess."

"James? He's not for you, Sarah. He's too rich, and he has been too accustomed to having his wicked way. I've heard some of Zanthe's stories, too, and although she makes them funny, I don't doubt they are true."

"Like the one when she caught him lying on top of an unnamed female in his garden? He tripped, he says, being an ungainly sixteen-year-old, and the girl cushioned his fall." Sarah laughed. "You're right, though. Her outrageous criticism of him is very much brother and sister, and speaking of which…" She glanced sideways at Charlotte. "Sometimes, I rather think you resemble him—though mainly in your coloring."

"Is dark hair and light eyes so unusual? Though, I wouldn't mind being his *sister*. I'm very fond of his family, but you can't sidetrack me so easily when I'm worrying about you."

"Don't. I know what I'm doing, and I won't be having my gown ripped at the supper dance. If I don't hear a proposal before then, I'll be most surprised." Sarah looked half malicious, half satisfied.

"Just don't do anything rash." Charlotte placed Sarah's hat carefully with the others. "Has he said he loves you?"

"He says he wants me," Sarah said defiantly. "But he's going to have to marry me first."

Charlotte threaded her fingers, trying not to worry. "If he doesn't propose, you will have plenty of other prospects. Your birth is perfectly respectable and with a great social success behind you, you will have your pick of the best."

She left for the drawing room where Mrs. Wishart planned to introduce her to a new housemaid. Sarah wouldn't needlessly ruin her reputation. Perhaps she was obstinate at times, but she had always worked with Charlotte for their respective futures. However, she mulled this thought until dinner that evening.

After dressing in her blue green-trimmed gown, she placed fresh flowers on the dining table.

Nick joined her downstairs, scrupulously dressed and so vitally attractive that her heart skipped a beat. She tried to look no more than coolly welcoming but out of all the feelings she had for him, welcoming featured low on her list.

"I presume Sarah is back. I saw Luke in town today, and he says everyone is."

"You spoke to him?" Charlotte pressed her hands together. "I hope you didn't accuse him of anything he didn't do."

"I told him you wouldn't need his escort any longer because I planned to be his stand-in. He nodded politely and said he would be glad to see me with my wife. From there, it was fairly hard to accuse him of anything but teaching me my place."

"Do you think James plans to marry Daphne?"

"Interesting change of subject. I've never given a thought to anything James might do. Why not ask him?"

She gave a reproving smile. "We don't exactly have the sort of relationship that would allow me to ask his intentions."

"I'd say any intentions he had toward a woman would involve either a bed or the removal of clothes. But if you wanted, you could have a relationship with him."

"Another prospective father for our children?" She clamped her lips, her veins flooding with ice.

He didn't attempt to veil his expression of horror. "Good Lord, no. I meant something else entirely."

"I don't want to know," she said, breathing unevenly.

He gazed into her eyes. Her skin prickled and she longed to glance away. She didn't want to fool herself into thinking he was about to give her a fond smile, or even a hug, bearing in mind the subject of the conversation.

"I'm not late I hope." Sarah stood in the doorway.

"Not at all," Charlotte said, relieved by the interruption.

Nick turned. "Welcome back," he said to Sarah. He leaned over and whispered in Charlotte's ear, "I don't want you bearing any child but mine."

Outraged, she gasped. The man would say anything at all to keep her off balance.

That night, she lay in bed with her fists pressed over her mouth. Having Sarah back in the house gave her convenient excuses to avoid Nick, who had spent the evening in his father's study catching up on business matters, while leaving the ladies the chance to gossip.

Apparently, he now objected to the thought of someone else playing with his very own toy, but despite his egregious statement, he wouldn't let her bear his child. If he thought his new stance would get him into her bed, he would be sadly disappointed. At this stage, only an avowal of love would achieve his aim, but she doubted he would be able to force such a word through his throat.

That night, she closed and locked her bedroom door.

Chapter 20

The full moon lit the night outside the window, and leaves quietly rustled in the dark. Sitting at his father's desk, Nick finished the accounts and leaned back, pleased. While for years he'd contributed nothing but disinterest, his father had kept him. Now Nick found great satisfaction in managing his inheritance. The improvements to the Stirling cottages, despite the expense, would not only add to the Alden workforce but also the wellbeing of many local hills' families.

Although his presence had not been requested by Charlotte, he rose, buttoned his jacket, and strolled into the drawing room where she and Sarah sat plotting the most expensive way to choose a husband for Sarah, interesting, but needless in his opinion. Other than the fact he would like to be alone in his house with his recalcitrant wife, he saw no reason to marry Sarah off.

Fortunately, biding his time with Charlotte had made her more tolerant of his presence, either that or Sarah's current snappishness was wearing her down.

"…but we'll want the rooms to look a little different," Charlotte was saying. She glanced up at him. On the side-table, which had been shifted in front of the long couch where she sat, lay color swatches, lists, pencils, paper, scissors, ribbons, and a plate of cheese and fruit.

Sarah sat on the window seat, swishing the lace window covering. "You're more interested in colors than I am. Why don't you choose?"

"Because yesterday you accused me of taking over."

"It's your money. Why shouldn't you?"

Charlotte glanced at Nick again, as if in appeal.

He settled beside her, peering from under his brows at Sarah. "She should. She has a talent for organization she shouldn't waste, but possibly she's expecting you to take a little responsibility, too."

"And I will," Sarah said, her face set. She dropped the curtain. "But I can't think of any way to decorate the rooms other than with flowers." She stood, rustled past him, and headed for the hall.

"Not exactly the outcome I wanted," Charlotte said wryly, staring at the empty doorway. "I was hoping she would offer to help with more of the practicalities."

"If it's too much for you, we could get Mrs. Wishart on board." He toyed idly with the ribbon tie on the shoulder of her gown.

"It's not too much for me." She lifted his hand away. "It's the sort of thing I love to do, but I want to take her mind off expectations of James getting down on one knee to her. If she wants to make herself into a desirable wife for a rich and spoiled young man, who apparently doesn't mind leading on the gullible in the hopes of leading one astray, she needs a few more skills than gallivanting around all day with other young ladies with the same silly ideas."

He laughed, pleased to hear her patience could be stretched. "I will happily shake her for you."

"You did. She's used to you taking her side."

"How positively stupid of me. So, James is a rich and spoiled young man, is he?"

"He's certainly not treating her with respect."

Nick leaned back. "I can't see him trying to lead anyone astray who wouldn't have a propensity to be led astray. I wouldn't have applied that description to Sarah who appears to have a very keen sense of self preservation."

"We're all fools for love."

He smiled, enjoying her new asperity. To prove his faith, he refrained from questioning her mysterious daily excursions and, his actions carefully casual, he cut himself a slice of cheese. "Do you do this plotting and planning all day as well as all evening?"

"Only when Sarah and I spend time together, which isn't during the day," she said, cleverly avoiding a subject that was, after all, none of his business. She began to pack up her lists and her samples.

He ate his cheese and broke off a stem of grapes. "During the day, I spend most of my time experimenting with new ideas for expanding my father's various businesses. The house in Stirling is fully furnished, but like here, sadly old-fashioned. Many of the furnishings would be thirty years old and some due for renewal, curtain fabrics, for instance. It seems to me that this is your province rather than mine."

Her gaze caught his. "I would enjoy advising where you want advice, but currently I have my hands full with Sarah's presentation and another project."

He popped two of his grapes into her mouth. "What other project?" He held his breath.

"A charity commitment," she said, between chewing and swallowing. "I'm going up to bed. I'll see you at breakfast." She stood.

He stood. "That sounds rather final. I'll come up to bed, too."

She inclined her head and led the way up the stairs. He followed, apprehensive. Although he could accept another rebuff, he didn't want one. He opened the suite door for her, and she headed toward her bedroom.

He followed. "Will you want help with your buttons and hooks?" he asked casually, stopping in her doorway.

She faced him, examining his expression, which he kept entirely impartial, and she turned, presenting her back.

He sauntered over to her, knowing he couldn't invade her bed after behaving like a jealous fool and expect to be received with open arms. Focusing entirely on the delicacy of her white nape, he stirred the soft curls with a deliberate breath while he dealt with her fastenings.

She shivered and he closed his eyes, loving her and wanting her.

"Are you sure you need to continue punishing me?" Almost afraid of taking the wrong step, he ran his palm from her shoulder to her neck. He felt rather than heard her intake of breath.

"I have never intended to punish you. I just don't like being judged by your standards."

"My standards are higher for others than myself."

She gave a tiny, reluctant laugh. "You're impossible. I know you want to bed me, but I know you are not exclusive."

"I am exclusive. I want only you."

She rested her cheek on his hand for a heartbeat. "And eventually your precautions against having a baby will fail and then what?"

"We will have a baby."

She turned swiftly and faced him. "And what if the baby is not perfect?"

He cleared his throat, as awkward as a sixteen-year-old. "I have no reason to believe that my children will not be as perfect as those of any other man. It seems I didn't father Clara's child at all." The confession hurt, and all the anguish of all the years ached through each of his bones. The truth, so new to him, had not been said aloud before and hovered between them.

Her brows drew together. "And this was a recent discovery?" she asked in a voice of suspicion.

He tried to hold her steady gaze but pity for his foolishness would be too hard to bear. "Mrs. Grayson led me to believe Clara's baby was fathered by her husband."

"So now you expect to leap into my bed." And with that she crossed her arms. "After all your accusations and mistrust?"

"I was wrong to accuse you of infidelity, and I'm deeply sorry for my ill considered words. And I am, of course, hoping for forgiveness sooner rather than later."

Her hand went to her face, and with a finger, she prodded the dent in her chin as Tony did during thoughtful moments. This tiny familial gesture hit him in the belly and made him smile despite himself.

"If that's all you have to say, later then."

"Perhaps we could shorten the process." He pushed his hands deep into his pockets. "We'll play cards. If I win, you'll accept my atonement of the past few days and we'll start anew."

She inclined her head to the side, as if considering. "You never beat me. Do me up again, and I'll give you a chance."

Unfortunately, she didn't. A former gambler, and his gambling was as former as his drinking, he was good, as Mrs. Grayson had noted. However, he didn't lose because his game had deteriorated. He lost because she cheated. With every card she dealt from the bottom of the pack, he knew she planned him to lose. She had no intention of being won with an apology. He realized a self-contained woman like her would naturally be more attracted to a man who had the same attributes, and he hoped she hadn't lost interest in him because of any lingering feelings for Luke.

Packing up the cards, he wished her a good night at her door and lay awake for an hour or so more. Even a former drunk with an inclusive taste in women could be reformed for the sake of love, and so he would show her.

* * * *

"Mr. Luke Worthing," Thomas said with an efficient smile as Luke entered the drawing room where Charlotte sat tying wrist ribbons onto dance cards.

"You are receiving visitors, I hope?" Luke ignored Thomas, who left. "And in a new and very smart room. Your touch?"

Although Nick said she wasn't to see Luke alone, she could hardly ask him to leave. She nodded. "Please sit. Are you recovered from the strenuous cricket matches and tea parties of Stirling?"

"I am. I wanted to make sure you are well. Nick said he hustled you away because he was concerned for your health."

She took her attention back to her ribbons. "What a fib," she said lightly. "He was concerned for his own. He missed me. Our plan worked, you see, but perhaps too well."

"He's been dogging me lately. I'm not sure why."

"Let's hope he is trying to renew your friendship after being so suspicious of ours."

Something clattered in the hall outside.

"Sorry," Sarah called. She arrived so quickly into the room that she almost skidded. Her skirts didn't quite catch up, and her crinoline bounced. "I dropped the card tray while I was counting the replies to our supper dance." Her voice sounded stiff. "Ah, Mr. Worthing. How delightful to see you here."

Luke inclined his head, rose to his feet, and waited until they were both seated before he spoke again. "I, too, received an invitation for your supper dance and will be delighted to attend." He smiled at Charlotte. "This will be your first function as Mrs. Nicholas Alden. I suppose you're rather nervous."

"This will be my first time as a guest of honor," Sarah said before Charlotte could answer. "And *I'm* not in the least nervous." Her glance at Charlotte was unreadable.

Charlotte tied another bow. "I'm enjoying the preparations. Yesterday I auditioned string quartets, three of them, a very lulling experience much needed as I'm having a rostrum built in the hall for the musicians tomorrow. I doubt we'll be able to hear ourselves think while the workers are here."

"It's fortunate I called today, then."

"We've invited a hundred people." Sarah gazed at the backs of her hands. "The house will be swarming with eligible bachelors."

Luke pulled out his fob watch and stood. "I'm sure you are both wishing me elsewhere while you're so busy. Glad to see you looking so well, Charlotte. Sarah."

"That must have been the shortest call in the history of calling," Sarah said as she watched him leave.

"He didn't come to gossip. He just wanted to make sure, um."

"Um, what?"

"Nick hurried me out of Stirling. I think people wondered why."

Sarah sat, unmoving. "Was there a reason?"

"He was alone here. That's a good enough reason."

"I don't know why you left him alone." Sarah stood, staring narrow-eyed at Charlotte, as if waiting for an explanation.

"Perhaps because I thought it might do him a certain amount of good to be left on his own."

"Well, in your case, absence did make the heart grow fonder. You have interesting ways and means of achieving your ends. I don't doubt I can adapt a few to my own purpose." With a tilt of her eyebrows, Sarah bustled off as quickly as she had arrived.

Sighing, Charlotte finished the dance cards, spent an hour in the kitchen, sampling, admiring, and rechecking the various dishes that were being organized for the supper dance, before changing into a walking gown. Harvey arrived at the door to drive her to the Adelaide Women's Hospital, where she toured the long, stark birthing ward.

During the next few days, acceptances to the supper-dance piled high while Sarah managed to be elsewhere most of the time. Nick was supportive without interfering. If possible, he had grown more appealing. His bronze hair gleamed, his skin glowed with health, his eyes shone with mischief and his fastidiously cut suits showed the rakish elegance of his honed body. She looked forward to his presence at dinner each night where he entertained her with comments about the alphabet tastings.

She didn't want to keep him out of her bedroom forever, and she knew she shouldn't fear he would expose the secret of her birth. He had as little reason as she did to want the truth known. However, the fact that he twice alluded to her parentage hurt. If he had any feelings for her, he would simply accept her for herself.

* * * *

After her morning ride, Charlotte washed her hair. In two days, a canopy would be set over the front walk to protect almost one hundred guests who would arrive for the supper dance. With the temporary rostrum built in the hall, the quartet chosen, the extra chairs hired, and the flowers selected, she sat at her dressing table and combed out her tangles.

She stared into the mirror, gazed closely at the slight darkening of the skin under her eyes, leaned back, blinked, and saw another face staring back at her. With her hair wet and flat, she saw familiar blue eyes, thick dark lashes, etched cheekbones, and a straight nose, but not her own. Yesterday, when James had come to call for Sarah, he'd removed his hat to greet Charlotte. His hair had been slicked back, as hers was now.

Virginia Taylor

All his features were hers, though his nose was stronger and his chin more square. He had a tiny dent in his chin. Sarah had mentioned a likeness, but Charlotte could see more. She could be his twin. And James looked very much like Tony.

She covered her suddenly dry mouth with her hand and put together certain numbing facts. Tony had tried to keep James from courting her. He had questioned her friends about her family, and he had tried to question her. After her marriage, he had been inexplicably kind. He had given her a valuable horse from his stables. Clearly he knew, as Charlotte didn't, that they had a parent in common.

Nell knew, too. More than a month ago, Nell had taken her to St. Luke's Church where her grandfather had once presided, ostensibly to make a donation for the repairs to the nave. Charlotte hadn't left the brougham, afraid to show too much interest in what was, after all, a simple stone building. Possibly, Nell had either hoped to spark a confession from her or to confirm the truth.

Charlotte buried her Hawthorn face in both her hands. She had accepted Nell's friendship without considering an ulterior motive. The fashionable wife of a wealthy property owner had no need to recognize the nobody who had married a friend of her husband, no need to draw her into a special relationship—unless she wanted her cooperation. Nell would, of course, not want Charlotte to flaunt her reprehensible parentage, and Charlotte would grab the bribe of acceptance rather than a monetary payout. She had left herself open to complete humiliation, which she could possibly bear—but not for Sarah, too.

Poor trusting Sarah had always accepted Joseph Davies as Charlotte's father, and she wanted to marry James. The wealthy Hawthorns wouldn't consider a bride related to their illegitimate half sister. Naturally, because of this knowledge, James assumed he could have Sarah without marriage as his father had assumed he could have the parson's daughter, Adelina Dunbar, without marriage.

Because of Charlotte, Sarah wouldn't have the opportunity to wed the man she loved. All her life, Charlotte had prevented Sarah, by no means deliberately, from achieving her goals.

She pressed her cold fingers into her flushed, shamed cheeks. Never would she be able to put herself in Sarah's place as a poor, well-born relation. Sarah had been brought up in a home where she was second to a baseborn cousin whose wonderful future had been perfectly orchestrated. Charlotte couldn't change the truth, couldn't give Sarah anything but a come-out party where the world would laugh at her if they knew of Charlotte's shameful birth.

She sat blotchy and dry-eyed with no solution. Eventually, she rang for Vera to help her dress, and she went down to breakfast long after everyone else had finished. "Is Mr. Nick in?" she asked Thomas.

"In Mr. Alden's study with Mr. Wickerby."

"I won't disturb him, then." She could wait until after his father's man of business had left to make her full confession, hoping that Nick would… what? She couldn't tell him the full truth, not until after the supper dance. If, too ashamed, he canceled the function, her cousin would be left with nothing.

She consoled herself with the thought that the only difference between today and yesterday was that she now knew her mother's secret. The Hawthorns had not confronted her with the truth, which meant they were prepared to bide their time. And so, to bide hers, she resignedly settled her skirts in the drawing room, reading the musician's suggestions for tomorrow's program when Thomas came to the door. "The dressmaker has arrived with Miss Sarah's gown."

"I think Miss Sarah is still in her room. Take the gown to her, please."

Within five minutes, Vera appeared in the doorway. "I can't find Miss Sarah anywhere. We wanted to do the final fitting of her gown this morning."

"She must have an engagement elsewhere. Let the dressmaker go. I can fit the gown this afternoon, if need be."

"T'ain't right. You'll have enough to do finishing off your own."

"I might do that now. That will be all, Vera."

Not willing to be annoyed by Sarah's casual attitude toward her gowning, Charlotte went to her room and inspected the dress she planned to wear tomorrow night, the blue currently decorated with rows of green ribbon on the skirts and shoulders. She wanted to look severely plain at the supper dance, for she planned to wear her diamond necklace.

Within half an hour, she had removed the ribbon and given the gown a comprehensive examination. With long white gloves, she would look elegantly matronly, a good contrast for Sarah's soft peach skin, stunning apricot hair, and glimmering white gown.

Still Sarah didn't arrive home. Nick had finished his business and disappeared, and with a feeling of reprieve, Charlotte asked Thomas to call Harvey with the brougham to the front door. The weather had turned dusty. Dressed in her burgundy gown and a lime green hat tied with a burgundy bow on the side, she gathered up the four tiny baby gowns she had made and asked Harvey to drive her to her house in Stepney, where four unwed mothers and their babies had settled two days ago.

The door was opened by the youngest, a sixteen-year-old, and the others stood back shyly. After they had settled in the parlor, she set her bag on her knee. "Now, you've all seen the work room?" she asked, handing out her gifts.

They nodded, each examining their baby gowns, cooing and smiling.

"I don't intend to send you out to earn your board, but I thought if we could somehow earn our way, we could help even more women in your position."

"Seems only fair, ma'am. No one else would give us a place to live, not fallen women like us. While we live together, we can take turns baby-minding while the others work."

"You've already discussed this?" Charlotte beamed at the girl, Peggy. "Later, I'll teach you hat-making, and we'll see where we can go from there."

"We just need a start," said the tallest, a nineteen-year-old with a bad leg. "We won't want charity forever."

Charlotte hauled in a breath. The charitable contributions she hoped for would not be forthcoming if she were to be exposed in society as the bastard daughter of Herbert Hawthorn. Likely her generous allowance from Alfred, one of Herbert's contemporaries, would be stopped. Refusing to feel sorry for herself, for she had snatched the bed she lay on and she would somehow work this out, she spent the afternoon discussing various craft ideas with the mothers.

The best she could do for the women at this point was to teach them to take advantage of their situation while they could. And she would take advantage of her own while she could.

* * * *

Nick leaned back against the ropes, sweaty, gazing at the youngster who had challenged him to a round. "You did well. Practice," he said, "stay off the drink, and try again next year." He grinned, and the youngster, his face shining with suppressed joy, untangled himself from the ropes and stepped out of the ring into the back slaps of his energetically encouraging peers.

The group moved off, and Nick rubbed his face with his towel.

"Stay off the drink?" Rossdale Luscombe, a red-faced bully at school, who had developed a paunch since marrying an heiress, rested a hand on the ropes. He had stripped for a bout with a punching bag. "Only a month or two back, you were drunk in every tavern in town. It's all very well to beat lads, but how would you go with a real man, eh?"

"You being that person? I think we found that out ten years back."

"And you're afraid of a rematch?"

"There's a time and place, don't you think?" Nick slung his towel over his shoulder.

"I have time now and this is the perfect place."

"I'm expected home," Nick said, surprised to hear himself say so. For the first time in years, he was expected to be present for meals, and he found great enjoyment in being part of his family.

Luscombe chortled. "And you wouldn't want that nose of yours pushed out of joint. I'd say it already is. Ask Worthing."

Nick laughed. "He hasn't managed that yet. Nor will you." He untied his gloves.

"He's doing it right now. I went past his place not an hour ago, and your wife was steadying her horse slap outside his door. She might have been heavily veiled but everyone knows that horse of Hawthorn's."

"If I were you, I wouldn't be spreading stories about my wife."

"You and Worthing both like the same sort of easy pickings," Luscombe said, his slack upper lip curled.

"Easy pickings?" Nick asked, looking down his nose. "If you heard tales that I had your wife before you, they're not true. She didn't make my list." He waited.

Luscombe tried to vault over the rope where Nick stood, but overweight and angry, he tripped. Nick didn't need to touch him. The hoots from the youngsters ended the bout before it began.

Chapter 21

Nick rapped with the brass doorknocker. Luke lived in rooms off his office on the ground floor of a bluestone Georgian construction on North Terrace, entered into from a private gate on the side. Luke opened his door, a gray hat and a pair of gray gloves in his hand.

"Just home?" Nick asked, edging through the doorway.

Luke moved back, a wary expression on his face. "Just about to leave. But of course, if you want to chat…"

"I hear Charlotte came to see you today." Nick pushed his hands into his trouser pockets, his reflection flickering in the tall mirror above the hall table, flanked on one side by a rack holding a buff collared greatcoat and an umbrella.

Luke frowned and he shook his head. "Who on earth told you that?"

"Rossdale Luscombe," Nick said with a hard smile. "I saw him in Dixon's, and he was certain you were entertaining my wife."

"This is a gentleman's residence. I don't entertain ladies here as a rule."

Nick rubbed his jaw. He had expected a denial. "He was also sure he recognized her horse."

"He doesn't know a horse from an ass. Charlotte hasn't been here. The man was always a fool and you know it." His face stiff, Luke indicated the front door. "Now, if you've finished throwing uninformed accusations at me, may I go about my business?" His glance flickered.

Luke's defensiveness puzzled Nick. Barely two weeks ago, he had edged his way around the subject of his wife and Luke having an affair, which even now he could not believe. "So, on the word of a gentleman, Charlotte has not been here today?"

"On the word of a gentleman." Luke placed his hand over his heart. "I don't know why Luscombe would want to start such a rumor, but that was always his way. He used to taunt you about being as pretty as a girl and he'd throw a punch at you, hoping he had distracted you enough to get a hit in."

Nick nodded. Luscombe and creatures of his ilk had initially been the cause of him learning to box. Later, after he'd made the sport his own, they'd done their best to beat him, giving him the elating task of trying not to damage them. Although he enjoyed his champion status, now achieved, he used his fists during exercise only. He turned to leave and noted a flash of bright color on the skirting board under the greatcoat. Very slowly, he bent and picked up a long single curled emerald feather.

"From your Sunday best hat, no doubt?" he said in an aching breath.

Luke shook his head, his voice awkward. "Believe me, I don't know where that came from."

Nick took one step forward, and with gritted violence threw a punch at Luke's jaw.

Luke fell back into the table. Dazedly shaking his head, he straightened, spread his feet, and raised two clenched fists in front of his rigid face. "Try that again. I could give you more competition than almost anyone."

Nick made a sound of contempt. "Even drunk I could lay you out quicker than I could take my next breath. The least you could have done was tell me the truth."

Luke dropped his gaze and his stance. Nick slammed out of the hallway.

In the busy thoroughfare outside, he flipped a coin to the lad watching his horse. "There's another for you if you can tell me if a lady on a tall chestnut was here earlier."

The lad nodded, his dirty face solemn. "'er 'orse was sidesteppin' bad. She lost her 'at and the critter walked all over it. On purpose, I'd say."

"Did she stay long?"

The lad shrugged. "An hour, I reckon."

Nick pressed a gold coin into the lad's hand, swung onto his horse, and maneuvered past various carts, carriages, and street vendors, making his way home as quickly as possible. Charlotte had long curling feathers exactly the same color on her riding hat which was, incidentally, heavily veiled in black and her idea of making invisible the most visible woman in Adelaide.

* * * *

Charlotte removed her hat and jacket in her bedroom.

Vera bustled in. "Miss Sarah is home. The dress fits perfect, and so we won't have any alterations to do." She took the coat and hat into Charlotte's dressing room.

Charlotte tidied her hair and went to see Sarah, who sat hunched in her bedroom chair, her lower face covered by her two palms. She barely lifted her head when Charlotte entered.

"I expected you to be at home for your fitting today. Vera says the gown is perfect."

"It's lovely."

"And yet you don't seem happy."

Sarah showed a pale face with red-rimmed eyes.

Assuming from her cousin's expression that James's proposal had not been forthcoming, Charlotte reached out to squeeze Sarah's shoulder while seating herself on the bed. "All is not lost," she said, sympathetically. "We have the supper dance tomorrow, and the house will be full of eligible bachelors, as you said."

Sarah lifted a wan face. "I did, didn't I? How pointless when there's only one eligible bachelor I'm interested in."

"But you can't have him. It's my fault and I'm sorry, but I can't change the situation."

"Nor can I." Sarah's mouth lifted on one side. "I tried, but he won't have me." Her eyes glossed and filled. Tears spilled down her cheeks and dripped from her chin. "I've made such a fool of myself. I don't know what I can do now."

Charlotte rubbed Sarah's arms. "James can't marry you, but not because of anything you did. It's because of something his father did."

"James? I don't care who James marries, and I don't care what his father did. I want Luke. I wanted him from the moment I met him…. The day Lady Grace sent him to escort you to her picnic."

Charlotte frowned. "Luke? I thought you wanted James."

Sarah swiped a palm over her tears. "I let you believe that because I knew Luke was in love with you."

"Sarah, this is crazy. Luke and I have never been more than friends."

"You might think that, but he doesn't. He loves you and he always has. Anyone can see the way he looks at you. I didn't know how I would get him, but I was thrilled when you accepted Nick. I thought that with you out of the picture, I might have a chance with Luke." Sarah laughed bitterly. "But although I got him to the point of saying he wanted me, he refuses to marry me."

"Let him go, Sarah."

"You were caught with Nick in a compromising situation. So, I tried compromising Luke this afternoon. Not too long ago, Nick said you can lead a horse to water without letting him drink only so often before he slakes his thirst elsewhere. I went to Luke's rooms and told him he could make love to me."

Charlotte gasped.

"Oh, don't worry. He very kindly re-dressed me and told me to go away."

"But you wouldn't have been compromising him. You would have been compromising yourself."

Sarah gave a half-hearted shrug. "I left a note for Nick asking him to call on Luke. He was supposed to catch us in bed together. But Luke had me out of the house before any of my plan could be put into motion."

"Nick's not home yet. I can get the note back."

"I've already done that. I put your hat back, too. I needed a black veil so that I wouldn't be recognized, about the only smart thing I did today."

Lost in thought, and still clasping Sarah's hands, Charlotte said, "What should we do? Luke will be at the supper dance tomorrow night."

Sarah rose to her feet, as if concluding an interview. "I certainly hope he doesn't show his face."

Charlotte looked up, her brows drawn together. "One thing. You walked into his house to offer yourself and... Where did you undress?"

"In his bedroom."

"How did you manage to undo the fastenings by yourself?"

"He managed them."

"And so he helped you off with your clothes and put them back on again?"

Sarah hung her head.

Charlotte's mouth tilted. "That was extremely noble of him."

Sarah glanced at Charlotte's expression. "Very," she said slowly, "for a man who refuses to marry a woman who *let* him take off her clothes."

Charlotte laughed and covered her mouth apologetically. "If he *wants you* but won't take you without marriage when he has a perfect opportunity, that is a great pity because tomorrow you will outshine all, and he will be extremely sorry."

"Do you think we can manage to make him sorry?"

"Hm." Charlotte stood. "And that's a very definite *hm*."

"What did James's father do?" Sarah asked as Charlotte reached the doorway.

"He fathered me, too."

Sarah took her bottom lip between her teeth, and then she nodded. "I wondered. I don't suppose he'll let on, though."

Charlotte swallowed her astonishment and realized that Sarah would have to be very gullible to imagine that Charlotte's mother, a vitally attractive woman, would have been enough interested in seventy-year-old Joseph Davies to allow him to give her a baby before marriage. She took a deep breath and let out half her apprehension with a whoosh. "That's what I'm hoping."

* * * *

Nick arrived home after midnight. Thomas had waited up, which infuriated Nick, who hadn't had a drink and didn't need an escort to his room. "Touch me and you'll find another job," he said, his voice icily clear.

Tonight he hadn't primed himself with alcohol or found an amenable female to forget the realities of his life. Instead, he spent his evening at Dixon's, in vague, restless conversations about politics, the criminal justice system, and the needs of the poor. His treacherous, unfaithful wife had changed him into a respectable citizen, and he resented her influence as much as he resented her disloyalty. He'd grown accustomed to being her escort and belonging to a greater community than the bottle. He'd had an extended family for the first time in his life.

Thomas nodded and dimmed the lamps as Nick walked up the stairs. He entered his sitting room in darkness, struggling out of his jacket, which he tossed at his bedroom door. His cravat followed, and he undid his waistcoat as he approached Charlotte's room. The time he'd come home drunk, she'd been awoken by him bumping into furniture, but tonight she didn't stir as he invaded her bedroom.

"Sorry I'm so late," he said, sitting on the side of her bed and removing his shoes.

She rolled over and opened her eyes. In the moonlight, her thick hair in one long plait and just aroused from a deep sleep, the woman was so heart-stoppingly beautiful that he understood why his friend had betrayed him.

He stripped off his socks and stood to unbutton his trousers.

She cleared her throat. "You're in the wrong bedroom."

"You're my wife. I belong in your bed. I deserve you, don't doubt it." He lifted the bedclothes and, naked, lay on his back, palms behind his head.

"You missed watercress soup," she said, inexplicably.

"What?"

"The last of the alphabet tastings."

He laughed without amusement. "You've shaken my esteem today. Am I so repulsive? Clara, ever the lady, trapped me with her husband's get while you have gone to great lengths to find the least suitable lover you could. Or do you actually have feelings for Luke?"

She sat up, leaned back against the headboard, and crossed her arms. "I'm desperately in love with him. That's why I married you."

His head reeled. "You married me because you couldn't have him?"

"You see, he wasn't drunk. I couldn't trick him."

"You didn't trick me, either. It's just that I can't resist little sluts. I wanted you from the moment you ripped at your bodice, but you didn't want a real marriage, not with me. When you discovered we could couple with a condom, you left me."

"You didn't want a real marriage. You kept your mistress."

"I got rid of her for you, and I tried every way I could to crawl back into your bed. I even left you to go your own way until you were ready." His thoughts fell apart. "I won't bother any longer. You're free to do as you like. I no longer want you. You're a whore just like your mother."

Charlotte gasped. "You didn't know my mother."

He rolled to the side, taking the bedclothes with him. She tried to snatch her blankets back, but he held the bulk twined around him. Confusingly, she pressed her warm cheek against the skin of his back. Her hand threaded across his ribs and she sighed out a soft breath.

Not about to be influenced by her female wiles, he stopped her hand with his, but she took her palm to the warmth of his abdomen. Without a qualm, and with complete disregard of his insults, she spooned her body against him. He forced a sound of derision.

"You want it from me now, do you?" Indicating his despicable need, he shifted her hand to his erection. "I didn't find a woman tonight, as you can feel, not when I remembered I had my own little harlot at home waiting for me. And you have been waiting, haven't you, my precious bloom?" His hand left hers as he rolled over, facing her.

"I've been asleep. Still would be, but for you."

He lay with his head on the pillow, eyes open, waiting for a credible thought. "If you didn't want me, you would have thrown me out. Ergo…"

He lifted her wrists above her head, taking both in his left, undamaged fist, while he rolled atop her. Without using as much as a cursory touch to ascertain her readiness, he forced her legs apart with his knees. His face above hers, he positioned himself and plunged into her. Unprepared, she jerked but instantly reacted with a surge of moisture. He despised her for her lack of discrimination and himself for being glad. Holding her in place by the power of his thighs, he continued to thrust.

When she reacted by winding her legs around him, he instantly changed the rhythm of his thrusts, penetrating deeply and withdrawing slowly, watching her face crease with frustration. Then he made his strokes short, fast, uneven, and shallow, teasing her with his lack of purpose. He knew her body as well as he knew his own. He had no intention of letting her reach fulfillment.

She butted his shoulder and so he slid out of her, holding her knees together so that he could roll her away from him. He heard her moan of anguish, and she began to sob uncontrollably. Against all reason, he took her into his arms. His hand stroked her hair.

"Love me, Nick. I want you to love me."

He rolled out of her bed, gathered up his clothes, and left.

* * * *

Charlotte drew air into her lungs, huddling, awash with tears that swelled and blocked her nose and dribbled from her chin. She cried for her mother who died without being offered respectability by the man she loved. She cried for Sarah who chased the man she wanted while losing sight of the fact that he might catch her if she stopped. She cried for Luke who was so determined to be cautious that he might miss the prize. She cried for Nick who simply could not believe in love.

When her whole body ached with weariness, she cried for herself. Nick had come to her bed, not in love and not in drunkenness, for she couldn't smell alcohol on his breath, but in stark, cold rage. He'd meant to show her his lust couldn't overcome his disgust of a wife who'd had an affair with another man, which he still, ridiculously, believed. She wiped her face, still shuddering with sobs.

She couldn't live her life under the rule of constant jealous scrutiny. A man who couldn't trust, couldn't love.

* * * *

After a night with only a few hours of sleep, Charlotte arose and dressed in her black riding skirt. The riding hat Sarah had borrowed looked squashed. One feather was missing and the other two broken and crushed, echoing Charlotte's mood so completely that she almost wore the darned thing.

However, she had planned today for a lifetime. She had married Nick so that she could have today, the day when she would show society that birth, legitimate or not, didn't show the worth of a person. She had been trained for today—educated with her father's annuity to her mother. This was the day when she would fulfill her mother's every wish.

Society would see her as a woman, not necessarily as a lady, strong enough, tough enough, and smart enough to plan and execute an event that would honor her husband and her father-in-law and give her cousin an opportunity to shine with the best. She would prove she was as good as *anyone, no matter how rich or wellborn.*

Therefore, she would begin the day the way she meant to end it, properly dressed and showing her proudest face. Instead of her bright green riding jacket, she put on her blue jacket and the hat she had decorated with red silk roses.

Outside, she heard hooves on the drive and knew Red Robin had arrived, as usual. She skittered down the stairs and met Harvey at the front door. "Is Rob ill?"

"Nah. I thought the walk would do me good. Drivin' all day makes a man lazy. My, that's what I calls a hat," he said with an admiring glance.

"It's cheerful." She forced a smile as she took the horse's reins.

"Watch her. She's testy this morning. Tried to nip me."

Charlotte ran her hand over the mare's neck. "That's unusual. I know she's mischievous some days, but she's never mean."

"I 'spect she's upset about yesterday. She didn't like being taken away from her oats."

"Who did that?"

Harvey shook his head, dolefully. "Miss Sarah wanted to ride her."

Charlotte moistened her mouth. She'd never baulked at sharing her clothes with Sarah, but she hadn't planned on sharing her horse with someone who didn't understand horses and wouldn't appreciate the finer points of riding one as high bred as Red Robin. "How did she manage?" She didn't meet Harvey's gaze, not wanting him to see she was upset.

"Couldn't say. Came back a couple of hours later, Rob says, both in a bad mood. Miss Sarah must have offended the 'orse, bad."

Charlotte stroked her horse's nose, her throat thick. "Never mind, Red. Like me, you can't depend on having everything your own way."

She spent one gloriously irresponsible hour riding in the park before going home to a house that bustled with importance. The canopy was almost erected when she arrived back. After changing, she took breakfast with her swollen eyed cousin.

"Vera says I'll want cucumber on my eyes before tonight," Sarah said, glancing at Charlotte's face. "You look a little peaked, too."

"I don't have time to be peaked. I can already hear the sound of deliveries. I'll start with the flowers and get that job out of the way, that is, unless you want to do the decorations."

Sarah shook her head. "I'm supposed to count glasses, of all things. I can't imagine why a maid can't do that."

"The maids will be fully occupied, don't doubt it. There's more to organizing a sizeable function than you can imagine."

"Well, keep me occupied so that I don't have time to be nervous."

Charlotte nodded, sure she wouldn't have time to be nervous either, and certainly no time to worry about Nick, or what she could say to a man she had begged to love her, who couldn't because of his lack of faith.

The line had been drawn. She suspected that nothing would make her cross it.

* * * *

Nick deliberately ate breakfast late. He didn't want to face Charlotte. He left for his club as early as he could, knowing the supper dance would be better arranged without his participation. Likely, the night could as well.

Deciding not to take a horse to stand all day in the club mews, he sent for Harvey with the brougham. As usual, the man couldn't keep his annoying mouth shut. "Wonderful thing the mistress is doing," he said as he let down the step.

Nick grunted, assuming the man alluded to the damned supper dance.

"Rare treat to have her in the brougham every day. Hats! Each day a new one. Everyone stares. Not another lady in the whole city what is as clever with hats as our lady."

"The cleverest little shopper in the whole of Adelaide," Nick muttered, stepping into the vehicle.

"Mind you, she needed a new one this morning for riding. Miss Sarah made a right shambles of the black one yesterday, I heard tell. Made Red Robin a bundle of nerves, too, yet Mrs. Alden didn't turn a hair when I told her."

"I doubt any other man in Adelaide is regaled with gossip about ladies' hats first thing in the morning. Your job is to drive. Take me to Dixon's without another word."

Harvey backed away and took the driver's seat. The stiff set of his shoulders spoke volumes about the rebuke. Nick didn't want to know anything about Charlotte's hat, having recalled that the green feather came from her riding hat—*the one that Sarah had made into a shambles yesterday*. "Harvey." He leaned forward. "Did you say Miss Sarah had Mrs. Alden's hat and horse yesterday?"

Harvey clamped his lips.

"You may answer when I ask you a question."

"She did," Harvey said in a surly voice.

"Although I know my wife is doing many wonderful things, to which were you referring earlier?"

"I can't say, being as how I'm no gossip." The carriage jerked as Harvey sped up the horses.

Nick waited until the brougham stopped outside Dixon's. "You take my wife out every day. Where does she go?"

Harvey leaned forward, tied the reins to the brake, and stepped down from the driver's seat. "Mrs. Alden visits friends, and she works for her charity, a very worthy cause, in my 'umble opinion," he said, carefully letting down the steps. "The lady is an angel, a true angel of mercy, and I wouldn't gossip about her. Not never."

"I have offended you and for that I am sorry. With which particular charity is my wife expending most of her energy?"

"I 'spect that's for her to tell you." Harvey gave a stiff nod of his head, rolled up the steps and took his place back on the box.

Nick walked to the front of the carriage and fixed his coachman in his eye. "Since she hasn't, and I'm in blissful ignorance, I would like you to tell me."

"The house she bought for unwed mothers."

"Where?"

"Stepney."

Although Nick kept his expression no more than politely interested, he'd been overloaded with information that conflicted with the facts as he knew them. Rather than instantly react, he decided to clear his head before investigating for himself more thoroughly.

He read the morning papers at the club, he discussed politics, he ate a luncheon, he parried comments about the supper dance, and his apparently amusing reasons for being out of the house, and he stripped for a round or two of boxing. Then, via Charlotte's house at Stepney, he returned home.

The long, wide hallway floor of Alden House had been polished to a high sheen. A single table stood at either side of the dining room entrance, holding rows of sparkling, empty glasses. At the end of the hall, beside the wide curved staircase, columns twined with gold silk leaves separated the platform for the quartet from the dancing floor in front. More gold leaves trailing from tall vases had transformed the drawing room on the other side. The furniture glowed with lemon-scented beeswax, and mirrors gleamed in the gaslight. A faint tuning of strings began.

Somewhat imbued with the moment, he bounded up the stairs. His sitting room was redolent with the scent of roses and his bedroom fresh with laundered linen. Thomas awaited him with a perfectly starched shirt, his evening suit set out, and his shoes polished. Charlotte set as high a standard for the servants as she set for herself. Nick's insides crawled with regret.

Apparently, Charlotte had dressed and was with Sarah. He could hear giggles and a few odd words. Ready and stiff with shame, he took himself downstairs. While maids carried bottles of champagne to the hall and placed them in buckets of ice, he kept his eyes on the staircase, watching for the ladies to appear.

A carriage pulled up in the drive, and he prepared himself to greet the first guest alone, but Charlotte and Sarah, two visions of loveliness, sped down the stairs laughing with joy. Thomas moved to open the door, slightly flustered.

"There you are," said a familiar voice. Alfred stood waiting in the doorway as the two ladies threw themselves at him, laughing and talking at the same time. "I couldn't miss this. Yes, of course I meant to come. Now, now. Let me be. I must go upstairs to change for our function."

Chapter 22

As Nick waited in the long receiving line of guests, he knew he had avoided his former life for too long. Acquaintances from his youthful past waited to be greeted, and his smile became genuine long before he had completed his stance of duty. Charlotte, beside him, stood serene. Among the nods of approval, he noted glances and raised eyebrows expressing surprise he had won such a diamond.

His most careful moment came when she was faced with Luke. Her greeting was polite, extraordinarily so, which in Nick's opinion meant the man had displeased her. Luke, in turn, evaded her gaze, which confirmed Nick's deductions of this morning. He hoped, in doing so, he could find some sort of redemption for himself. Lately, he had made too many mistakes about too many relationships. Now, he believed in Charlotte's complete innocence. Perhaps on the trail to the whole truth, he wanted to know why he'd been misled and if Charlotte was complicit.

The reveal would in no way change his feelings for her, other than to regret he had given her no reason to trust him. However, tonight wasn't the night to confront her, not while she still owed him a good shaking.

After the hordes of guests had moved past into the dining room and sampled the food laid out, the quartet began to play dance tunes in the vast hall. Nick had the honor of leading Sarah onto the floor for the first set while his father partnered Charlotte. Conversing during an energetic country dance was impossible, and he didn't try.

Moreover, he enjoyed dancing with Sarah, who looked exceptionally lovely tonight, her burnished head simply dressed, pearl earrings her only adornment with the cream satin gown. More than one young man, who may well have not noticed her before, took interest, and Nick knew her dance card was filled soon after she left the floor.

James was only one of her admirers. Nick hadn't believed she was hoping for a proposal from him. From the start, Luke had been her focus, and Nick had never been convinced by her faked disinterest. He'd warned Luke off, but apparently Luke hadn't heeded him, either that or Sarah was determined to have her way. Nick didn't care how the couple played out their romance, but somehow Charlotte had been involved. Now that her name had been bandied about at the club, Nick was involved, too. He wouldn't let anyone implicate his wife for his or her own ends.

Although rigidly sticking to his self-imposed role of the perfect husband and dancing with those left without partners, he didn't lose sight of Charlotte during the evening. Few could. The simple, elegant lines of her gown, her glittering necklace, both took second place to the purity of her beauty. With her appearance overshadowing her accomplishments, few knew of her sterling qualities, Nick least of all. She'd given him a resounding lesson in humility these past months.

Now, rather than tossing her on her back, he wanted to nurture her, hold her in his arms, laugh with her, tease her, and be her protector when she needed him, a role he hadn't been encouraged to take, but a role he would assume this evening.

Finally, he saw Luke pat his pockets and head behind the quartet toward the conservatory at the back of the house. Nick waited and saw Charlotte and Sarah glance at each other. Charlotte nodded, and like a wraith, Sarah followed Luke. If Sarah were about to be compromised, Nick wondered who her witness was meant to be. If Charlotte, she, too, would be compromised, and he couldn't allow his wife to be involved yet again. Her night would come tumbling down and all her hope of social success dashed.

When he saw Charlotte slip away, too, to the garden beyond the conservatory, resigned, he followed the trio out into the fresh night air where the half-light from a few lanterns winked along the path to the pond, lit more brightly. He couldn't see Charlotte, but Sarah had managed to accost Luke by the glistening water, where two small green frogs sat on a drifting lily leaf awaiting the insects dazzled by the lamplight.

Unfortunately, Nick couldn't hear the conversation, but he saw Luke stub out his cheroot and turn to leave. Sarah screamed and Nick moved. "This is my cue, I believe."

Sarah stared at him, her eyes narrowed and catlike. "He was about to take advantage of me."

"You'd best rip your gown, then."

Her jaw opened. "This was expensively made by Millies' Mode," she said with indignation. "I would be a fool to ruin it."

Luke made a sound of derision and crossed his arms. "Don't, not for me. I won't be forced into any marriage."

"I'm sober now and a credible witness," Nick said, holding Luke's gaze. "As you were once."

Luke narrowed his eyes, but his foursquare stance said he was listening. "It would seem too coincidental to have cousins marrying for the same reason. Sarah will look foolish if she goes on with this."

"Is that what you want? For Sarah to look foolish? None of us are drunk tonight, and so I suggest we play this more reasonably."

"When I marry, it will be on my terms." Luke jutted his jaw.

Nick laughed with genuine amusement. "I think I might have said that myself, once, and thought I had decided on the terms. I have since discovered that it's best not to tie oneself too tightly."

Sarah's shoulders eased. Face plumped with relief, she moved to him and attached herself to his arm. "And so, without further ado, we will leave this cad to his sad and lonely view of the female gender."

"Excuse me for intruding." Charlotte moved from the shadows of the wall into the light where moonbeams played across the elegant bones of her face. "But the noise you people are making will be heard inside if we're not careful." She eyed Sarah. "So, Luke was about to take advantage of you?"

"Not so." Luke clamped his mouth. "Despite being given multiple opportunities. Sarah doesn't seem to understand that when I decide to marry I will also decide on the bride and the time."

"He took my clothes off yesterday." Sarah gazed up at Nick, her expression limpid. "He ought to be gentleman enough to propose because of that alone, without putting me to this trouble."

"I'm here to make sure he does marry you." Nick patted Sarah's hand.

Luke frowned at Nick. "Naked or clothed, I have not taken advantage of her."

"I can't know that because yesterday I arrived too late to see anything," Nick said politely. "She had already left."

Luke examined Nick's expression. "Yesterday you told me I was with Charlotte."

"The evidence pointed in her direction."

"How so?"

Nick pushed Sarah forward. "Tell him what you did and why."

"*He* removed my clothes, not me." Sarah glanced from Nick to Luke. "*He* placed them on his chair."

"Then what did I do?" Luke asked, his tone sardonic.

"You certainly looked your fill."

"I helped you on with your clothes, and I sent you home."

"In the meantime," Nick said, persevering, "leaving Charlotte hung out to dry by the gossip."

"What gossip?" Charlotte asked, looking for the first time at Nick.

"I heard at my club that you spent the afternoon with Luke in his rooms."

Charlotte's expression froze. "And your knowledge of me told you that was true?"

Nick pushed his hands into his pockets. "As a matter of fact, no, but after questioning Luke, I had to conclude it was. Well, Sarah? Don't you think it's time to explain?"

"My plan went awry." Sarah's tongue flickered across her lips. She blinked hard, her mouth turning down, and if she tried for more sympathy, he would shake her. "You were busy when I went out, and so I left you a note. You were meant to read it, leave straight after, and catch Luke with me. Charlotte knows about that, but she doesn't know the note said *she* was with Luke. I didn't think it mattered because after I arrived home, I realized you hadn't read my note and so I grabbed it back." She twisted her fingers together. "I wasn't sure you would care if I were to be compromised by my own deliberate actions. I thought you might leave me to stew in my own juice, as it were."

"So that's why you took my horse. I wondered." Charlotte stared at Sarah, her eyes stark.

"You wore her hat, and you took her horse," Nick said, using a judgmental tone. "You left the mare outside Luke's house for anyone to see."

Luke frowned. "That was underhanded, Sarah. I'm sorry, Charlotte. I had no idea."

Nick maintained Luke's gaze. "Now you understand why I was somewhat annoyed." He stood straighter.

Luke nodded slowly. "Again, my apologies. It seems I've been rather dense. Since I appear to have ruined Charlotte's reputation rather than Sarah's, I suppose I'll have to"—his querying glance met Nick's and loitered while he considered—"make restitution?"

Nick let the moment expand while he eyed his wife. "You will. You need to put this right.... *The only way possible,* remembering you are a man of honor and Charlotte is blameless, words I remember you saying the night of the Hawthorn's ball." He drew in a deep breath, which he held, hoping Luke understood.

Luke eyed him, rubbed his jaw, and then creased his forehead. "You'll need to have your marriage annulled before I can marry Charlotte," he said, his voice uncertain.

Charlotte gasped. "We wouldn't be granted an annulment." She looked over at Luke, her face a picture of shock.

Luke's glance flickered to Nick. "After a forced marriage of four months? I think you would."

Nick shook his head. "Not a chance. The marriage has been *consumed*. Do you know a tame judge?"

"One or two."

"Consummated." Charlotte stared at Nick, and kept staring, two lines forming between her brows.

Nick waited, his heart pounding with hope. "If you can't forgive me for my unfounded accusations and my jealousy, I'll leave you to follow your heart."

"What about me?" Sarah asked, her voice hesitant.

"This is about Charlotte, for once." Luke sounded inflexible. "In this instance, you've made life difficult for her, and Nick and I must come to an arrangement. If she has nothing to say, I'll take her silence as being amenable to a change of husbands." His mouth relaxed, and his eyes gleamed. Nick knew he had his old friend back. "Let's leave these two, shall we, Charlotte?"

Charlotte cleared her throat and faced Nick. "I do forgive your accusations, especially now I know you would have every reason to think the worst. Perhaps Sarah owes me an apology for implicating me."

Sarah chewed her thumbnail, apparently not about to back down. "I'm sorry, of course, but in the end it makes no difference. Luke still prefers you." Her lips thinned.

Luke drew himself up. "I know you don't like being compared to Charlotte, but she would never have done the same to you. She has supported you no matter what. As to whom I prefer..." He shrugged.

"I don't care."

Charlotte took a step forward. "Yes, you do, Sarah."

"I hate him."

"Me? And yet you were willing to trick me into marriage. I'm not terribly rich, terribly handsome, nor terribly clever. Why would you want me?"

Sarah crossed her arms.

Charlotte took a step forward. "Tell him you love him, please, Sarah. Otherwise I'll have to marry him."

Sarah lifted her chin, her expression outraged.

Luke inclined his head to the side, considering. "Before Charlotte and I leave, I need to be sure Sarah hates me. It's hard on a man to be lured and rejected and then easily passed over to her married cousin." He advanced slowly toward Sarah who stood, her expression changing to wary astonishment when he snatched her into his embrace. His mouth closed with hers as Charlotte glanced at Nick.

He shrugged. "He needed to know why she implicated you."

"She thought he loved me."

"Excuse us," Luke said, apparently satisfied with Sarah's response. "I'm taking this wretch to the back of the garden for a moment. I think I'm about to propose." He took Sarah's hand and hurried her off. The sound of a soft laugh echoed in the darkness.

Charlotte lifted her elegant chin. "Fortunately, you said 'consumed.' If you hadn't, I would have thought you were serious."

"I knew you would pick up the cue. That's one thing I love about you—your quick wit." He advanced on her, hoping his role would be as easy to play as Luke's.

She put out a stopping palm, shaking her head. "Did you know that Luke meant to marry Sarah? A few hours ago you thought he was romancing me."

"He took off all her clothes, he dressed her, and he sent her home?" Nick shook his head with admiration. "And you think he didn't mean to marry her? It takes great fortitude to reject an interesting offer from an appealing young lady, and Luke would only refuse a lady he meant to marry. He'll make a worthy husband, don't you think?"

She nodded. "I suspected that if he didn't want to marry her, he would either have taken her, or he would have sent her home still wrapped."

"Wrapped." He laughed. "I suspect he came here tonight to propose. And I'm here now to make a proposal to you."

She stood perfectly still.

"I want to start again." He took another step toward her.

"No."

"No?"

"Tonight is my night. Most of my life has been a preparation for tonight. I married you so that I could take my chance to bask in the warmth of society's approval. If you will excuse me, I'm going inside to be with our guests." As he watched, she straightened and walked off, chin raised with pride.

The night hid her, and he strolled to the back of the garden, preparing Luke and Sarah with a cough. Perhaps Charlotte didn't want him after all, but only the shield of his name. He sighed, not yet abandoning hope. Regardless, he had the responsibility of making sure of her continued success tonight.

* * * *

Charlotte noted the speedy return of Nick and Luke to the supper dance, a satisfied grin on each face and laughter lurking. If society had been gossiping about Luke and her today, Nick's demeanor alone would prove the lie. Since her marriage, these two men, lifelong friends, had suffered an amount of antipathy for each other, and the reversal heartened her. Nick deserved all back he had lost during the past few years.

With Nick to help Alfred as host, Charlotte had a chance to make sure the youngest maids had been sent off to bed and that the plates of food were refreshed. Cook had retired some time earlier, having to be on duty in the morning, but Mrs. Wishart was keeping an eye on the food, the consuming of which had almost ceased.

"I think we can start to serve the ices now," Charlotte told her, and the maids circulated with the refreshers instead of champagne.

Sarah arrived a good half hour later, her hair freshly dressed and her face aglow with happiness. Now that Sarah's marriage had been proposed, Charlotte didn't need to keep the secret of her birth much longer. She wished she could tell Nick tonight, for her concealment seemed more of a lie when used for her own advantage. If Nick wanted to start again with her, he needed to start with the truth for anything less would be dishonorable.

With a heavy heart, she danced, she laughed, and she moved through crowds remembering everyone's name, everyone's position in the world. Alfred retired just after midnight, giving the guests a hint that they might leave, too, and by the time the last guest did some two hours later, she knew her supper dance had been a great success and that her own part had been noted by the most important of the hostesses. If Nick wasn't proud of her accomplishment, she was.

She told the servants to leave the rearrangement of the rooms until tomorrow, and she headed toward the main stairs. Nick was sitting at the bottom, a silver tray beside him holding tiny cakes, fruit, cheese, and a tall chilled bottle of apple cider.

"You are ready to retire, my love?"

"If my tired feet will carry me up these stairs."

He stood. "I will do so. I'll come back for the food and wine." Almost swooping on her, he took her into his arms and, as if she weighed no more than a child, he carried her up the stairs. At the top, he set her on her feet. "I suspect you've barely eaten tonight," he said, smiling. "And so now I'll retrieve our provisions."

"I'm too tired to eat. I'll say good night here."

"Not a chance," he said, steering her into their suite. "I've been waiting all night for a word with you, and I don't want to wait until tomorrow."

"You won't get any sense out of me tonight," she said, unbearably nervous. If he wanted to say he had grown to like her or that he respected or admired her, she would shrivel into nothing when she knew she had lived a lie with him from the start, hiding her true birth from him and his father.

"I don't want sense from you, my love. Frivolity would suit me better, as a role reversal of sorts." He opened the door.

"Did Luke give you an idea of their wedding arrangements?" She paused near his bedroom door.

"He and I settled for a quick wedding, next month if possible."

Charlotte heaved a sigh of relief. She could unburden herself after that. "The costs?"

"He will bear them. He quite understands that Sarah is penniless, and he doesn't see why you should continue to sponsor her. She said she would be happy to be married in Stirling, which will suit us all. So, your duty is done and your brief is fulfilled. Now we have our own marriage to discuss."

She backed toward her own bedroom. "Not tonight. Let me sleep and then we'll…"

He took her arm. "I was no prize when you took me on, and I was determined not to change. I had seen Clara's desperation turn to retribution, and I had learned from that not to let a woman get under my skin." He gazed at her, slowly kissing her fingers. "I thought I was protecting myself, but instead I was living a half-life."

She nodded. "I understood. Good night."

"I have insulted you and misjudged you." He settled her into a loose embrace. "Your standards are so high that I know without a doubt your mother was no whore, and I apologize for the insult."

"Accepted."

"I apologize for every cruel and thoughtless word I have uttered to you. You have never done so to me, although I deserved your scorn. Not now, I hope, because you've changed me."

"I have?" She glanced into his eyes.

He cupped her face in his palm. "You've also changed my life. My home is comfortable, well run, and happy. The servants hum while they work. I swear I heard Cook singing in the kitchen tonight, despite having worked harder today then she has for years."

She dropped her gaze. "I tricked you into marrying me, and so my side of the bargain was to be a good wife to you."

"You've been a perfect wife. You're an amazing woman, courageous and independent, loyal and generous, although perhaps a little too generous with your allowance."

She tried to pull out of his hold. "So, this is about my spending?"

"Not at all. This is about your confidence in me. You have little. You have not shared certain aspects of your life with me, and I wonder why. Have I been parsimonious?"

"Not at all. You know you've been nothing but generous from the beginning."

"Why so secretive, then?"

"There are certain aspects of my life you wouldn't approve."

"How could you know that?"

She closed her eyes, afraid of his response. "You have taunted me with my birth despite the fact that my mother was legally married," she said in a low voice.

He looked aside. "That was unfair of me. I can't excuse myself, and I hope you will forgive me for that, too. Would it help if I told you I love you so much that I don't care if you were born under a hedge?"

Her breath caught in her throat. "You love me?"

He hugged her so tightly that she needed to push back a little.

"More than my life. I wouldn't let you go even if I discovered you were using your allowance to support unwed mothers."

She gasped. "You know?"

"Unbelievably, I only found out today. I could have found out at any time if I had ever bothered to talk to Harvey, and let me say now, I will make sure I talk to Harvey every day of my life henceforward."

"Do you mind?"

"Only that you struggled alone. I would have been delighted to help now that I don't spend my money on gambling."

"I love you, too," she said, leaning back to look into his gleaming eyes.

With mock shock, he staggered back into his velvet chair, taking her with him, slanting urgent kisses across her mouth. She returned his passion, opening her lips to his tongue.

He lifted his head. "I haven't finished my confession." He rested his cheek onto her hair, and she felt him shake. "You are the only woman I have ever loved," he said, barely above a whisper.

With her face in his neck, she unbuttoned his shirt and he rose to his feet, tipping her off his lap. His hand on the small of her back, her hurried her into his bedroom.

* * * *

"I know the name of my father," she said a good hour later.

They'd made love on his bed. She adored his wicked ways, but this evening, sharing his bed like a respectable married lady had been a new beginning. In his room, which she planned to share, he somehow used less expertise and more love. His tenderness excited her just as much as his previous words of carnal lust and choice of terrifyingly risky locations. Not that she would give up one for the other. Either would do when the occasion demanded.

He stretched his powerful frame, while she sighed with admiration. He'd been given his strong handsome face. He'd earned his splendid body.

He picked up her hand and gazed at her fingers. In a slow, thoughtful voice, he said, "I know the name of your father, too."

She tightened her fingers on his. "That's very sweet of you, but it's not who you think." Leaning across, she covered his lips with hers.

"It's not?" he murmured, tangling her hair in one hand and rising onto one elbow above her. "That's a shame, and Tony will be disappointed not to be your brother."

She caught her breath. "Really? He doesn't mind?"

"We thought you could be a long lost cousin. He thinks he can find a Davies on the family tree. Let's play cards. If I win, we'll stay in bed all day."

"Don't be silly. You never win."

They stayed in bed all day.

Meet the Author

From art student to stylist, to nurse and midwife, Virginia Taylor's life has been one illogical step to the next, each one leading to the final goal of being an author. When she can tear herself away from the computer and the waiting blank page, she immerses herself in arts and crafts, gardening, or, of course, cooking. You can visit her website at www.virginia-taylor. com, and tweet her @authorvtaylor.

Be sure not to miss Virginia Taylor first book of the *South Landers* series

Starling

An aspiring dressmaker, orphaned Starling Smith is accustomed to fighting for her own survival. But when she's offered a year's wages to temporarily pose as a wealthy man's bride, she suspects ulterior motives. She can't lose the chance to open her own shop, but she won't be any man's lover, not even handsome, infuriating Alisdair Seymour's...

To prevent his visiting sister from parading potential brides in front of him, Alisdair has decided to present a fake wife. He lost his heart once, and had it broken—he doesn't intend to do it again. But stubborn, spirited Starling is more alluring than he bargained for, and Alisdair will risk everything he has to prove his love is true...

Set against the sweeping backdrop of 1866 South Australia, *Starling* is a novel of cherished dreams and powerful desires, and the young woman bold enough to claim them both...

Starling on sale now!

http://www.kensingtonbooks.com/book.aspx/31133

Chapter 1

Adelaide, South Australia, 1866

"Straighten your collar, girl," said the sharp-faced clerk guarding the office door. His olive jacket faded into the green-papered walls of the anteroom. "Mr. Seymour don't like to see his employees looking scruffy."

Starling Smith fingered the starched white cotton around her throat. She didn't look scruffy in the Seymour's Emporium uniform she had worn with pride for the past two weeks. She looked neat and anonymous in the plain gray. Any female lucky enough to be employed selling fabrics should be nothing less than tidy—and diligent, too.

Yesterday, when the owner, Mr. Alasdair Seymour, had toured the emporium he stopped to inspect the materials she had ranked using the rainbow color scale, a new idea of her own. He had taken her name from the department manager, and now he possibly meant to commend her.

His office door opened. "Miss Smith?"

Remembering her place, she leapt to her feet.

He glanced at his clerk. "I'm not to be disturbed. Come into my office, Miss Smith." Broad shouldered and tall, he looked younger than he had the day before, under thirty and handsome enough to deserve those sighs from the shopgirls.

Starling's knees wobbled as she hastened past him through the doorway.

"Take a seat," he said, taking his own. He wore his dark hair fashionably collar-length.

She perched on a carved chair upholstered in dark green brocade. The hovering red of sunset shone through the tall windows dressed with swags of yellow-striped silk. Sparkling motes floated to his desk where he sat, picked up a pen, and tapped the end on his blotter. His forehead was smooth, his nose precisely chiseled, and his jaw firm.

"Do you enjoy your job?" He looked straight at her. His eyes, an assessing luminous gray, sent a shimmer of panic through her.

She quickly lowered her gaze, trying to regain her breath. "I do." Her voice sounded embarrassingly husky. "I like working with fabrics."

"You worked in a hotel before you came here." He scrutinized a page lying on his desk. "They gave you no reference."

She had thrown away the crumpled piece of paper that described her as "a good worker," hoping she could gloss over the six weeks she had been employed at the Star Inn, mentioned in the South Australian police records as a site of gambling and prostitution. "I didn't think a temporary job would matter when I was waiting on the Seymour's list for more than a year."

He glanced up, his gaze again causing a strange jumble inside her. "You've had a small amount of education? That is, you can read and write?"

"Yes, sir. Or I wouldn't have applied here."

"Unfortunately, you've been annoying my customers." He set down his pen.

She drew a surprised breath. "I sell them what they want, sir."

"You sell them what you think they should have."

Shaking her head, she stared at her fingers knotted in her lap. "I sell them what they need. It wouldn't be right to sell fabrics not strong enough for their purpose or too heavy or the wrong color."

"And it seems you have decided on the colors they should have."

"I advise them on what might...suit."

"I don't pay you to advise my customers to buy cheaper fabrics than those they choose or less material. I pay you to make money for me."

"I do, sir." She leaned forward. "Just the other day, a young lady came back to buy more fabric. She said I'd given her just the right material for her ball gown, and she wanted me to help her again."

"Mr. Porter thinks the fabric department can cope without female staff."

"Female staff?" she queried, shaken. "But he told me I'm a quick learner."

He shrugged. "I'm sorry but I am not going to keep you at the emporium."

"You're going to get rid of me? Oh, no, you don't mean that. I get twice as many sales as Mr. Porter."

He shook his head, placing his pen in the holder. "I can, however, offer you a different position." He aligned his blotter with the edge of the desk. "In my home."

A quick shake of her head dealt with his offer of a maid's job. "I won't advise your customers about colors. I was wrong, and I'm sorry." Her voice rose with hope. "I would accept a position in any other of your departments."

"I don't have a position in any other department. I *do* have a list a mile long of women wanting to work in the emporium, as you know." He evaded her gaze.

Focusing on her weary black shoes, she exhaled her last hope. She'd loved measuring the soft fabrics, feeling the quality, and sliding the sharp scissors across the width. She'd loved working out the profits. She stood, not caring that her shoulders drooped.

He pushed out his chair and stood, facing her. "You could earn quite a bit of money if you accept my alternative. I'm much in need of a woman like you."

She straightened. *A woman like her?* "If you don't want me, I will get a job at Harris's."

"Unlikely, given that they don't employ females *with* or with*out* references. I won't beat around the bush." Pausing, he eased his black cravat with a forefinger. "You look respectable. I need a woman to pose as my wife for a couple of weeks."

Aghast, she took a step back. He didn't want a maid. He wanted to tup her. "I don't know what gave you the impression that I might do that, but—"

"Money." His lips tilted cynically. "Now, what would you say to five pounds for the two weeks?"

"No." Her jaw tense, she backed to the door. "I worked as a laundress at the inn. Not a prostitute."

He raised his eyebrows. "You only have to *pretend* to be my wife."

"I'm not good at pretending. I never have been." She opened the door and walked out.

Cheeks hot with humiliation, she strode past the clerk and down to the fabric department where, with shaking hands, she grabbed the cloth bag holding an apple, a clean pair of cuffs, a handkerchief, and a few pennies. Tying her shawl across her shoulders, she took the staff exit leading to a narrow alley off Rundle Street. She didn't have time to weep.

First, she would need to retrieve her belongings from the emporium's boardinghouse and next find accommodation for the night. The Star Inn might let her use the laundry room. If not, her friend Meg would find her a safe place.

Starling's chest hurt and her eyes prickled. As she pulled the heavy door, she noticed the purple haze hovering over the sunset. She stood staring, her dreams shattered and her life in pieces. Gathering her bag under her arm, she hurried down the cobbled alley, chased by the aroma of fresh horse manure and settling smoke. A hot wind whipped her hair across her face, forcing her to pause. Blinking hard, she tucked the strands behind her ears.

Dashing the back of her wrist over her eyes, she cornered into Rundle Street. Mr. Seymour stepped in front of her. His high-crowned hat cast a shadow across his features.

"This way." He seized her elbow.

She wrenched her arm out of his grip. "Let me be. I don't want your money or you."

"I have to have you tonight." He drew a deep breath. "I'll give you six pounds."

She backed away, disgusted. "I know at least three women who would accept your proposition. Go to the Star Inn and see which you would prefer."

He shook his head. "I wouldn't be standing here with you if I hadn't already tried that. None could pass as a lady."

"So, now you want a lady? I thought you said a wife."

"My wife would, of course, be a lady. I spent the last two weeks interviewing whores and actresses. Then I looked at my staff yesterday, and there you were with your careful speech, your background at the Star Inn, and your neat and plain appearance."

"Neat and plain." She firmed her lips.

"Good Lord, girl." His voice softened. "I'm offering you real money, far more than the fourteen shillings a week you earned here, to live a life of luxury for two weeks. You don't need to look at me as if I'm Satan. I'm giving you the greatest opportunity of your life."

"I had the greatest opportunity of my life—a job as a shopgirl." She blinked hard. "And for reasons of your own, you've taken my best chance from me."

His brow creased. "I'm offering you a better one."

"I have plans that don't include being anyone's wife, real or not."

"Two weeks, that's all I ask," he said in a long-suffering tone. With a sweep of his hand, he indicated she could move in the direction he wanted her to go.

She folded her arms.

He gave her a sideways glint. "I'll pay you *twenty* pounds."

"No." She wet her mouth.

"Perhaps you *won't* suit," he said, shrugging. "Mr. Porter said you were intelligent, but you are acting like a simpleton. I have offered you more than half a year's wages, and all you can do is persist in your belief that I want to bed you."

"Mr. Porter said I was intelligent?" Her voice rose with hope.

He raised his eyebrows.

"So, why can't you put me back in the fabric department?" She brushed down her sleeves, stalling while she thought. "I'm good at selling materials because I like selling materials."

He didn't want her as a maid, and he didn't want to tup her? She didn't understand what he wanted.

He heaved a monumental sigh. "And I'm sure you'll like pretending to be my wife because if you make a convincing job of it, I'll give you *forty pounds*."

Her mouth dried. Forty pounds! That was double twenty. For twenty pounds she could hire a little shop of her own. For forty pounds, she could not only buy stock, but also employ at least two other *Birds* from the orphanage. Robin and Nightingale would be her first choice.

Her breath fluttered. "You don't want to bed me?"

He looked her up and down. "Do you think you're my type?"

She put her hand to her hair and, blushing, quickly brought her arm down again. A gentleman who owned a number of emporiums, proving a head for business, wouldn't invest more than a few shillings in an untried, drab bed partner. He could take his pick of women.

"Well, what would the job entail *exactly*?"

"Just doing whatever wives do. Having breakfast with me in the morning, arranging flowers, eating cakes, drinking tea, sitting in the drawing room doing whatever you please until I tell you otherwise."

"What might 'otherwise' be?" She eyed him narrowly.

"Standing by my side and agreeing with every word I say while smiling pleasantly at my guests. You can smile, I suppose?"

"I'm not sure."

He gave her a suspicious glance.

"The job can't be as easy as you say." For forty pounds, there had to be a catch.

"It's as easy as you want to make it. I have a household that runs perfectly already."

"Then why do you want a wife? Other than to idle away the day."

Pushing aside his unbuttoned jacket, he slid his hands into the pockets of his biscuit-colored trousers. How he maintained a fit, broad-shouldered physique while sitting behind a desk all day was a mystery to Starling. Although she'd met no other rich men, she had assumed they were those with barrel bellies. "Last week my sister notified me she is bringing a lady with her, a lady she is sure I would like to see. She arrives from Victoria tomorrow."

"I don't understand."

"I don't like my sister's plan. She has tried this matchmaking before." His mouth tightened. "I told her I wouldn't marry any of her hopefuls."

"You don't need to marry the lady simply because your sister knows her."

"Nor do I need to have prospective brides presented to me so often that I give in out of sheer self-defense."

"Life is hard for rich men," she said sweetly.

"Exactly." He nodded for emphasis. "If I present you as a *fait accompli,* I will stop my sister in her tracks. So, are we agreed?"

She caught her bottom lip between her teeth.

"My deadline is today. I need to present a wife to my household by tonight. And, since I doubt you own suitable clothing," he said, averting his gaze, "we'll pick out a couple of gowns and, er, the trimmings before the emporium closes."

She deliberated. "I only have to smile, idle the day away, and agree with you?"

He nodded. "I want you to be as meek, quiet, and respectful as a good wife should be."

"And I will be a wife in name only?"

"That is our agreement."

Growing hope straightened her shoulders. Perhaps her dream was not lost.

He began to herd her along North Terrace. "I expect it will be worth forty pounds to prove my point," he muttered.

"That you won't ever marry? Are you a lady-man?"

His eyes widened momentarily. "A lady-man? Do you mean...? You do. Don't use gutter terms around my guests, or you'll be out of the house without a penny before you can sneeze. Of course I'm not bent. I simply want only one woman."

She could but wish. If she'd thought he only liked men, she could relax. "But isn't that a reason to marry?"

"I'm not sure intelligent and smart are the same thing. Enough. You have agreed to our bargain. The lady I want is already married, and it's time you became the sort of wife I require."

Starling nodded. He had specified a wife with a neat, plain appearance. She was neat and plain. Ordinary. Her body was slender, her skin was sallow, and she had brown hair and eyes. No male had ever glanced at her twice. At the inn, her plainness had been her best protection. Meg had told her she could be pretty if she tried, but she had no need to be pretty. She didn't want or need a man. In fact, her plan depended on her remaining single. No husband would let her follow through with her business idea. Married, she would blight more lives than her own.

She had nothing to lose by doing as he asked and had gained instead an opportunity to earn a great deal of money. She would obey Mr. Seymour's every edict. Opportunity had knocked, and Starling Smith only had to widen the door to reach her goal.

Half a pace behind Mr. Seymour, she passed the lawyer's offices, the pastry shop, the tailor, and a saddlery. The main commercial thoroughfare of Adelaide was familiar to her: the old wooden sheds, the new Georgian buildings, the constant grind of carriage wheels, the thump-thump of hooves, the bustle of people, and the push of their presence. Not only had she worked in the city, she'd lived nearby her whole nineteen years, watching the adornment of the newest constructions with ornate pillars and pretty plastered curlicues. She couldn't imagine living elsewhere.

Mr. Seymour pushed open the front door of his emporium. Dimly lit, the shop was preparing to close. He led the way to the ready-mades area upstairs and stood waiting for attention. The floor manager bowed from the waist.

"Miss Smith needs assistance," Mr. Seymour said.

The manager clicked his fingers for a shopgirl, who hastened forward. Starling knew Jinny, the red-haired assistant, from the boardinghouse.

"Three new gowns. Nothing gaudy. Help Miss Smith choose. I'll be back in half an hour." With that, Mr. Seymour strode away.

Jinny widened her eyes at Starling, who smiled and shrugged. Jinny moistened her lips and bustled about finding ready-made gowns while Starling stood by her left shoulder, pointing out those she wanted. Brown, being the cheapest dye, had been the color for the foundlings. She had worn brown her whole life until two weeks ago, when she'd exchanged that color for the gray of the Seymour uniform. Knowing neither flattered her, she decided that because this handsome man had chosen a plain woman for his bride, she should not try to change her appearance.

She kept on the last gown she tried. Patterned in a jaundiced green and brown, the high-buttoned fit was as unflattering as the other two she'd chosen. Continuing her disapproving silence, Jinny parceled them and Starling's uniform. When Mr. Seymour returned, he took the purchases, cramming them with a few other parcels into a new holdall. Next, he let Starling choose a plain brown hat. She wore that, too, certain she looked even more thin faced wearing a flat-brimmed poke with a long ribbon tie.

Finally, he took her to the jeweler's shop and bought her a plain gold ring. Keeping her face expressionless, she slid on the circlet. How she would pass as the wife of a gentleman, she didn't know. Nor did she know why he thought she might. She could only hope that the colors she had chosen to wear would merge her into the background, as she didn't plan to lose the forty pounds before she'd seen a single penny.

When he marched her outside the shop again, she totaled his purchases: one pound for the ring and more good money for a hat and gowns. He had shelled out a tidy sum to deceive a sister who merely wanted to see him happily married. Starling hoped she could play her unworthy role.

She kept pace with him, her bonnet ribbons fluttering as she moved closer to her goal. Eagles might soar. Starlings took chances when they saw them.